RUNNING HOME

A Novel

By Frederick Murolo

Frederick Murolo

Printed in the United States of America

ISBN-9781983118371

To my editor, business partner and wife, Karen, without whom this would be impossible. We should all have a Lisa in our lives.

BOOK ONE

Finding Something

CHAPTER ONE

Anybody who tells you he planned his great running streak is a lying shit. Don't waste your breath on this fool.

Underground Runner's Guide – Anonymous (reprinted without permission)

Harmon Willow thought he was a runner. He lay in bed and thought this. But he was full of shit. Sure, he'd done some running. Who hadn't?

All the way back in tenth grade he had been in the intramural cross-country race after football season. They'd shortened the course to a mile and a half, taken out the biggest hill. He knew he could do that short run. How hard could a mile and a half be? Just mind over matter. And then there he was rumbling in, red-faced and wobbly, sprinting the last fifty yards past Pete Vincent, some oversized freshman footballer, to grab popsicle stick number 14. His friend Will Whitson played soccer, and he finished third, got recruited to the cross-country team by Mr. Sharp. Coach Sharp never called on Harmon; he stayed with football.

Then there was that day senior year when the football team was flat in a preseason scrimmage against Trinity. Coach Johnson called them into a huddle to yell and say they were soft. Then he lined them up to run sprints. Sideline to second hash mark, 34 yards, then cruise it in to the far sideline. Then turn and listen for the command. "Set. Go." And run it back, another 34 yards and coast 17. No pause, no catching breath or drinking water. "Set.

Go." After ten, Harmon could feel his throat burn, felt the metallic taste come up. After twenty, Tommy Marion bent almost to the ground and hurled. Others were coughing, going slower. "Set. Go." Harmon went. By thirty, he felt better, like it might not be his body doing this, like he was watching this group of red-faced boys running, coasting, stopping, turning and doing it again. His breathing eased, even as the sprints continued to 50. He was in football shape. Good football shape. But he was no runner.

In college, he had flirted with running. Summer after his sophomore year, he and Greg down the street started running in the evening after working the roofing job for Greg's brother, Arnie. They put on cotton gym shorts and tee shirts and used bandannas for headbands. They laced up low-top canvas Chuck Taylors. They ran for an hour or so, a big loop, estimated 7 miles. Arnie hated the fact that they ran. He thought they were cheating him out of their energy the next day. Convinced that they would be too tired to carry shingles up the ladder or fill up the dump truck with the debris from a roof rip-off for $3.50 an hour. But they got stronger, worked better, so eventually he shut up.

By the time he was back to school, Harmon had run 60 days in a row. 60 consecutive days of running. He kept at it a few more days, till that Grateful Dead show in New Jersey. They parked on some residential side street, walked miles into the place, listened to music all day into the night, walked all the way out and bunked at Wally's parent's house. There was no running that day, and then no running the rest of the fall semester.

And then there was the marathon, of course. The summer after junior year, Harmon started running again, sometimes with Greg, sometimes alone. He read a little about running and thought he would run a marathon his senior year: the New York Marathon. He started running farther, bought a pair of sort-of running shoes at Shoe-town, the discount shoe place. They had no name, but they looked like running shoes, and the Converse basketball shoes did not.

He entered his first road race to see what it would be like, a 20-kilometer race in New Haven. Harmon didn't know how fast he might go, whether he would be faster or slower than the people around him. Whether he would be a natural—out front. He found out he was average, after all. Ran miles at 7:15 and then slowed to 7:30, then slower. Finished in 90 minutes. Bill Rodgers won. He ran 62 something. In the post-race interview with the local newspaper, the reporter said Rodgers would run again that afternoon.

As the days cooled, Harmon ran more—two or three hours each weekend day. But he never really figured out how to enter the marathon. He just acted like he was in. Acted like it so much, he got his sister Faith to drive to Staten Island to drop him off early one morning in October, and he ran the marathon. With no number. Wore his cotton shorts and tee shirt and bandanna headband through the streets of New York, watched the guys pee off the bridges, heard the cheers of the crowds, suffered in Central Park, chafed his nipples raw, till faint red lines ran down the front of his tee shirt. He ran right up to the finish line in 3:52, and ran into a cop. He was there to turn away bandits. Harmon pleaded a moment, said he'd run all that way, said the crowd was too thick to duck under the rope, said he should be allowed to cross the line. The cop pointed, and Harmon edged into the crowd 20 yards short of the line. The marathon was over. He took the D train up to his sister's apartment, ate a pint of Hagen Dazs and drove his VW back to school.

He had read that you are supposed to run the day after a marathon, so he ran three miles the next day. Then he didn't run again till spring.

Three years went by. He ran, he even raced sometimes, but he was not a runner.

One day he was in his thesis adviser's office talking running. The adviser ran and he asked Harmon how fast he was. Harmon said average. The adviser asked what his time was for a five-mile race. Harmon replied honestly, 36 minutes or so. The response was a mixture of incredulity and disgust no greater or less than if Harmon had announced that he had crapped in the professor's wastebasket. The professor changed the subject, something about Faulkner and long sentences.

And this running/not-running life chugged along to the day Harmon lay in bed thinking he was a runner. Of course, he was a runner. He had run for two and a half hours just two months or so ago, before his knee hurt, and he took time off. Like a runner would. He had run races, run a marathon, run the day after a marathon. Like a real runner.

* * *

Harmon looked over. Long brown hair was splashed across the other pillow. Paige lay next to him, turned toward the wall. He might have thought about how all this came to be: how this new woman was in his bed.

Six weeks ago, it would have been Lana. Who was Luscious Lana in college, curvy and far too good looking for Harmon's average looks. Who had had a summer fling with Harmon when they were both nineteen.

Fourth of July weekend, on the way to D.C. to visit Jim, Harmon stops at a rest stop to call Lana—just a friend, Lana—from his dorm last year. He casually invites her to come down to D.C. to party. And she says yes? They are so cool. They're friends. And the beer and wine flow and there's the reflecting pool, and Jim falls in chasing a frisbee. And there's a shopping cart in an alley and they're pushing each other and then she's staying over and they're sleeping on blankets on the floor and they're together, and he's falling. Falling. Falling like twice in a lifetime falling, right then. And it is great. And scary.

Back at college Lana had been part of Trip and Lana, the power couple of the dorm. Trip—Felton Wystan Martin III—preppie sophomore from somewhere outside of Cleveland. Trip, who had perfect dirty blond bangs and played lacrosse, who drove a used BMW, who danced ballroom and jazz, whirling the freshmen girls around. Trip, who would enter a room of partying guys and say things like, "Are you guys hallucinating right now? Do you see elephants; do you see space monkeys?" Drawing out the words for effect. Trip, the consummate douche. He had hooked up with Lana, the leader of the freshman pack, and they had dated practically all year. Then he refused any talk of certainty or commitment before heading off to Europe for the summer break with a tepid, "Have a nice summer."

Back to school, after a summer backpacking in France and Belgium, he had just assumed it would fall back into place. He was up for an excellent junior year with his excellent girlfriend. But Lana had choices. She had poor Harmon following her around with love in his eyes; she had cocksure Trip willing to pick it back up.

Like the girl who owned the world, Lana dropped Trip and scooped Harmon up and kept him that fall. Lana, who had essentially lived with sophomore Trip the previous year, then essentially lived with Harmon. Lana taught him college co-habitation—sex every night (including foreplay, and how she could finish on top after he was done), extra tooth brushes and clothes in each other's rooms, venturing down or up one floor to the bathroom—the logistics of serial monogamy that college girls had figured out. Lana was the kind of girl with all that vivacity, who ten years after they broke up would be the subject of a query from a sister or aunt. "Ever hear from Lana? I really liked her."

But they had stayed at it long after it flamed out as it does with 20 year-olds, and the sex was once a week or less, and the trespasses and missteps started to accrue. Old girlfriend Liza and crazy Phoebe (who slept with everybody and never came) right from their circle of friends. And Randy and then fucking Bill. Bill, who was Harmon's friend, supposedly best friend, but who followed Lana around like a sad dog. Bill, who took student teaching just because Lana did. Bill, who if he had a journal was surely writing "Bill and Lana belong together" over and over. With little hearts. Bill, who was always encouraging Harmon to break up with Lana and go out with . . . well, anybody else. Bill who moved to Washington after graduation, where . . . Lana had gotten a job.

They had carried it through graduation, Lana's job in Washington, and Harmon's grad school and then into the second year of grad school, by this point the relationship a ghost ship drifting along. They could remember the good things; they really liked, even loved each other, but the best things were gone. Just the same, Harmon couldn't let it go, stunned and gratified that someone so attractive and full of life had found him worthy, had turned her love light on him.

Then there was Paige. She had started grad school with Harmon. Probably the cutest woman of the first-years, standing outside of Professor Messier's mandatory research seminar during the break, bumming a rumpled cigarette, kicking at the gravel, full of existential ennui. She had gone to Smith, and she was not a natural beauty—too short, too pale, nose too big—but she had something, a languid standoffishness that fascinated the guys. Harmon was afraid to talk to her. She only dated second-years or older, like Mark Henny with the bedroom eyes, who recited "To His Coy Mistress" to all of his dates (conquests), or Ed Tait, who had been around for about 6 years and was finishing his dissertation or even Rich Rennerson, the philosophy major who would invite her to talks on Heidegger or Schopenhauer. She went to parties, all the department parties, with her long straight brown hair down, except for a red ribbon braided in a strand of hair on the left side.

And she was a darling of Professors, writing on the tragic sexuality of Heathcliff or disguise in Shakespeare's comedies. Then in the fall of second year, she was in Harmon's Joyce seminar. She wrote on the feminism of Molly Bloom, and of course Professor Ferry, with his tinted glasses and extra-long brown cigarettes, praised it and suggested she work it up for possible publication. Of course, she demurred. But she started talking to Harmon at the class break, and only Harmon. She laughed at his jokes, made word play of her own. Harmon borrowed records from her to put on cassette for his car. He asked her: "Got any Kinks?" Her eyes danced. "You'll have to find out for yourself." Before the fall term ended, something was happening.

She started showing up at his office cubicle in the tutoring lab with candy or a story about some hapless freshman's malapropism. Then she was there one night when Harmon was alone, working on a paper. Then they were making out and she took off her shirt and pressed her pink nipples against his chest, all cherries and cream, and they had sex right there in the English lab chair, her hair draped over him.

Harmon went home and his head was swimming. Then she showed up again and they did it again. The next week, she said, "I want this. I want us." When Harmon protested that Lana was coming to try out living with him the following week, what was he to do, she said, "That's your problem."

It was his problem. Lana was over. Paige, whom he hardly knew, was beginning. Then Lana moved to town (keeping the place in Bethesda), and he avoided her and then drove her out with indifference, back home. That day he ran for two and a half hours was not a triumph of athleticism. It was him avoiding spending time with her on a Sunday afternoon, while she went for a drive with his roommates Jim and Emily. Harmon was a coward.

Just before Thanksgiving when the fall term had ended, they had the talk. Lana was ready to go back home to stay, saying she had seen this coming before she moved. Harmon was sad, but they both knew the relationship had really been over for years.

Harmon considered that he might take it slow. But here was Paige in his house, in his bed. She wanted this.

He might have let all this wash over him as she lay there in his bed. Might have considered that this could be a huge mistake. It was. That he was connecting with a depressed, disagreeable, self-absorbed woman just to connect with someone. Just because here was someone who wanted him. But he was not that contemplative. He did wonder though. He wondered if she would have sex if he woke her. He stroked her shoulder.

The answer turned out to be no, one of many noes he would collect.

But he was also thinking about running, the running that was yesterday, the running that would be in the coming year. He had made a resolution for the coming year. He would run at least 300 days. He would cover at least 1,000 miles. He had a pocket date book to keep a log. He marked down the run for the 30th and thought he should run on the 31st as well to keep things going.

He was busy that day: went to Acme for groceries, to the beer distributor for a case of Stroh's, provisions for New Year's Eve. It was 4:00 and he hadn't run. The sky was grey-white and the first flakes of a snowstorm were trickling down. He put on his jockstrap and big grey cotton sweatpants and a grey hoodie, gloves and a hat. He laced up the Tiger Montreals over cotton tube socks. He eased down the hill, rather than the way he had gone yesterday, took a right under the bridge for the bypass toward Lewisburg, and then right on the narrow country road. He wasn't sure, but he had an idea this way would curl around and come out on the main road farther up. There was no traffic in the gathering gloom. The lane got narrower and went by farms. Harmon felt his breath grow heavy and short, could feel the sharpness, like a sore throat. He could taste salt in his throat.

The snow got heavier and made the world even quieter. His shoes made crunching sounds in the gathering snow as the miles clicked slowly by. With satisfaction and anticipation, he thought of running and the promise of the year to come. The error of his jumping into a relationship with Paige tickled his mind, but it was something he would consider down the road. Tonight was for celebration.

The lane turned left and left again, a big horse shoe. At about 50 minutes he came back out on the deserted main road, about a half mile from the house. He turned off the main road up into the little subdivision and into the driveway, past his Volkswagen and Jim and Emily's Datsun. Paige's big old Chevy was on the road in front of the house under a blanket of white.

Harmon had the feeling of something beginning. He had run yesterday. He had run today in the snow in the gathering dark. He would run tomorrow, even with a hangover. Next year would be a good running year, not like every other. If he could just stay true to his resolution. 300 days. 1,000 miles.

After six beers and a champagne toast, he slept till 10 and awoke with a fuzzy headache. Again, Paige lay next to him. Again, there was no sex to close out the old year or look forward to the new. Again, he got up and put on the jockstrap and sweat pants. Before breakfast he went out in bright sunshine and ran three and a half miles through the town and out to the highway on what would become the standard route. The shoulder of the roadway was slushy and the sunlight was blinding. It was day three, and his legs and wind already felt a little better. When he got back, Jim met him in the yard in front of the pile of pole length oak they had bought to heat the house. Jim and Harmon were comfortable with each other. They had gone to high school together, then different colleges, but the friendship had always been there. Jim had started a PhD program in the Anthropology department a year before Harmon went to grad school at the university. Harmon had followed in part because his friend went there. Harmon knew Emily well too. They had met in DC when she started dating Jim sophomore year of college. Now Jim and Emily were headed for marriage. The plan had been for Harmon and Lana to share a house with them, but the plan had changed.

Jim and Harmon looked at the pile that the delivery guy had dropped months earlier on the front lawn of the rental. Jim had the chainsaw and cut about six lengths. Harmon grabbed the maul and split wood for today and tomorrow. They brought the wood in through the garage to the wood stove in the finished basement and stoked the stove. Then they walked upstairs, turned on New Year's bowl games and finished that case of Strohs. Somewhere along the way, Paige drove back to her apartment near the University. Harmon had invited her to stay the night, but was relieved. He would sleep alone.

CHAPTER TWO

Every asshole who ever had a running streak knows that the first couple of months are the hardest. You have to develop a habit, a lifestyle of running, out of nothing. Then it will practically run itself. For a while.

Underground Runner's Guide

The New Year's resolution was in the front of Harmon's mind through January. He knew he could take days off, 65 days off, but he thought that would come later in the year. Those days were in the bank, to be guarded.

January fell into a rhythm once school started again. He taught at 8:00 a.m., driving the frigid VW Bus over the hills to school. 75 minutes of teaching English 20, the art of persuasive writing, then back home to run before his own classes. He ran the 3 1/2 mile loop so many times he felt like there should be a groove worn in the road. Rain, sleet, snow, and cold. Numbing cold. Jock strap, baggy cotton sweats, tube socks under the Asics. Tee shirt, hooded sweatshirt, ski hat, a pair of red knit mittens.

Paige hated the mittens, made fun of them. She pretty much hated everything: Jim and Emily to be sure, the wood stove, Harmon's bed—just a mattress on a homemade wooden platform. The house with the wood piled in front. She hated the food he ate—mostly pasta and homemade pizza from scratch—hated the beer he drank (Strohs: too lowbrow), the optimistic tone of his voice. As near as Harmon could tell, the only things she really liked were Mars bars and gay disco night downtown with her Italian friend Lucia with the crooked teeth. Lucia, who held her cigarette between the third and fourth fingers, rolled her r's and spoke even more languidly than Paige.

But running was good and getting better. Sometimes (often) running was a pleasant escape.

Then cold turned colder. He bought a blue windbreaker from the running store clearance rack for $15 and put it over the hoodie. And it worked until colder turned colder still. One Saturday, it was just bitter. He almost stayed in, but he had to split wood anyway, so he dressed as usual and did a shorter run—two miles. The breeze bit right through the sweats, right into his crotch. Later, at home, he curled up in pain. He made a wardrobe correction going forward in the cold, a pair of cotton gym shorts over the sweats for an added wind guard.

Still no days off, and spring was coming. He treated himself to a new pair of Asics and a six-pack of polyester tube socks from the Ames store on the highway. The cotton ones had distorted and discolored. He had read somewhere that you should alternate shoes, so he did, using the old and new. At the running store he found race entry sheets and he entered one, first week of April in Indiana, PA, a ninety-minute drive.

Running totals for the first three months of the year: 106, 98.5, 129.

CHAPTER THREE

Yes, Einstein, you will set all your pr's when you run every day. It's not magic; it's because you're running every day.

Underground Runner's Guide

That first race during the streak, the 90-minute drive to Indiana on a Saturday morning to run a 10k, almost didn't happen. It turned out that Paige didn't want Harmon to have running, to have this thing that he liked and did daily. She wanted him to skip this distraction, because. Because she wanted him to. They bargained. He would try to be more something . . . attentive or fawning, would buy her more Mars bars. She would come with him and sit in the park for the race. She seemed to fear that some runner girl would scoop him up, and the offer to attend mollified her.

It was sunny and about 50 degrees. The race started and ended in a local park. Paige sat on a bench in the sun away from the runners, looking bored. She had a John Barth novel at her knee. Harmon wanted to go over to her, wanted to talk and apologize again, wanted some peace.

The Race Director started talking through a megaphone about turns and course markings, and Harmon turned away. He grouped with about 200 runners, mostly guys, mostly young. A middle-schooler sang a screechy national anthem while runners waited, some bouncing, others flexing knees or jogging back and forth to stay loose.

Then a 5-second countdown, and they were off, winding through the park, then out into a neighborhood and to the edge of town, then back to the park. The course was marked with flour arrows on the pavement at the turns. Harmon had no trouble navigating as he followed a string of runners stretching out before him. The fastest guys, the skinny former cross-country runners, pulled away in a cluster of about 6. The rest of the field tried to keep up and about 20 formed a second group, the fit guys who were not whippets and two women.

Harmon was about 30 yards behind the second group trying futilely to keep contact. Just as he settled into a rhythm, they sped by a sign at the edge of the road that said "1 mile." A young woman was staring down at a stop watch reading times. Harmon could hear "6:31, 6:32 . . . 6:37, 6:38" and he passed the mile mark. He felt great and a little high. The race was moving fast, and his breath was in a three-step rhythm, all mouth breathing, three steps in, three steps out. His step cadence was high, the Montreals slapping the pavement audibly.

The second pack faded from view, and Harmon ran alone. Two miles in 13:25, and a water station. He gradually slowed for miles 3, 4 and 5, with another gulp of water at mile four. Two people passed him in that time and he passed no one. He seemed to be running in a little open area, not fast enough for the second pack, faster than the 7-minute milers. He hit mile 5 in 33:42. He was still cruising, but the pace was edging up. Three guys came by, and he started to feel the end coming. He latched on to these runners and raced for the finish, hair flying, throat burning with the increased effort.

He could hear a megaphone at the finish line. He poured on everything he had left. He couldn't swallow to ease his throat. Spittle stuck to his lower lip and chin. A trickle of snot came from his right nostril. He heard the timer shout 41:22, as he crossed the line and entered the chute. He was in the first long chute delineated by ropes with triangle flags like at a used car dealership. As he edged forward to be processed through the chute, he alternately shuffled forward and stopped and put hands on knees. Everyone was panting, some guys coughing with a dry hack. The first woman was about 8 places ahead.

A man at the end of the chute shouted out Harmon's number to a woman with a clipboard, told him he had finished in 36th place and dispatched Harmon out to the finish-line food and water. He got a cup of water, two orange quarters and a banana. A table had flavored Dannon. He passed. At another folding table was a trove of race entries for area races in the coming weekends. He dug in; he took one of each.

He turned and looked over at Paige's bench. She was reading, barely 150 feet from the finish line, oblivious to the action around her. He walked over. She looked up. "I want to go."

"We should stay for the awards, see who won."

"I want to go. Now."

They went.

Halfway home, with not-too-loud music in Harmon's VW bus so as not to annoy Paige, with barely any talk, Harmon's stomach started to clutch. Then it turned; then cramped. He folded up and kept on to home, where he curled up on the couch, knees to his chest. Now, Paige wanted to do something. Go for a walk. Drive into town for food or a beer. Something. Harmon wasn't going anywhere. Paige left.

Harmon was still down and out, but Jim and Emily came into the living room with Paige gone, and they talked and eventually drank a few beers and had pasta for dinner. Order was restored.

Later that evening, Harmon considered the day. On diet: he hadn't eaten anything before the race. He felt fine while running, but his stomach cramped hard on the orange and banana after the run. It had taken hours for his stomach to recover. On the run itself: Harmon was elated. He had felt light and quick, finishing strong. His time was a 6:40 mile average, better than he had ever done at any distance. And he felt he could get faster. On the personal side: it was a mistake to allow Paige to come along. It was a distraction for him and not pleasant for her. He was relieved when she left. On the future: Harmon was excited at the number of race entries he had gathered. It was going to be a busy spring and summer.

Sunday morning, Harmon had his first post-race streak run. He did the three-and-a-half-mile loop, slowly, through the center of the small village. He was never winded, babying his tight calves and hamstrings as he cruised along feeling like a hero. The run took 35 minutes. When Harmon returned home, Jim was out in the front yard cutting up the last of the oak. Harmon took the maul out of the garage and helped. He split the last few lengths, and they stacked the wood along the side of the foundation. The lawn looked pretty beat up, but it would recover. Maybe now the neighbors would stop giving them funny looks.

Harmon's shoulders and diaphragm felt sore from Saturday's effort. Swinging the maul had been tough. His balance seemed a little off as it arced up and over his head. He was glad the day's run was over.

Before the men walked inside, Paige's old Chevy pulled up, and the tension resumed. Jim and Paige argued over the Times crossword; Emily retired to her room. Harmon tried to make peace, making pasta and sauce for everyone for an early Sunday dinner. Paige complained, and they drove into town where she could get a burger while Harmon had a beer. Harmon didn't eat burgers, hadn't since undergrad days. The afternoon melted into night.

They stopped back at Paige's house in town. She shared housing with two other grad students: Myra, the unofficial den mother of the second-years, and Chris, a quiet, sincere woman who dated Nora, the frizzy-haired lesbian, who drove a town bus, dressed wild and had six earrings. Myra was home with her sometimes lover Sylvia, the bi-sexual heartbreaker. As far as Harmon could tell, Sylvia was simultaneously "seeing" Myra, Adam, another second-year, and Harmon's friend Jacob, who was a third-year and sometimes runner. She got away with it; she had boy-cut hair, wore tight black clothes and walked with a sashay that made men and women want to cry with lust. She operated in her own world because the world came to her. Over and over. Just now, Myra was waiting on her, trying to interest her in dinner.

They all parked in the living room, on the enormous ragged couch and the easy chair with the tapestry draped over as a cover to keep the stuffing from squeezing out. Beer was served—Paige's Heineken—and they drank, except for Myra, who said she was tired, but she rarely ever drank.

Harmon was tired and wanted to go home. He found his eye drawn to Sylvia; she drew eyes to her. He wanted to look away, to drive away. He wanted nothing to do with Sylvia. When they were in the kitchen to get chips, her hand brushed his. He ignored it.

His beer empty, Harmon left. Paige stayed, with Harmon's promise that he would bring her back out to his house to get her car after he taught in the morning. Her class was at 2:00.

And so life went. Harmon loved running, loved running every day. There was something to the rhythm that spoke to him. Spoke to him daily. But Harmon had woman problems. He just let the days flow by. He and Paige were an item in the English department. Men and women mentioned it to him. Myra took him aside.

"You know I love you, Harmon. I love Paige too. I would only want the best for each of you. Do you think Paige is the right person?"

"I don't know. We just sort of fell into this and we're seeing where it goes. We like each other."

"You should give it thought. Find the right person. It shouldn't just happen. You're a great guy."

"I get it. I understand."

"Do you?"

He didn't. But life went along anyway. He and Paige stayed together and explored sex in the way of 20 something couples. She didn't want to be licked, and she wasn't going down there. She did like to finish on top. Sometimes. She liked her nipples touched, caressed. Sometimes. Sometimes she just wanted to do it and finish it and go to sleep, and wanted Harmon to just be grateful that it happened and not try so hard and not ask questions. Harmon had more desire than she did, much more. He would be happy to do it every day, and he set out to please her. But he found she wanted less sex and less talk.

Two weeks after the first race of the year, he found himself at the starting line of another 10k. This one was on campus, sponsored by a fraternity for charity. Harmon was slightly hung over after a night of many beers with Jim. The race was crowded. Every undergrad who had ever run cross country seemed to be in the field. He saw no packs form, and though the race spread out as it traced the fields by the Ag college and the stadium, he was always in a stream of runners. As he crested the last hill, a lone trumpet player was repeating the theme from Rocky. Harmon hustled it home, though the race felt like one long semi-sprint in the big field. He finished in a wave of runners and his placement was well over 100. He was not happy, but the time was a little lower: 41:10. He stayed around the campus, had the banana and orange slice and a bagel, then tried to do some work in his cubicle in the basement of the English department building. He got disabling stomach cramps again. He bought a coke from the machine outside the office room. The big burp helped, but he had to go home to lie down.

* * *

Harmon needed to get faster. He had books by Sheehan and Fixx and he wanted to unlock the secret of increased speed. The answer was speed work, in addition to the everyday runs. There was a park near the center of town with a paved oval path in the middle, probably a little less than a quarter mile. Harmon started walking down there on Tuesday and Thursday evenings. Then he would run fast laps with one-minute walk breaks in between. He had no watch, except an old analogue Gruen that had been his grandfather's. The first day, he did 10 circuits. Paige was there and for the first few she ran across the middle to meet him in the backstretch and then again at the finish. Her long hair was flying, her cheeks pink. She was having fun. She looked great. After 4 or 5 laps, she tired and waited on a bench for Harmon to finish.

"How many are you doing?"

"Ten. Like, I said."

"How many is that?"

"Seven."

Sigh.

When they were done, they walked through the neighborhood home. It was a warm, clear spring evening. Life was nice enough.

Another two weeks and another 10k race, this one in Altoona. Paige did not attend. The field was smaller. The lead pack flew out of the start. Harmon tried to hang on to the second pack, but it eased ahead. He was next to a smallish runner with black hair and a green singlet with a shamrock on the front in black. The runner nodded; Harmon said, "Hey." They stayed together for about 3 miles. Then as Harmon tried to hang on, green runner steadily pulled away. At the finish, Harmon was in 26th, at 40:52. Green runner had barely cracked 40 minutes. Harmon wanted that. Bad. But he was almost a minute away.

Later, at home, Harmon on the couch, Jim asked about the race.

Harmon said, "It was good. Best yet. But this little fucker in green. I couldn't stay with him."

Jim laughed: "Little fucker? What, you hate him?"

"Nothing like that. Seems like a good guy. But I want to stay with him. Beat him."

In the next two weeks, he ran every day and did speed work on Tuesday and Thursday evenings. Paige stopped coming. Harmon wanted a sub-40. He just needed to go out fast and hold that speed. He knew he needed 6:27 a mile. He mapped mile times for his ideal sub-40 race: 5:55, 12:15, 18:40, 25:15, 31:45, 37:55, 39:20. It seemed so right on paper.

The next race was in a state park in the woods. There were about 150 runners. They parked by a lake. Got their numbers under a pavilion. The runners murmured about the course: a mile out a dirt road, a left turn across the wooden bridge and then up a killer hill. Killer. A solid half-mile long, relentless hill. From the two-mile mark, a few rollers, then gentle downhill almost all the way to the finish back at the lake. Harmon half paid attention. All he could think of was the sub-40 he had come for.

The race started, and the lead pack took off, but not as fast as expected. Harmon was in the second group, and it seemed too slow. He got in the gap between the groups. They wound down the dirt road. The volunteer at one-mile shouted 5:53 as Harmon went past. He felt a surge of power with this speed. He headed across the bridge, feet pounding on the wooden deck.

Then the hill. It was killer; it was relentless. Harmon leaned in and pushed on up, but the second pack came by, the little fucker in green with them. Harmon was already gassed, less than two miles in. His lungs burned as he panted. His legs were leaden. His shorts plastered against his legs and felt constricting. He folded the waistband to shorten them. His face burned; his hair prickled. Just past the top of the hill, the volunteer was yelling: "13:01, 02 . . . 13:10, 11." Harmon passed the mark, drenched in sweat, dizzy from the effort. He felt like walking, but he kept the running turnover as best he could and felt the breathing and speed coming back on the gradual downhill. The flow of passing runners stopped and he passed two or three. After hitting the three-mile mark in 20:10, he settled in and caught another two runners on a short uphill. There was nobody shouting time at the four-mile mark, but it didn't matter. Harmon was in a zone, feet fap-fapping the pavement on the steady downhill. Mile five in 32:40. He saw the little fucker in the same green singlet in the distance. He felt like he was gaining. Between them was one runner, a tall guy who was built like a football player. Must have been 6'5", broad shoulders and weightlifter's arms. Harmon was bearing down, but they both sped up. The last mile seemed to take a minute; there was no time to make up the gap. When Harmon first heard the finish line timer, he was shouting 39's. By the time he crossed the line, it was 40:13. He folded over in the chute gasping for air. There were quick handshakes with the little guy and the big guy and "good run" exchanged. The big guy said, "Man, that hill." Harmon could only say, "Yeah," between gasps for air.

It was over. That close. As he ate the orange quarters and the banana and drank a water, Harmon thought: "fourteen seconds."

Later that afternoon, Harmon again on the couch, Jim talking, "Yeah, I know that park. We had a dig out in that area first year. The department summer picnic is at that lake. How was the race?"

"The little fucker beat me again. And there was a really big guy just ahead of me. I couldn't catch either of them."

"A big guy? The big fucker?"

"Yeah. Big fucker. Really big fucker."

"So there's a little fucker and a big fucker and you can't beat either one? Did you beat anybody?"

"Yeah, I finished 22nd. I beat lots of people, just not those two fuckers."

"Are you happy?"

"No. I want to beat the two fuckers. And my stomach feels like I ate glass. Again."

"Take it easy. You're doing this for fun. I think you've gone pretty far down the rabbit hole."

"Did you even read Alice in Wonderland?"

"I saw the Disney movie. Hey, come help me adjust the valves on the Scout. I gotta get rid of that ticking sound."

"Sure."

Harmon felt better just being up and about and not thinking about the stomach. Paige came over late in the afternoon and they had a peaceful homemade pan pizza dinner with Strohs. They both had school work that evening and went to bed at 11:00, making sweet and soft love. Paige finished on top and then curled next to him, head on his shoulder, her hair splayed across his arm and the pillow. Everything felt right as he drifted to sleep. Maybe this could work?

The next two weeks, Harmon was finishing up a paper on justice and mercy in Book One of the Faerie Queene, completing his French translation for the language requirement and reviewing student papers. He ran every day with additional speed sessions on Tuesdays and Thursdays, but otherwise, he was not focused on the quest for sub-40. He also spent two evenings trying out for the department co-ed summer softball team, the Ablative Absolutes. He would start in center field.

Paige, for her part, was similarly busy. She had her own students and her own French translation. They were in the same class. She was also working on a paper on Thomas Hardy—something about Jude the Obscure. No doubt her prof would love it and suggest she work it up for publication.

They hardly saw each other and she spent only 4 nights at his house the whole time. They got along great. Sex was sublime, tensions were manageable. Paige even seemed to get along with Jim and Emily. Less exposure, less conflict.

With less Paige time and less Paige mood management, Harmon ran more. The morning run would cover 5 miles. The speed sessions were 12 fast laps at the park. He felt the extra miles, but he also felt stronger and faster.

Although the quarter was coming to an end and he was still busy, he drove to Centre Hall for a 10k on Saturday morning. It was cloudy and humid and the course was hilly. The big fucker and little fucker were there; they both beat him, as he rolled in with a 40:22. He had water and banana and a bagel at the finish and never got the cramps. Could post-race oranges be the problem? He was disappointed in the time, but distracted. He probably should have skipped this one.

He had to get right back to his cubicle after the race. His chest was tight from the frenzied breathing, but he was happy that the stomach was okay. From the vending machines outside the office, he ate a Snickers and washed it down with a Coke. He finished a draft of the Faerie Queene paper and walked to the computer lab to log in and type it. A little after midnight, he had 16 pages of printout, including endnotes and sources. He tore the pages and assembled the paper for submission. Tomorrow, he would have to finish correcting the final student papers and submit grades, but the quarter was basically over. He walked out into the spring night to the edge of the deserted campus to the VW bus and drove the 5 miles home.

A note on the counter said Paige had called. Three times. Harmon went to bed. In the morning he ran 5 miles, and she was at the house when he returned. She met him in the front yard.

"Where were you after the race yesterday?"

"I was at the office finishing the Spenser paper. I thought I would see you there."

"I tried to find you."

"Sorry. I was at the office. I had to finish the paper. It's due today."

"I was looking for you."

"You should have looked at the office. Then I was at the computer lab. Look, I have 12 more papers to correct, and then I have to turn in grades. Do you want to get dinner later?"

"Let's go out."

"I don't have any money. I'll eat something here; then we'll go out and you can get a burger and I'll have a beer. I'll come over to your house when I'm done with my work."

She turned to go, and he went in to shower.

And so it went. Harmon got A's; Paige got A's and accolades. Spring quarter ended, and there was a break before the summer session. Harmon would teach English 10 in the summer, the basic expository writing class, to students who were starting school early and were not great writers.

He would take no classes, but would commence work on his thesis. He was writing on humor in Vonnegut's novels. His thesis adviser was one of the younger faculty members, Cat Reilly. She made her own clothes, and she often looked like she was wearing repurposed drapes or tablecloths. Although Harmon had never had her in a course, she was the obvious choice because she was the only professor in the department who taught and cared about contemporary lit. She accepted as his adviser, and recommended he bury himself in the background work for the summer: reread all of Vonnegut's novels and take notes. Read all criticism of Vonnegut to find articles that touched on his humor style. Read seminal studies on humor and the nature of what we find humorous, starting with Bergson and Freud.

So, as the summer term unfolded, there was teaching, there was thesis, there was running, there was softball. Or running, softball, thesis, teaching. And Paige. And Paige's happiness. Which was no sure thing.

And so he found himself sitting in the back of the van on June 13th, taking off a long sleeve tee shirt, leaving the red cotton singlet, the blue cotton shorts, the Tiger Montreals. He was somewhere south of Williamsport, in a town park near a subdivision that snaked up toward the ridgeline to the south. The race was called the Up the Down Mountain 10k. Rain was pelting the van and it was about 60 degrees. Harmon stepped out and was immediately chilled. Puddles dotted the parking lot. He and about 75 hardy runners trudged up to the banner over the dirt driveway to the parking area, the start-finish line. The race director was giving final instructions. The course was marked with flour, but he was concerned it may be washed out. He would try to have volunteers at turns, but described the route in detail, just in case. There were many turns. He pointed to a huge puddle just after the start line. "We are going to walk up around that puddle and start on the other side. You will have to run through it to finish, but no sense starting off in a puddle. Okay, let's get going."

The runners walked up past the puddle and grouped together, bouncing and rubbing arms against the cool rain. Harmon had done no warm-up; he had just sat in the van to keep warm. In the driving rain, goose bumps broke out on his arms. His clothes soaked almost immediately. He rolled the waistband of his shorts to shorten them, so they wouldn't bind. The race official walked up to the line and shouted over the rain. "I will raise my arm. When I drop it, go. Be careful out there and let's have a good race." Almost immediately, he raised his arm, dropped it.

The first 100 yards were dirt and gravel. Powering down the driveway, Harmon and the other runners kicked up mud, till they turned right onto a paved road. The lead pack moved off, as always. There were maybe 6 or 8 guys. The second pack formed and Harmon stuck to it. The little fucker was in there. The green singlet danced in front of him about three strides. Harmon had no watch. There were no mile markers, no volunteers shouting time. There was the course and the runners around him. They ran parallel to the ridge line, climbing slowly, then turned left up a steep hill, then left again along the ridgeline, slight downhill. Another left and they plunged down a steep paved road. They stayed to the middle because a river was running down the gutter by the curb. Right turn at the bottom and then another right up a longer, steeper hill, and up along the ridge line even higher. Harmon was breathing hard, his arms swinging madly, trying to stay in this group. He never overheated; he barely warmed up, rain coming down harder, hair plastered to his forehead. Finally, they turned off the ridge and went hard back down toward the park. Harmon felt like he was flying, despite the rain, the sloshing of his feet on the pavement, the weight of his soaked shoes. The green singlet was just in front, maybe ten feet. And despite Harmon's pushing, charging, running for all he had, it pulled away as they approached the finish. He smashed through the puddle that was ankle deep on the dirt driveway and went under the banner as he heard "38:17." He came out of the chute and the volunteer in a rain poncho said, "14th place."

Harmon talked to no one. He got a banana and nothing else. He retreated to the van, put on a dry tee shirt and windbreaker. He emerged for the quick awards ceremony. He heard the winning time announced: 34:05. Harmon walked to the van, drove back to the house.

His mind was churning. He had just cracked the 40-minute barrier, really cracked it. But the course was about 100 feet short because of the race director's choice to avoid the puddle at the start. And that little guy in the green singlet. That guy was too fast always. For now.

Harmon got home and felt at peace with this race. He had sub-40 on a full course right in front of him. Next time. He ate some toast and peanut butter. He worked on the Sunday crossword with Jim. In the afternoon, when the rain stopped and the sun peeked out, he ran a slow two miles to air out his sore legs. This would become a habit. Paige was busy in town. Harmon and Jim drank some beer and hung out. Emily wanted to watch Friday the 13th on tv, and they had a nice night of old friends just hanging out together.

Harmon's class for the summer session started at 10:30. He got into the habit of running in the morning. At first, he felt slow and lethargic. Breathing was strained. Afternoon runs had been smoother, faster. But the schedule favored the morning, and he kept at it. Soon, it was get up, brush teeth, have a cup of coffee, run. Either the 3.5 or 5-mile course. By 9:30 he had his run in for the day. If he ran again, great. If he had speed work at the park, great. If he did neither, it didn't matter. It was literally another day of running in the books, or book, the appointment book that kept his miles and race times.

Harmon went back to the running store. The clothes were out of his price range, but he found a pair of last year's Nike racing flats in the bargain bin. They were so light and felt like slippers. They had no lugs, no hard rubber, just the spongy midsole material sculped into a few waves for supposed traction. They were $20; Harmon bought them.

The first softball game was on Tuesday. Paige came and watched. The rules specified 4 women on the field at all times and not more than 2 men in a row batting. The English department had an advantage, being blessed with a plethora of smoothly athletic lesbians. Jodie, the shortstop, looked and dressed like a twelve-year-old boy, but she played as well as any of the men. She fielded her position and hit line drives all over the field. Ed Tait, player coach and responsible for the team name, had her batting second and Harmon third. Harmon hit two homeruns with her on base, and the team won 9-4. After the game, Jodie chucked Harmon on the shoulder and said, "That second blast. I've never seen a softball hit that far." Harmon nodded thanks, and thought how comfortable it was to play a sport he knew. Years of little league, senior league, school teams, varsity, even college club ball had led him to this ease of proficiency, and he loved the explosive grace of the sport of baseball. It felt great to get a compliment from such a good player. But just the same, he was consumed with something he knew very little about; he was consumed with running. His next thought was of the missed speed session.

As he walked back to the VW, he thought about the missed workout, and he wondered—would it be better to do Wednesday and Friday this week, or just do one set of intervals on Thursday. In the end, he chose the latter. There was an 8k race on campus Saturday morning.

The 8k race was small: about 80 runners, including a very pregnant woman and a 30-something guy with a golden retriever. It started and finished at the fieldhouse, over by the lion statue. At the start the lead group of about 5 guys took off. Harmon hung on to the second group of about 10, wearing the Nikes for the first time. The little fucker was absent, but the big guy was there near the front of the second group. Just behind him was the guy with the dog trotting along off leash by his side. It was bright, and the morning was cool, but it was already heating up at the 9 am start. The race traced the outer access roads of the campus, mostly in direct sun. Harmon's goal was to run 6-minute miles for the 8k, which was just under 5 miles, so a little under a half hour. He passed one mile in 5:40, two in 11:40. The second pack started to fracture after three miles in 17:45. Harmon was feeling the speed coming off a little rise by the stadium just before mile four, and he carried that momentum past the guy with the dog and right up to the big fucker's heels. They turned right along the main road and crested a gentle rise up to the last right turn and the uphill finish.

The pace was cracking both of them. The big fucker's footfalls were slaps, his breath like a steam engine. For his part, Harmon was moving along in the Nikes, feet splayed out with every step, leaning forward with his last desperate surge. He passed the big fucker like two trucks on a hill, edging up and then by him. The finish loomed, and Harmon reached for one more gear. About 50 feet from the line, he knew the big guy would not come back. They were locked in place, Harmon to the left of and about two full strides ahead of him. Just then, from his left, Harmon saw the man with the dog fly by, the dog's tongue lolling in the rising heat, the man gliding smoothly. Then the finish. For the dog, 30:04, for Harmon 30:06, the big fucker 30:08. There was a short chute with a volunteer shouting out places to the runners. She pointed to Harmon. "11."

Back at the house, Jim talking: "So you lost to a dog."

"It was a fast dog. Really fast. Golden retriever."

"But, an actual dog?"

"Yes, Jim. The dog beat me. To be fair, it had twice as many legs. But I finally beat the big fucker. Took him on the last hill."

"And you beat the pregnant woman."

"Hey, she was fast. Really laid it down. If she weren't pregnant, I think she could have beat me. But she was pretty pregnant."

"Okay. I'm just giving you a hard time, Harmon. You seem to really like the running. Have you even skipped one day this year?"

"Nope. Almost half a year, every day."

"That's good. Really good. Hey. We need to talk about other stuff. You know I'm getting married on August 14th. I want you to be the best man.

We'll have a reception at Smith House on campus, and you can give a toast."

"Wow. Yeah, I would be honored. You don't want one of your brothers to do it?"

"No. Emily and I talked about it. You're my best friend. You should do the honors."

"That's really nice. You look like you're about to say something else too."

"Yeah. The other thing. We're not staying in the house for next year. We're going to move into an apartment. So, if you want to stay here, you'll have to figure out something else."

"I'm okay with that. I kinda want to move into town, anyway. I love it out here, but I should be close enough to ride my bike to the campus. So, it will be fine."

"Good. It's nothing to do with you. We'll be married."

"Something to do with Paige?"

"Nah, Emily isn't crazy about her. But it's no big deal. When we're married we should live by ourselves. Like married people."

Harmon paused. Jim had been his roommate through two years of boarding school. They had discovered and summarily memorized early Dylan together. Highway 61 Revisited had sat on their turntable for weeks sophomore year. They had gone to their first concert together—Jethro Tull. Had smoked their first joint together, had learned to drink together, trying scotch and bourbon, neat, to prove their manhood at 17. And now he was getting married, joining the adult herd. Harmon was nowhere near that and knew it. His relationship with Paige felt no more mature or advanced than what he had with his high school girlfriend, Jackie, who had told him what was cool, ordered him around, and literally spat in his face when he declined to follow her orders late one night at the ski house in Waitsfield.

Harmon put his hand on Jim's shoulder, for just a moment. "I think it's great. Really."

When Emily got home from her job at the art store, Harmon gave her a hug and said, "I'm proud to be the best man. I'm really happy for you guys. You definitely should get a place, just the two of you."

Jim wasn't done: "While we're talking, Harmon. I'm not sure how long we're staying around the university. There were 13 tenure-track positions open in Anthropology in the whole country last year. I don't see the point of spending three more years on a PhD for nothing. I can take a masters right now and move on when a decent job comes up."

"Woah, things are moving kind of fast. Weren't you the one who told me the value of a graduate education. You even said the education was an end in itself. That's been my mantra."

"Yeah, the education is good, but things change. You know my brother Stan trades bonds? He got a five-million-dollar bonus last year. Five fucking million. One year. I'm 26. I need to join the real world."

"I see it." (He didn't see it.) "And I am really happy for you." (Five million? Shit.)

And he was happy enough for them. Nobody needed the tension in the house. It was time for them to move on. Harmon would find a place in the vast student marketplace. It turned out to be an unfinished basement in the house he had lived in first year, a brick duplex right in town. He could live in the basement for $125 a month, plus a promise to do five hours of work each month for the new owner. He would move in when the lease was up on the house at the end of August.

But there were more races to run as the summer wound on.

July third, he was in Jersey Shore, a town along the west branch of the Susquehanna River, apparently named after cows along the shore. It was drizzling and cool. The race advertised itself as flat and fast. It had the best giveaways—a singlet of sheer nylon with mesh below, with the race logo over the left chest, and a pair of sheer polyester running shorts. Harmon would wear them for every race of the year after that day. He talked to no one, as usual. He ran a little to warm up and went to the start under a big banner. There were about 300 runners.

The race started on a short downhill, and the crowd started to divide. As always, the front pack zoomed off. Harmon stuck to the second pack of about 12 runners. The drizzle was steady and cooling. The pace was hot: 5:25, 11:20, a turnaround on the wide road, and then halfway in 17:45. Harmon was right at his red line, tucked in and flying back to the finish, the little fucker right at his side. When he got back into town, past 5 miles, the course turned right, then left parallel to the start and a block past it. Then left again, and a steep uphill. Harmon, who was in the thick the whole time, faltered. The hill killed his pace, and he was slogging along by the top. The pack with the little fucker deserted him when he died on the hill. Then a left turn and steep down to the banner. He heard the call: 38:14. A personal best, but it could have been so much better. As he stood in the chute, hands on knees, gasping, he thought, "Who was the evil bastard who laid out this course? What the hell?"

He stayed for the awards. The winner ran a 32:20. He had finished 28th. The course was fast, but the hill was killer for Harmon. He knew it was a good sub-40 on a full measured course. But he felt it could have been so much better, felt he had a 37 flat in him that day. But no. And he would never run a faster 10k.

He drove back home, head swirling with success and failure.

The summer wound on. The softball team charged to the playoff finals where they lost. Harmon read Vonnegut and practiced then delivered a short, mumbled best-man speech. But mostly he ran and raced. East to Williamsport, Montoursville, Milton. West to Tyrone, Butler, Shanksville. All 10k's, all over 38:30 and under 40:00. He beat the big fucker every time he showed up; he could never catch the little guy.

Harmon was covering more miles. He had run just over 900 miles in the first half of the year, but during the summer, he grabbed a race entry for a marathon in October and decided he would try to qualify for Boston. The Boston Marathon was by far the most famous in the country and it required a qualifying time of 2:50 for open male runners, just about 6:30 a mile. On paper, that seemed doable. Harmon was running 10k's at about 6:10 – 6:15 a mile, and he felt like he had more to give.

They cleaned up the house and moved out. Paige stayed with her same roommates. Jim and Emily moved to an apartment off the main road beyond the stadium. Harmon moved into his basement in town. He hung tapestries from the exposed floor joists to close off his area from the furnace and the rest of the basement. He moved his platform bed and small dresser in, and he was satisfied. He envisioned a monastic existence as he wrote his master's thesis and trained for the marathon.

But first a start of school party at Paige's house. Everybody showed, even Jim and Emily for a while. The whole softball team was there. The music was rocking, and women were dancing with women, Paige with Lucia. Myra was playing hostess, cleaning up empties and serving chips and dip. Sylvia was alternately close-talking with her and then sliding into another room to talk to Jacob, who was nursing a beer and talking to Cecil Duwalter, Harmon's cubicle-mate in the grad student office. Jacob was a wiry 5'8" with balding blond hair. Cecil stood 6'2", hunched a little with light brown hair and halting speech laced with a North Carolina drawl. He was quiet and sincere, and he and Harmon had no problem sharing space in their cubicle.

Harmon walked out the slider to the back patio that was deserted in the warm late summer night. He stood holding his beer and just letting his mind wander. Then Sylvia was there.

"Nice night." She touched his shoulder; she was a toucher.

"Yeah. Beautiful." He always felt on his guard with her. Never sure what she would say or what she meant.

"Ready for another school year? Another crop of earnest freshmen. More classes with cynical profs."

"Less course work for me. I'm writing my thesis this year. It could be my last here."

"You're not planning to become part of the furniture like Ed?"

"Nah. I'm thinking of going to law school. Someday I might need a real job." (Where did that come from?)

She was right next to him. He could hear, could feel her breath on his neck. Then she turned smoothly and kissed him, her tongue pushing in, searching. He didn't push her away; he didn't pull her in.

She backed up maybe six inches. "Don't worry. Your girlfriend is dancing with the Italian chick." She raised her brows conspiratorially. "Myra's playing hostess. We're alone."

"And Jacob?"

"You think I'm going out with everybody. He's talking to Cecil."

She moved in close again. Kissed him wet and slow, tasted of beer. Harmon kissed back, thinking, "This is a mistake. This is a huge mistake." She brushed a hand across the front of his jeans, subtle but deliberate.

"We should get together sometime. That would be nice."

"I don't know Sylvia. That seems dubious."

"Harmon. You're nice. You and Paige are such a bummer couple. Why are you even with her? You are someone who likes life. She's the kind of person who's happy when she's unhappy. You should have some fun. Life is not a hair shirt."

She kissed him again. Placed her hand there and held it. Felt him growing. Her eyes danced. "I like you. I'm getting the feeling you like me." Suddenly, it was so warm on the patio.

Then she was gone. Harmon was on the patio alone, looking at the half moon, body tingling, head swimming, an empty beer in his hand.

He stayed over at Paige's. The next morning, their sex woke the household.

Half an hour later, they were drinking coffee at the kitchen table. Sylvia walked in and headed toward the refrigerator behind Paige's back. She smirked at Harmon and gave him an exaggerated wink. He tried to ignore her. Didn't Paige notice any of her come-ons? "Wow. Great morning, huh?" she purred.

As soon as he could extricate himself, Harmon walked the half mile home to run. He went 18 miles through the backroads and corn fields in 2:15 and felt good, no great, the sun weaker this time of year and the light breeze gently cooling. He felt so ready for the marathon, still a month away. He would wear the Nikes. He would run a steady pace 6:30 or a bit less.

The whole time he ran, and later as he lay on his bed, Sylvia intruded on his thoughts. She was so sexual, such a tease. She was also provocative, blunt. "Why are you even with her? She's the kind of person who's happy when she's unhappy." Why was he with her? Still with her and she with him in a chronic miasma of recriminations, anger and depression. Why could he not let this relationship go, not let any relationship go? Why could he not just fly away?

* * *

This part was planned, but still not easy. Dad and Faith, his oldest sister, dropped him off. They helped him make his bed, put away clothes. New clothes: jackets and ties and shiny shoes like he had never worn before, clothes that he would have to wear now, as if this day he was joining the adult world. They set up the blotter on his desk and the tensor lamp. It was still early afternoon. His roommate was on his own bed across the room, tall, skinny, shock of blond hair, Matt or Mike or something. He had already forgotten.

Then Dad said it was time for them to go, for them to leave him there, in that room that was not his room, with this other person, whom he did not know. And where was his mother? No one would say. She was gone this last week, or was it two? Just gone, and Faith or Hope taking care of him in the days leading up to school. It was all wrong. He put his face in his pillow and cried and cried. He was 11.

And each day unfolded and passed. He learned to tie a tie, wear a sport jacket. He had no defenses. He just tried to get along, get people to like him. Talking to his roommate, a skinny blond, Mike Ronan. Mike, from Greenwich, where apparently everyone lived in a mansion. Mike on his third boarding school, so worldly, compared to Harmon. Mike: "Yeah, Ronan's Irish, but my dad says not dirt-farmer Irish. We were the people who owned the land and rented to the farmers. The rich Irish. Willow. That's English, right?" Harmon: "Well, my dad says it's really Italian. His dad came from Italy. When he got here, he said his name was Guglielmo Villano. The customs agent said that wouldn't do, now that he was coming to America. Gave him a proper American name, Will Willow. Then he married an English girl, Harmony Parrish. She died having my father, so my Grandpa named him Harmon. That's where I got my name." "So, you're named after your grandma?" "I guess so. My dad, too."

About a week later, Davey Wilson, one of the popular kids on the football team, and Jeff Salisbury, a tall thin soccer player, blocking a deserted hallway as Harmon comes by. Jeff: "Hey Gi-woppy." Davey: "Yeah, Gi-woppy." Harmon: "What?" Jeff again: "You're Italian. You're a Guinea, and a Wop. And you're named after your grandma. Pussy. We're going to call you Gi-woppy." Davey: "Yeah." He chucks Harmon hard with his open hand on Harmon's shoulder, causing him to flinch, but not make a sound. Mr. Nevins, the math teacher walking around the corner just then and the boys melting away. "Everything okay, Harmon?" "Yes, sir."

Another week later, after three more confrontations, harder hitting on the arms and shoulders. Harmon on the football field for a scrimmage. He's on defense, a linebacker. Davey a running back. Davey taking a handoff and hitting the hole just to Harmon's left as Harmon slides past the defensive tackle, slips the guard's block and wraps him up. Harmon planting his helmet right between the two and the three on Davey's chest and driving him back, legs churning. And it's a momentum standoff for a split second and then Davy giving way and Harmon pinning the crown of his helmet on Davey's sternum and driving him into the ground. Hearing the satisfying, long "ooof" of escaping air as he knocks the wind out of Davey when Harmon's full weight comes down on him. Harmon up and walking slowly back to the defensive huddle, never looking back. Ignoring his own feeling of electricity running from his neck down his arms after the hit. No one saying a word on his side of the ball. The offensive players gathering around Davey convulsively gasping on the ground. Then, minutes later, Davey up and walking over to Harmon's back: "What the fuck!" Rising intensity of voice. Almost crying. Harmon never turning, never looking at Davey. Coach Stanton: "Hey, hey. None of that language in my practice, Wilson. Nice hit Willow. Why don't you save it for the Rumson game on Wednesday. That guy's your teammate." Harmon not wanting to save it; wanting to do it again right now. Maybe harder this time, till Davey stays down.

Then another week later, the letter comes from his sister, Hope, the middle child, who had just started college in Boston. First, out of the envelope falls a water-paint and ink sun, heavy orange face with jowly cheeks, like the most depressing sunset. And then the letter: "You might not understand this. Mom moved to Philadelphia. She and Dad got divorced. She married Darren. They live there now. I love you. Don't worry. It will all be okay."

He didn't understand. Darren? The guy who used to be her high school student? The dorky one who played the accordion? Who just got out of college? Married him?

He might not understand. Might not understand.

It was not okay. It was definitely not okay.

He was on his own. He would have to rely on himself.

Mom was 38. Darren was 21.

Harmon was 11. Alone.

Eleven, it turns out, is not too young to learn things. When they tease, never show emotion. When they hit, never make a sound. Never give anyone the satisfaction of seeing your pain. The playing fields are your equalizer. And never, never ever, share anything about yourself. To anyone. Never let them in. Because you can never trust them. He might make friends later, but at eleven, these were the rules.

By the end of the month, Dad was there on Saturday afternoons, even though Harmon was not yet allowed to go home on weekends. He would get in the car and Dad would drive onto the dirt roads around Salisbury or Millerton. They would drive up into the hills, find new connections, always on dirt roads through fields high with corn, through woods, road dust on the lower leaves. Few words were spoken. Dad never said what Harmon thought—that this was a huge mistake, and that Dad, this great lawyer who could represent clients in trials in courts, could and would save him, would undo this injustice, would bring him home. Dad drove the dirt roads. They found connections. Few words were spoken. Harmon would get out of the car in the dying light and mumble a goodbye, never turning back to let Dad see the tears in his eyes as he strode up to the school building.

Thanksgiving came. He had not seen his mother since August. They had talked on the phone. She had cried; he had not. He was done with that. She arranged for him to take a bus—alone—to Port Authority in New York, and from there take another bus—alone—to Philadelphia where she would pick him up at the bus station and take him to her apartment. Where she lived with Darren. He was in dental school. Hope and Faith came to the apartment.

Mom said it was a little game. Hope and Faith were to pretend that she was their older sister. After all, she wasn't that much older, was she? Especially when friends were over. Sisters, because Darren had just turned 22. Hope left, just left. It seemed like Faith cried all weekend. It was just a little game. These were Mom's sisters, Harmon's young aunts?

On Sunday, Harmon would take a bus back to New York and another bus upstate to where the school would pick him up. Mom bought him a ticket all the way through, a three-layer piece of paper with destinations on it. The driver ripped off the top piece in Philadelphia, leaving the second piece and the base receipt. In New York, he didn't know how to find his bus. He stood in the middle of the bustling terminal, everybody seeming to know where they were headed. Out of the crowd came a boy just a year or two older than Harmon, brown skin, short hair, tee shirt under a ratty jacket. "You lost?"

"Just trying to find the bus that goes to Millerton."

"Let me see that." He snatched the ticket from Harmon's hand, looked at the big board. "It's upstairs. Follow me."

Harmon followed. They emerged on another level with more numbered gates. "Right there. 38."

"Thank you."

"How much money you got?"

"Umm, six dollars."

"Shit. All you got is six bucks? Give it to me."

"But that's all I got."

"Give it to me."

Harmon pulled a five and a one out of his right pants pocket. The boy grabbed it and was gone. Harmon walked over to the gate, handed the ticket to the driver, who tore off the page, hardly looking, gave back the receipt. Harmon climbed on the bus with his small plaid cloth suitcase. He added another lesson to his learning: never look lost, never get lost, never ask for help, never let anyone help.

He was almost twelve.

CHAPTER FOUR

You may think running every day and having a little success confers some level of wisdom on you. In truth, you know nothing. Either stay humble, or this sport will humble you, buddy. You feel like you're one step away from breakthrough success. You're a half-step away from crushing failure.

Underground Runner's Guide

Harmon was consumed with the marathon. He ran long and researched what he could at the library. The key was to be smooth and steady for the entire 26.2 miles. The whole year of speed and racing and now long runs was building up to this.

But first one more time trial. He put the magic Nikes on for a 5 miler in a steady September rain in Juniata. About 90 runners took off from a parking lot in a town park down a gravel path and then around town. Bits of mud were flying from the runners' heels as they sped out at the start. Harmon was flying. Everything felt right and the times were just like on paper: 5:25, 11:25, 17:25, 23:40, and then Harmon accelerated, running away from the second pack and the big guy to a 29:35. He got to the end of the chute and the official said, "nine." He had cracked the top ten, had run what felt like the perfect race. After watching awards, he walked back to the car, wiped flecks of mud from his legs and clothes and hair. Talked to no one. Toweled off and drove home.

A perfect 5 miles. The marathon was going to be great.

Two weeks after the perfect five-miler, Harmon stepped off a school bus at a business park in a small city about two hours north. He and Paige had driven up the night before and stayed over. She was waiting by the finish. He had had toast and coffee for breakfast because he'd read somewhere that Rodgers ate that before a marathon.

He had the Nikes on. He had the nylon singlet and polyester shorts. It was 7:30 and about 60 degrees; the forecast was for a high of 75. His running streak was 277 days.

He sat on the lawn under some trees in front of a squat brick office building. He stretched half-heartedly, as he observed other runners jogging, doing strides, leaning against trees to loosen their Achilles tendons. His prep was mostly in his head: steady pace, 6:30 per mile or a little less, smooth and even from start to finish. The effort would increase but the pace would stay steady. He visualized crossing the finish line in 2:48.

Another school bus stopped off to his left and disgorged runners. He saw the big fucker step off. Harmon looked down and continued his preparation. A minute later, a shadow passed in front of him and he looked up. It was him.

"Hey man."

Harmon replied. "Hey."

"I've been seeing you at races all over this year, but I didn't think you would be up here."

"Yeah, a long way to drive for a race."

"I would say the rules are different for a marathon. Hey, I'm Tom, by the way." He offered his hand.

Harmon stood and shook hands. "Harmon. Are you at the University?"

"Harmon. Cool name. Yeah, I'm studying kinesiology. You could say all the running is in my field."

"I'm in the English department. Running is definitely not in my field."

He laughed. "So, any plans for today. Other than kicking my butt?"

"No. I think I'll just go out and see how I feel," Harmon lied. "No real goal," (except that Boston qualifier and 2:48).

"Me too. Could be a little warm later. Well, good luck, man. See you around."

They shook again, and he walked away. A few minutes later, Harmon was lining up near the front of a group of about 300 runners. The big fucker—Tom—was about 20 feet farther back, his head above the crowd.

After some megaphone instructions, a recorded national anthem played. Then there was an actual starting gun and they were off.

Harmon felt perfect. The Nikes had no weight; the morning shadows kept him cool. He strode quietly, with ease. He had bought a new Timex digital watch for the occasion, and it told him the miles were right on. First mile in 6:20, easy. Five miles in 32:28. Ten miles in 1:05 flat. He felt so good; he tightened it up a notch. Half marathon, still cruising: 124:20. As the miles continued in the teens, the effort rose. The day was warmer, the course sun-drenched. Heat rose from the pavement. The breeze ebbed to nothing.

By mile sixteen, it started to degrade. His stride shortened and his feet slapped the pavement. He stopped at the 18 mile water stop and drank a full cup, poured another over his head. He continued, slower yet; people started to pass. He passed no one. At 20 miles, he looked at the watch: 2:18. He had blown up and given up all the morning's good running.

He ventured on at a jog. Walked. Jogged again. It felt like the whole race was passing him. At 21, the big fucker glided by looking smooth. "Hey," he said. Harmon grunted and tried to fall in behind, but lost him within the minute.

A car drove up: a race official. "Are you okay? You look very hot." Harmon waved him away.

"I'm okay."

He continued with a mix of walk and jog, beaten down, just trying to finish. Finally, he was in the last quarter mile, and he picked up the pace. He ran across the line in 3:20:40. He bowed his head. A half hour: he had missed the goal by a half hour—even a little more.

He drank water, ate a banana, orange slice, yoghurt. Drank more water. He walked to the van, dejected. Paige was there reading a book. She barely noticed. "Can we go, now?

"Yeah. Let's go."

The next day, he was wrecked. His quads throbbed with his heartbeat; he could not walk down stairs. His feet were blistered and felt like they had been split apart. But he ran. He laced up the Montreals and went 3 miles in 30 easy minutes. By the end, he felt better. He felt like he needed to be better; he decided that he wouldn't use the 65 rest days he had planned. It was October and he would just carry the daily running to the end of the year. And he did, racing three more times and then just getting back to easy daily running, no races, no speedwork for the winter.

CHAPTER FIVE

So you've run every day for a year. You think that's so great. It's just the beginning. Think of walking the stairs in a skyscraper. You are on the first landing. It's not nothing, but it's a long way from the top.

Underground Runner's Guide

The end of the year, Harmon was on the phone with his sister, Hope. She lived in a small shoreline town near the Cape. She was a runner. His running streak was 367 days.

"You ran every day of the year? Like every day?"

"Yeah. Every day."

"Is this a thing you are trying to do, like a thousand days in a row or something?"

"Maybe 10,000 days in a row."

"Seriously?"

"No. I made that up. I don't even know how long that is." (He did; he had just done the math that day.)

"So, you're going to run every day next year too?"

"I don't know. I ran today. I plan to run tomorrow and into the future. That's as far as I know."

"Do you really think it's good for you to do that every single day with no days off?"

"Yeah. I really do. That way, it's easy. Either I'm in it, or I'm not in it. Right now, I'm in it. And I've run faster and gone farther than any other year."

"How far?"

"2,141 miles. By far my best year."

"Be careful, honey. Don't hurt yourself."

"Honestly, I think this is the best thing for me."

"Do you ever wonder why you're doing this? What's making you run every day?"

"No. No wondering. Just doing. Run every day, like brushing teeth."

Harmon wasn't completely honest, even with his sister. He wanted 1,000 days. He wanted 10,000. He knew that was about twenty-seven and a half years. He still had no idea where this was going, but he wanted to run every day through the rest of his twenties, his thirties, his forties and into his fifties. That part was all laid out in front of him. He would run farther and better, get faster and reach some level of mastery of the 10k race.

Maybe not the marathon. That stood out as a failure in a good year. He was not in a hurry to run another. Maybe two marathons would be enough.

He went down the open basement stairs to his room. The furnace hummed in the corner. He lay looking up at the joists, listened to the winter creaks and cracks of the old house.

He loved Hope, thought that she understood him at least a little. Her opinions were important to him. "Do you ever wonder why you're doing this?" He wondered. He wondered what made him want to run every day on into forever.

* * *

Dad was the man and Harmon knew it from the beginning. Not always there, but always the man. The boozy breath whispering nonsense in his three-year-old ear. "Cuppity, cuppity, cuppity." The bearlike frame and big hand dwarfing Harmon's as they walked together. The booming voice in public places making people turn. He was the only lawyer in their little town. Whenever Harmon was with him, Dad was greeted warmly by people. And he always knew what to say. He told jokes and people laughed. He could sing, and people would applaud. He had worked his way through college as a singing waiter. He still had the voice.

Harmon as a little boy watching Dad shave before going to court. Harmon with a green plastic army man, holding the body in his hand, pretending that the rectangular base was a razor. Lathering soap on his cheeks and shaving it off. Like Dad.

He wasn't always there, but he was the man in every situation. And he was usually there to see Harmon play baseball. Harmon would look in from center field and there was Dad in the stands. He would put his big arm over Harmon's shoulders and walk him to the bus, talking about the game, showing that he had watched every play, every pitch. "If you choke up a little, you can get good wood on the inside pitch. Like the one you grounded to second." That time up at Huddleston Academy, when Harmon hit a double to right-center and then came up and hit another one to straightaway center when they shifted. Walking back, he patted Harmon on the back. "Those were two good shots. Hit 'em where they ain't." That booming laugh.

That long afternoon at the father-son golf tournament when he was 15. Harmon so hopeful that Dad would be proud, not disappointed. Playing well as a best-ball team till the sixth hole, an uphill par three. Lying 2, Harmon leaning over a putt on a fast green, about 18 inches and above the hole. Striking it weakly and watching it curve and slide past the hole, now 4 feet away on the low side. Dad striding up and striking it with authority right up and past the hole, back 18 inches on the high side. Harmon nursing it again and sliding it 3 feet past. Dad hitting it in and laughing that laugh. Touching Harmon's shoulder as they walked to the cart. "Well, the boys won't think I brought in a ringer." They finished third, despite that 6. Won a sleeve of Titleists. At the end, Harmon was overcome, having held it in the whole afternoon. Wanting so much to play well at a game his father loved, but he hardly knew. He just couldn't go in and eat a sandwich at the buffet, couldn't hang with the other boys he didn't know; he had to walk out of there and all the way home 3 miles along crappy County Road, declining two rides along the way. "No thanks. I just feel like walking." And he did.

Dad, who married Rita, his legal secretary, after Mom left. Everyone, maybe even Harmon, knew he was dating Rita, before Mom took off. In the end, it was okay, better than okay. Rita was nice, and although he was in the way and not really part of anyone's plan, she reached out to him and made sure he was part of the family. Loved him like a son. Wouldn't use the word step-. Cooked the best Italian food he loved. Rita had a daughter, Deana, two years younger than Harmon. She loved him too and looked up to him. Harmon wasn't always there; he was at boarding school. But when he was home, now Dad was there, and that same miserable ranch house had become a happy home. As long as it lasted.

* * *

There was a hum in the room, almost like a party atmosphere. Small talk was everywhere, people in twos and threes, people sitting and standing, but no laughter. Harmon wanted to be back at school, wanted so bad to be back at school. He had a baseball game today. He should be starting in left field against Milford. Dad was in the front of the room, in a snappy dark grey suit. Looking like a lawyer, well-dressed and serious, a little paunchy, ursine, long straight nose, full head of salt-and-pepper hair. Harmon headed for his father. Slowly. About ten feet away, he was intercepted by Auntie Carol. "You have to help your step-mother. She's not doing well."

Harmon became aware of a deep moan from his left, almost a growl. It rose to an inarticulate wail. Rita was trying to say something. He kept his course for the front of the room and there was his father. In a casket. And people were all around, speaking in hushed tones. "Harmon is here," and, "I'm so sorry for your loss," "So young." The air in the room was thick and hot. He could barely breathe.

Then Rita was talking, addressing a tall man who was approaching: "Doc, make him get up." Pleading, her voice broken and slurred like someone very drunk or stoned. "Doc, make him get up." Imploring. "Doc! Doc! Make him get up!" Just screaming. Wailing. Uncle Dave held her and sat her down again. She slumped.

To Harmon, it was pointless. He wasn't getting up. He was dead in a casket. Tomorrow they would bury him in the ground. Forever. Dad should be 48; he was 48. Harmon was 17. And he was so sick of people saying how sorry they were. How could they know?

* * *

He knew why he did it, but it was no one's business. When people asked, he would shrug his shoulders. He would run forever and live forever. Not be Dad.

So he ran through another winter, even as he slogged through the master's thesis, and Cat Reilly crushed every bit of fun out of Vonnegut. By the end, Harmon concluded that what he had thought was funny must be something else: tepid irony, simple metaphor, amateur philosophy. The study of the very premise of humor, followed by the painstaking rehash of the Vonnegut canon, left him with a level of appreciation of the subject and an acceptance of all the hours he had put into it, but he wasn't laughing anymore. He couldn't remember if he ever had been.

As Harmon was logging miles in a second date book, he was thinking about the future. Bill Dieter, the sweet hitting third baseman/outfielder from the softball team, finished his dissertation on restoration drama. He was stonewalled in his job search, finally getting an offer to teach technical writing in Idaho. It seems no one was looking to hire a guy who had read and catalogued seven hundred 17th century British plays.

Witnessing Bill's struggle and aware of his own dismal prospects in the coming years, Harmon applied to law school at his home state's university. He had been accepted out of undergrad before he elected to go to grad school. He was accepted again, to start in the fall.

In March, at the end of the winter quarter, Jim and Emily left town, headed for Florida and a career-type job for Jim. All of a sudden, Harmon only had running, the English department and Paige, and it was winding down.

Into all this he sprinkled the occasional spring race. In April, he was down in Amish country for a half marathon. He remembered the smooth first half he had run in October and thought he could do thirteen miles at a 6:30 pace. He was reminded again that it was easier to plan than to execute. Nobody he recognized was in the big field though he ran in a crowd the whole way. He did a steady first ten in 1:04:50 through the gently rolling hills with the big barns and Amish families standing by the side of the roads, then lost it a little to finish in 1:26:05. He was 91st out of 750 runners. He thought again how hard the longer races were.

Then he had a chance to go back to the 10k at the lake with the big hill. Now that he knew the course and the hill, he was confident that he could go sub-40. He tried to push from the start, easing into the second pack and trying to push the pace. But something held him back. He hit the first mile in 6:15 and then slowed as expected for the hill. Despite another strong recovery, he crossed the line in 40:22, slower than the previous year and disappointing. He had waited a year to beat the course and ended up with nothing.

He decided to stop racing until he finished the spring quarter and got all of the final classwork and the thesis off his plate.

As the spring quarter wore on, there was Paige. Their relationship fell into a pattern. They spent nights together. But not every night. They had good sex about once a week, always, always initiated by Harmon. Paige railed against her stupid students, ridiculing their earnest optimism. Even as Harmon felt he had become a good teacher, Paige resisted teaching at all. Similarly, she hated her own teachers, lampooning their silly pedantry and ego, even as they were surely fawning over her.

Then the end came. The thesis was finalized and accepted. Grades were in. Harmon had had a short article accepted by the Hemingway Review. He was elated, but it was time to take his master's degree back to New England for summer work and then law school. He was in a college bar sitting across a pocked wooden table from Paige. She was crying.

"So you think we should break up?" (Was he hoping?)

Face down toward the table, head shaking.

"You think we shouldn't break up?"

Hesitant nod.

"Okay." (Oh, man.)

They didn't break up. They talked on the phone. She visited him near the end of the summer. They talked on the phone some more. Through the distance, they got along well.

Harmon ran every morning before carpentry work, sometimes again in the evening, longer on the weekends, with the occasional 5-miler or 10k on Sunday mornings. He ran the fourth of July 5-mile race in Hope's small town: 32:30. He ran the Colchester 10k and stalked and ran down a guy who had been ahead of him all race, only to find he was about 40, with a pot belly: 40:32. Lackluster.

Then he took his running streak of 612 days to law school, where the people were more ambitious and successful and less intellectual than in grad school. His grad school friends could weave beautiful tales of the ways life had slighted and cheated them. Law school students had connections, scored great seats, got the best deals. And while the classwork beat him down—torts, contracts and civil procedure taking the place of Milton, Joyce and Melville—he would run every morning and most nights to clear his head and be ready to do it all over again the next day.

Paige visited him in November. His housemates (three males) thought her pretty, ethereal and distant. (She was.) They saw each other over the holidays, then were going to spend months apart over the winter. Harmon completed year two of the streak and started on the third year.

Law students started hooking up, but not Harmon. He went to all the parties, danced at two-for-one night at the Oakwood Café, studied with guys and women. But everyone knew he had a girlfriend in grad school.

One Sunday just before finals in May, Harmon ran a hungover 10k in Hartford, cracking 40 minutes for the first time of the year. He was feeling good when he called Paige's house that evening. Myra answered and said Paige was not home. Harmon was ready to just leave a message, when Myra said, "Harmon, maybe you and Paige are not really right for each other." Pause. "Maybe she's not a very good person."

It was Harmon's turn to pause. "Is she going out with someone else or something?"

Long pause. "You need to talk to her."

She called later that night. No, she didn't want to break up. Yes, she was seeing someone. It just sort of happened. No, she wasn't planning on telling him. No, it wasn't really serious. It doesn't matter who it was. It doesn't matter. You don't really want to know. It was Cecil Duwalter.

What? Cecil fucking Duwalter, hulking with bad posture and a mealy drawl. Shy, earnest, Cecil? It was fucking Cecil. Apparently, fucking Paige.

The next day Paige was there after a frantic drive. Contrite and desperate. Apologizing through sex, even oral sex. (Was this the first time she went down on him?) She would do anything Harmon wanted. She was ready to leave school, hated it anyway, leave the state, come live with Harmon.

In his head Harmon said No, No, No, a thousand times No. Just let this disaster end. Here. Now. This is not worth it. What he said: "Okay."

After exams, here he was making a grand gesture, driving the VW bus out to the University one more time, to fetch Paige, to bring her back to live with him in New England. They were at the house in town, loading the van. Myra was there with a wan smile for Harmon, no words for Paige. Sylvia was there being Sylvia. She insisted on helping carry Paige's stereo speakers to the van, then dumped one on the sidewalk, picked it up and dumped it again, with an "oh, well" look and a shrug. She placed it in the van with exaggerated care and said, "I'll get the other one."

Paige said no and rushed into the house.

When just he and Sylvia were out by the van, she started talking. "What the fuck are you doing, Harmon? Do you even think about your life at all? You know where she was the night before you came? His apartment, where she was all year, when she wasn't fucking him right here, right after she got off the phone with you."

"Do I need to hear this?"

"You need to hear this. She didn't just make a mistake and hook up with him. She was like living with him. They fucked in every room in this house and probably his place too. Probably all over campus."

"I don't need to hear this."

"You do. Listen. Listen. Take care of yourself. Take care of Harmon. Not Paige. She will be fine. Her deep, sad-girl act wore thin with me a long time ago. Maybe someday you'll see the light."

Later: Myra gave him a long hug, a good-bye hug. Sylvia walked up right in front of Paige and kissed him hard and long on the mouth. Still right in front of Paige: "Remember what I said: take care of yourself, take care of Harmon, nobody else."

"I'll see you, Sylvia."

"No, you won't. You're not coming back."

He tried humor. "Well, then, good bye. I'll think of you." This time, he winked.

"I know you will. Everybody does." (How did she always get the last word?) She pulled him close one more time.

When they were in the van, Paige said, "What was that? You and Sylvia?"

"I don't think you want to talk about us and anybody else right now."

She stopped talking. That subject sat. Forever.

And just like that, Paige moved in with him, at Rita's house for the summer, and then they got an apartment that fall in a town across the river from the law school, away from his friends.

Paige still hated the running and racing and he still ran every day, raced weekends when he could. She got a job in an office. She hated all the co-workers and bosses, except one friend, with whom she talked conspiratorially on the phone, making fun of the bosses for their ego and stupidity.

Harmon was at the apartment studying while Paige was at work. He looked in her desk for a pen. He found a pen, but also found over 20 letters, sent while they lived together at the apartment, from the University, sent by Cecil. His face burned as Harmon opened one then another and another. Read them all. His stomach clenched at this truth. Such yearning and flowery romance. Such sex. Cecil had indeed fucked Paige in every room and outdoors. He had violated her every orifice. He seemed perpetually erect. They had used various sex toys. He had bound her with silk ties, had spanked and dominated her. He had made her blow him in semi-public places around the campus, daring passersby to catch them. He longed for her touch again. She was his muse, his love, his whore.

Harmon's hands shook, his palms sweaty. He folded each letter, put everything back as it was, even put the pen back. He would say nothing. Things would change. Somehow, things would change.

That night, for the first time in two weeks, they had sex, rougher than usual. Paige seemed happy. Harmon was empty. He lay on his back, staring at the ceiling in the dark room. Water dripped in the kitchen sink. The refrigerator thrummed.

He would move back near campus for third year, let Paige find a roommate. They would still be together, but not living together. Not that anymore.

CHAPTER SIX

Doing the same thing over and over and expecting different results may be a definition of insanity. In love, it may be a prescription for disaster, but in running it is called persistence. It is a hallmark of eventual success. Eventual. Patience, runner.

Underground Runner's Guide

Harmon started running longer on weekends, going out for two hours or more. His mileage was creeping up again. 2245 the second year, then 2318. The streak was over 1,000 days. For the fourth full year, he wanted to try to run at least 50 miles each week, not just every day, but also every week with consistent distance.

At the suggestion of Hope, they both entered the New York City Marathon that year, and he trained through the early fall. He had moved closer to campus in a shared apartment, and he would run in the morning before classes, then hang out at school and run again in the afternoon on Tuesdays and Thursdays before his evening tax seminar. He wanted another chance to crack three hours.

Paige, Hope and Harmon stayed at Faith's apartment in the City the night before the marathon. Then, in the predawn darkness Hope and Harmon took the subway to the shuttle bus to the start. It was cool and clear, a nice day for a marathon. Harmon planned to run flat splits, just under seven minutes a mile. He was aiming for 3 hours. His running streak was 1,397 days.

He, Paige and Hope planned to meet up at the finish, then take the train back up to the Bronx. At the start, it was madness, wall to wall people jockeying for position. The race officials had signs for projected pace. He pushed up between the 6:45 and 7:00 signs. There were fat guys in basketball sneakers. There were all sorts of people who were not going to run under seven minutes a mile. They pressed in. Harmon tried to move forward and saw the same. Even worse.

The gun went off. He was crushed in a mass of humanity and could barely walk. He pushed forward up the Verrazano Narrows bridge to the mile mark. He hit it in 19:15. He hadn't run a step. His chest clenched in stress. On the down slope of the bridge, he tried to run, but the crowd was still too thick. Finally, he moved ahead. It wasn't until the 3-mile mark that he could run free. Through Brooklyn, he felt anxious, short of breath; he needed to catch up and pushed the pace hard, passing everyone around him.

He hit the halfway mark in 1:36, but felt his energy ebbing already. By 16 miles, he entered Manhattan with nothing left, his frantic pace slowed to a jog, then a jog with walk breaks. The crowd implored him to run, to push it. He had nothing to give. He wanted more than anything to just stop, eat something, maybe have a beer to get some energy. But he pushed on, jogging and walking until he reached the finish in 3:57, completely beaten from the frustration and effort. Maybe the marathon was meant to remain a mystery.

A volunteer put a thin mylar blanket over his shoulders, closed it with a peel-off sticker. He sat on a chair, cooled and started to shiver. The area was full of people in motion; he never saw Hope. He left the finish area and started to walk around in the park looking for Hope or Paige. Then he was out on Central Park West, thinking he would take the sweaty five-dollar bill pinned inside his shorts and get a train back to Faith's. It was later and colder and the shadows were long. He was underdressed and shivery.

Suddenly, he saw Paige hurrying, then running toward him. She hugged him and started to cry, words coming out in a jumble. "Looked everywhere. Saw no one. Afraid. Ready to give up. Frantic. So glad I found you." They took the train up to Faith's together. Drove home that night. He dropped her off at her apartment and drove back to his place. Slept alone.

Harmon came down with a cold after the marathon and stayed on his side of the river for a week. Then he got two kittens (Panda and Stripey) for his shared apartment and spent more time there. Paige stayed over some nights, but had to work in the morning.

Harmon ran a jingle bell 10k in 39:03 and felt good about it with all that had happened that year. He missed his mileage goal after the cold and came in with 2564. He thought that was about as much as he could run and remain healthy. On New Year's Eve, he reached 1463 straight days of running.

He started his final semester of law school, still with Paige, ready to get out of school. But would he ever get out of the relationship. He took courses he didn't care about, didn't regularly attend: business organizations, international law. He took a course he thought he might find interesting, but ultimately did not: law and literature. (It went fine until Harmon told the professor he was flat wrong when he said realism and naturalism in literature were the same thing. Then their relationship was frosty. The promise that the professor would help Harmon work up his final paper for publication melted away after the exchange on literary genres.)

He took a course that might actually relate to future employment: trial practice. The professor was an actual practicing lawyer, Stanton Willingham, who tried to impart some practical trial and practice skills. The class involved students delivering oral arguments and then being critiqued by the professor and peers.

Harmon was not a natural. He could write out a fine argument, but he would falter in delivery. He lacked the self-possession that made a litigator, had the habit of jettisoning key parts of the argument for fear that they would fall flat. One night, he argued dully in favor of increased alimony in a mock divorce case. He had planned an overriding theme, a recurrent metaphor, but left it out and argued literally in hushed tones. What he planned was inspired; what he said was underwhelming.

Professor Willingham looked pained. "Yes, yes, those are the nuts and bolts, but where is the persuasive argument? Where's the zing? You're trying to convince a judge. Don't plod, persuade. What if you said something like, 'Your honor, Mr. Smith was married to Ethel Smith for 16 years. He claimed irretrievable breakdown, but I can't help but note he's with a new Mrs. Smith now and has been for some time. He may suggest that his marriage just miraculously broke down on its own and he miraculously met the new Mrs. Smith afterward, but in my experience, a man swimming in the river of life doesn't let go of one log, until he is darn sure he has another log to hold onto.'"

Harmon's ears glowed red. The criticism piled up as the students echoed the prof. Harmon didn't care that much; he knew the argument was lacking. But the truth of what Willingham had said hit him: "a man . . . doesn't let go of one log until . . . he has another log . . . ."

After class, Harmon went for a 6-mile run, easing down suburban sidewalks, breathing easily. Was it as simple as that? A man doesn't let go of a log? Was he just like any other man?

Then it was the week before graduation. Finals were over, and Harmon was in a dive bar on a Thursday afternoon with Ben and Audrey, friends since first-year, who had started dating when they were matched as moot-court partners. Also along was Maria, a cute third-year, whom Harmon barely knew. She was one of the criminal clinic students, who spent all their time with one professor, going to court on behalf of indigent defendants. It was a club Harmon had no connection to. She was tall with ringlets of brown hair framing her face.

Beer flowed in pitchers. There were toasts to law professors and courses, to things learned and barely understood. At one point, Harmon left to make a quick call to Paige to say he would not be joining her for dinner. More beer flowed, and then everyone was sufficiently loaded, though it was still early evening. Harmon was standing by his car, contemplating the mercifully short ride, five blocks to his apartment.

Then Maria was in front of him. "Can I kiss you?"

Harmon nodded, and she did, long and slow. All of a sudden, it was warmer, the air close.

"Can I see you again?"

Harmon nodded again.

She handed him a scrap of paper with a phone number. "Call me." She kissed him again, longer, slower. Touched his arm. Then was gone.

Graduation was on Sunday. Harmon broke up with Paige on Monday. They spoke of a separation, a reassessment, during his summer of intensive study for the bar exam. Just talk. He knew it was never coming back together. It was streak day 1,601. This was a long time coming.

BOOK TWO

Losing the Groove

CHAPTER SEVEN

If you are serious about running every day, you will have to endure. There will be illness. There will be injury. Some cannot be overcome. Others are just tests of your dedication to the ethic.

Underground Runner's Guide

That summer, Harmon was a sometimes member of the law school softball team that played in a city lawyer's league. He was less dedicated than in grad school, but still played hard when he showed up. Two weeks after graduation, late in a doubleheader, Harmon hit a single to right center. He thought he had a chance of stretching it into a double and accelerated as he approached first base. He felt a pop in back of his left leg and fell to the ground. He got up and hobbled to the first-base bag and then took himself out and went home. He had a pulled hamstring.

It was day 1,612, and he thought it might be the end. Up to that point, he had run through a cold and the flu and an intestinal ailment that had him puking for two days, but never a real leg injury. He couldn't walk without a limp. His thigh would become a distorted purple in back.

The next day he tightly wrapped the thigh in an ace bandage and jogged a slow two miles through the neighborhood. It felt tender and really sore. He was dragging the leg. That night after bar review class, he went to the pharmacy and bought a neoprene leg sleeve. The following morning, he pulled up the tight sleeve and jogged another two miles. This was doable, and he thought he could make it through if he didn't reinjure it. Two weeks later, he pronounced himself 90% better and able to run normally again. Just the same he kept the sleeve on for another two weeks.

Maria had become his girlfriend. She questioned his judgment, but deferred to his commitment. "I know this means a lot to you. You'll work it out."

Later in the summer, when he threw out his back lifting a bundle of shingles while roofing on the weekend, he did another week of two-mile runs, before upping mileage again. He realized that he could power through most injuries. It was a matter of commitment, even if the refusal to take time off might lengthen the convalescence.

* * *

After the bar exam, he started work at a twelve-attorney firm and learned that working as a lawyer bore no relationship to law school. He knew nothing and spent long hours trying to figure out what he needed to know. He would run before work every day, often just three miles. Then he would work late and drink with other associates before going home.

He ran every day, but felt like he was losing something. Maria was working long hours of her own. They saw each other on weekends.

CHAPTER EIGHT

If you keep a running streak long enough, you will probably encounter someone who wants you to stop. Someone close to you, who may insist that you stop. For your own good. Run away from this person. She (or he) doesn't have your best interests at heart. And this is not about running.

Underground Runner's Guide

Harmon realized that the world saw him differently as a lawyer. People treated him as an adult. Women, who had never previously noticed him, were attracted. (If only they knew how little he made and how long his hours were.) With one of these women, although there was precious little sex, and there were various assurances, there was a failure of birth control and she announced she was pregnant. She wanted nothing to do with him; she was engaged to someone else. She set the ground rules. She would have the baby, and he would leave her alone and pay support. She would tell her son the truth and he could seek Harmon out on his own terms. Harmon acquiesced. He didn't really want anything to do with her either, but in the process he managed to miss the first ten years of his son Matthew's life.

He and Maria had cooled. Harmon mostly ran and worked, really worked and ran, averaging only 25 miles a week. Then he was visiting his sister Hope for the 4th of July race, and stopped in the bar she tended in the local seaside inn. A dark-haired beauty, Joan, walked up to him and picked him up, and before he had a moment to think, they were practically living together, and she was telling him what was what, what to do and how to do it. And, no surprise, he was doing it and he was doing it her way.

* * *

Live with her. Sure.

Love her daughter, Amber, and help parent her. Absolutely. With pleasure. Amber was awesome.

Stay away from Matthew, because she felt threatened by his mother's liaison with Harmon. Sadly, already a done deal.

Give up his job, take her state's bar exam and work there. Okay.

Get two additional cats because she didn't just want his cats. Four cats? Whatever.

Marry her when she decided it was time. All right.

Have one, then another child with her. Yup.

Have her mother live with them, to help take care of the kids and the house. Sure. (Her mother was nice.)

Make more money so they could afford a house. (That entailed him getting a better job back in his home state. Would she move? Sure. Then he got the job. No. No move.)

Commute two hours to another state to work, only coming home weekends, while she continued to live in her seaside town, so she could enjoy the beach. No problem. He could do that.

Make still more money so they could rent a condo for a week on Sanibel Island every year. Yes.

Cut down on that running thing. Yes. Even that.

Stop that stupid running every day. No. Nope. Not that. Not that last thing.

And so it would go:

On the way into the relationship: "You run every day? That is so cool. What a great way to stay in shape."

When it started to sour: "Stop the every-day running. It's stupid and selfish and it interferes with our life."

On the way out of the relationship: "You're an embarrassment. I can't even tell my friends you run every day. It's a mental illness. It's so stupid. I hate you."

* * *

There were times he despaired and cursed this situation, but he went along and went along. The bar exam was a breeze; the job was awful, one of those firms that advertised heavily on tv. The partners were millionaires. The associates were just workers, in cubicles, not even offices. They hated the partners, but they backstabbed each other to curry their favor.

Harmon ran in the morning before work, and again at lunch. Some days he ran with a title searcher from the firm, Nate, and then a stockbroker, who worked up the block, Greg Garrett. Greg was short and thick and fast. He had a habit of going out nice and easy and coming back at a killer pace. His favorite run was to take an extra hour and go out onto the country roads by the water, before turning and cranking the pace every mile till they flew back up the hill to the center of the city at about a 6:30 pace. Harmon loved it. His first regular running partner and a fast, driven guy.

That first fall, Harmon ran a marathon in Rhode Island. The idea was to go sub-3:00, because that was the new Boston qualifying time. He and Greg ran their guts out all summer and Harmon laid down a 38:20 10k on Labor Day to prove he was in shape. He was running good miles, could even reach close to 3,000 for the year. At the end of September, in a cold rain, he tweaked a hamstring again, but he thought he would be fine for the marathon, his first since New York.

He took off at about a 6:40 pace and felt great on a sunny, breezy day. The sun started to take a toll, and he slowed after 10 miles, reaching a series of rolling hills between 10 and 14 miles. He passed the halfway point in 1:29, and was slowing down on the hills. Greg came powering by and he never saw him again. Harmon struggled home in 3:27, still unclear on how to manage the marathon. Greg had run 3:15. At the finish line, Harmon was gassed. Greg looked like he could go another 26. Joan was there, bored. She said, "Remind me not to go to another marathon. This takes forever."

And then the running started to bother her. "Why do you run in the morning if you are just going to run again at work?"

"Because I want to run every day, and some days I can't run at work."

"It doesn't matter if you run every day."

"It matters to me. It's important to me."

"You should end the every-day thing. Then you won't have to worry about it."

And so on.

Then she said it was time they got married, so they did. But first, they had to order a custom engagement ring from a local jeweler. When it arrived, she thought it too small and hated it. Somehow, it was Harmon's fault: "I will never forgive you for that." The words hung on him like a millstone.

The day before the marriage, Joan to Harmon: "I don't know if we should do this. I don't think I'm enough for you."

"I think if anything, maybe you're too much for me."

Both turned out to be true.

The day of the marriage was Harmon's run streak day number 2,848. It was his first marriage, her third. Harmon was struck by the ritual, him on one side, her on the other, as if they were adversaries. It seemed their relationship was a points-gathering competition and he would always be behind.

That year, his run at the July 4th road race was faster, 31:35, but his time in the Rhode Island marathon was slower, 3:32.

After the marriage, Harmon chafed at work, decided to advance his career. He and Joan discussed him getting a better job back in his home state. She agreed. She would move there. He got a job. She decided not to move. So, he got a place in the town he worked in, an apartment in the back of his aunt's house, and commuted on weekends.

He started the new job on streak day number 3,214.

He would run in the early morning before the job, and then run on the weekend mornings, as well. Joan wanted this to end. "If you're gone all week, there is no reason for you to take off running on a Saturday."

"It's just a few miles. 40 minutes or less."

"You don't have to run every day. It's stupid."

"It's for my health. I need this."

But it was something beyond her control, and she resented it, hated it.

The day she went into labor with Iris, she called him early in the morning at the apartment and said it had started but wouldn't be critical for at least 12 hours. But he should come now. He got off the phone and ran 2 miles before getting in the car and driving the two hours to the apartment. Later she asked if he had run. When he replied that he had, she was so mad.

"I could have had to go to the hospital."

"You had just told me that you had 12 hours."

"You didn't know that."

"I did because you told me so."

The baby, Iris, was born the following morning, on running streak day 3,881, a full 24 hours after Harmon arrived.

Then two years later young Harmon was born. There was a battle over his name, of course. Harmon wanted him named after him and his father, and his grandmother. Joan wanted control. Ultimately, she agreed, but gave him a different middle name.

Joan's mother, Ruth, moved in with them and took care of the house and kids.

The streak went on, but yearly mileage dipped as low as 1,300 miles. Running was this thing that he used to love, a thing that made him feel alive, but it was more a memory than a daily reality. He would get up in the morning and go out for 3 miles, then shower and hurry to work.

Weekends were worse for running, as any run could be the source of strife. By 14 years into the streak, Harmon took to getting up at dawn long before anyone was awake and running no more than 45 minutes. Usually, when he arrived back at the house, everyone was still asleep, but it was not enough. If Joan was up when he got back to the house, she would be mad.

"Where were you?"

"You know where I was. I was running."

"Why?"

"Really? Because I like it. No, I love it. It's the one thing I have that keeps me sane."

"I don't see why you have to do it on weekends. We don't see each other all week."

"You were asleep. You weren't missing me."

"What if the kids woke up?"

"They didn't."

And so on.

By then, Iris was a 4-year old spitfire: ringlets of brown hair, flashing dark eyes, button nose, wide smile. He took her in a baby jogger whenever she would agree. She liked to speed on the downhills and made him stop by the lighthouse to find a perfect piece of white quartz in the gravel driveway. On running streak day 5,302, Harmon ran the 4th of July 5-miler in 44:05, pushing Iris in a baby jogger. She loved it. Near the 4-mile mark they passed Iris's pediatrician. He waved, and Iris stuck out her tongue and giggled. Harmon laughed.

Two weeks later, Harmon slept in his car in front of the house after Joan screamed at him until he left. Things were falling apart. He had these perfect kids, completely wrong marriage.

CHAPTER NINE

Sometimes a little magic will come into your life. The key is to know it, honor it and grab onto it. This magic will make your life better, may even make you a better runner, which you know you could use. Because in all likelihood, you suck.

Underground Runner's Guide

On running streak day 3,956 something happened. Harmon was on the main floor of Ricci & Connor, the 20-lawyer firm he worked at back in his home state, talking to another associate, Mary Freund. Mary primarily worked for the first-named partner, Rob Ricci. Harmon collaborated with her when Rob brought him in to work on certain files, usually ones that had the potential to go to trial, as Harmon had found a niche in trial work.

Con Connor (parents with a sense of humor) was walking down the hall with a young woman Harmon had never seen before. She was petite and shapely, with long blond hair almost all the way down her back. She was dressed in a typical dark lawyer's suit. Con buttonholed Harmon and pulled him into a meeting with the mystery woman.

"Harmon, come on into my office for a minute. This is Lisa Mueller. Lisa sent us a resume."

Harmon ducked into the office, sat in a chair facing Con's desk. Lisa was pretty, had striking green eyes to go with the blond hair. She was fielding usual interview questions from Con and doing an okay job, but Harmon could tell by the tone that this was all perfunctory. Harmon saw from the resume in his hand that she had attended an Ivy League law school. Con loved applicants from good schools. Harmon knew he was going to hire her if she would agree.

On streak day 3,991, there she was, carrying her framed diplomas into the small office in the basement. Con had a group lunch at the pizza place to welcome her, but Harmon was in court.

CHAPTER TEN

Running every day is an adjunct to your life, not the whole thing. There will be times, maybe years, that you have to focus on other things. Keep your toe in it. Run a few miles a day. Running will still be there when you are ready to recommit. In the meantime, you may find that the same dedication that you applied to running will make you good at other things. Maybe even very good, despite your obvious shortcomings.

Underground Runner's Guide

Harmon was no more confident in his personal life, but he could try a case. When he walked through the doors of the courthouse, he was a technician, a teacher, a storyteller. He loved picking the jury, spending two or three days interviewing prospective jurors in an intense dialogue. He loved the rules and techniques of the trial, the flow of witnesses, the question and answer. He especially loved closing arguments, fashioning long metaphors on perception, understanding, trustworthiness.

* * *

Ladies and gentlemen, you've heard all the evidence in the case, heard the expert testimony based on the physical evidence at the scene. And you've heard the testimony of the plaintiff. She is telling you to go against all of the evidence, the photos, the measurements. She wants you to believe in the phantom car, the dark sedan no one else saw, that she says was there and disappeared into the night.

Ladies and gentlemen, I want you to imagine being right here where you are, and imagine that you have been here all day and you don't know what the weather is. Well, imagine that the back door to the courtroom opens and in walks a man in a raincoat brushing drops off his sleeves. Then in walks a woman with an umbrella. She closes it and shakes the water off it. And in walks another man with a wet newspaper, and another in a raincoat, until the whole back of the courtroom is filled with wet people.

Now imagine the plaintiff takes the witness stand and testifies, looks you all right in the eyes and testifies that it is perfectly sunny, not rainy at all. All these wet people in the courtroom and she says it's not rainy. She says, "Trust me."

Well, you might shake your heads; you might be confused. But what I want to ask you all is: would you take your umbrella if you left the courthouse for the lunch break?

And that's what this case is. You know what the evidence points to, what it says. And you have the plaintiff saying disregard all of it. She says, "Believe me, not the evidence."

Ladies and gentlemen, it's painfully obvious what happened here and what your job is. At the beginning of the case, I told you that at the end I would ask you to go back in that jury room and return a verdict for the defendant. That time is now. Thank you.

* * *

He was successful at trial work, but success came at a price. He spent long hours at the firm, with nowhere else to go on weeknights anyway. He confined his running to early mornings, gained 20 pounds over the years, raced only 3 or 4 times a year. Fifteen years into the running streak, he was struggling to break 45 minutes in the 4th of July 5-miler. 10k's were over 50 minutes.

And so, one Wednesday morning, running streak day 5,580, he found himself in the large conference room of the firm at 7:30. He had run 3 miles at dawn. All the lawyers were there for the weekly meeting. Rob Ricci, the founder and driving force of the firm, was on a rant, not uncommon for one of the meetings. He was in equal parts brow-beating and encouraging the associates to meet the billing goal of 2,200 hours a year.

"If you work hard and do good work on your files, the hours will be there at the end of the day and the week and the month. Billing doesn't drive the work; work drives the billing. Just work hard and record your time. This is how we measure your value to the firm. This is how we decide on year-end bonuses. If you bill your hours, you can be a success here. If you don't, there is no place here for you."

Con, the number two in the firm, in his annoying smarmy voice, followed up: "What Rob is saying is that we always want to do what's best for our clients, but we also want to get paid and make money. It's important that you are conscious of both things when you work on these cases."

Rob again: "No, Con. Don't give this your negotiator treatment. It's not a negotiation. Don't be all nice nice and sing Kumbaya. This is the most basic thing. If you're not going to put your time in and bill 2,200 a year, there's the door. You can walk through it right now."

Twenty lawyers sat. No one moved.

Rob went on: "I could bill 2,500 hours, 3,000 hours, no problem. You just put in the time and do good work." (It was rumored widely that Rob billed about 1,000 hours a year, but he did put in long hours.)

Harmon looked across the table. Lisa was there. He caught her eye, looked at the ceiling and back. She smiled so slightly; her eyes flashed. Brilliant green. She looked smart in a dark grey lawyer suit with cream-colored blouse and glasses. Her blond hair hung past her shoulders, giving her a sexy librarian look.

The circus that was the Wednesday morning meeting turned up a notch. Stephen Bradford, who proudly traced his lineage back to the Mayflower, and who was partially deaf, chimed in with his atonal voice. "Rob, as you know, some of us are trying to kill more than we eat (this was a frequent Rob-ism about marketing). That takes a lot of time. Do we get credit for marketing? Is that part of the 2,200?"

Rob's countenance darkened. He furrowed his brow, looked down, as if in disgust. "No Stevie (he always used the -ie when he was condescending). This is how we make money. I need 2,200 hours on the dotted line."

He was gaining momentum, as if this had all not happened before. "Look, this goes for Stevie and everyone at this table." His gaze from the table-head swept both sides. Everyone avoided eye contact. "I built this firm. Built it from nothing. I mortgaged my house. There were months I took no money. And now I'm the most successful insurance defense lawyer in the state. That's no accident. I put in the work."

Steve had a blank stare, like he was looking off into the distance. He brought his right hand up to the side of his face like he was brushing his cheek or touching his ear, which had reddened considerably. He put the hand back down.

Rob's voice raised another notch. "And one more thing." Shouting now. "If anyone of you, Stevie or anyone else, wants to leave, there's the door. If you don't like it, start your own firm. Make your own rules. I'll just keep doing it my way."

Silence.

Still not done. Seething anger now. "Stevie, if you want to go, just put your files on my desk and I'll handle those too. I'll just work a little harder."

Silent-er than silence.

Con finished the meeting with some light talk about upcoming case issues. Rob just stared down at the file in front of him, his energy and bile spent.

Years later, when he was a superior court judge, Steve confided in Harmon that he touched his ears in meetings to subtly turn off his hearing aids. That morning, he had had enough of Rob's bullshit. Harmon laughed so hard that tears came to his eyes.

* * *

Lisa and Harmon had become friends over the years. She lived with her boyfriend, a court clerk, in a condo a few towns away, near the beach. She was quiet and smart and worked mostly with Con on big construction cases or Rob on insurance coverage issues. She was almost silent at the office, but at office outings or happy hours, after a few glasses of beer, her voice would rise in volume and timbre and she would hold forth on politics or law or any topic of the moment. She looked people in the eye and laughed out loud. In these moments, the whole office was smitten, the guys anyway. At some of these outings she and Harmon had had long conversations on law or politics or popular music or anything, and he loved her company. She was brilliant and witty and exuded such youth. She was fresh and her future full of promise.

At one happy hour after a trial win by Harmon, after 4 beers and two tequila shots, she had a long discussion with him about her intention to have green-eyed children. She batted her own emerald eyes and went on about blond hair and green eyes.

"But, Lisa Lisa, doesn't Tim have dark brown hair?"

She shrugged. "Who said anything about Tim? And, do you have to call me that?"

"I'm sorry. It just comes out. If Tim were here, I might call him Cult Jam."

"Well, he's not here, is he."

When she was flirting like this, Harmon felt a weight lift and let himself think that if it were just he and Lisa on a desert island, they would be great together. But the world had six billion people and life was complicated. It was just a passing thought.

Then she was dispatched to work with Harmon. An insurance company had taken a file from another firm five days before trial and hand-delivered it in three banker's boxes directly to Rob. Rob and his minions in turn took those boxes and delivered them downstairs directly to Harmon's desk, with the encouragement: "Harmon, you're the guy for this case. Go get 'em. Have Lisa help with support."

It was Thursday afternoon. Jury selection was to commence the following Tuesday. Harmon stayed till midnight going through the documents. For all the filings, the case was simple in form. A Hollywood casting director visiting family in an upscale town in the hills had pulled her rental car out from a stop sign, right in front of a local guy driving up the main road in his pickup. The impact was heavy and the local had dislocated his hip, requiring surgical repair. He had medical bills of over $42,000, paid by health insurance, and lost wages of $4,240. He would always walk with a small limp. There was $100,000 in available insurance and the insurer at first wouldn't offer it and then the plaintiff's lawyer wouldn't accept it, thinking he could get much more at trial. The casting director had her own personal lawyer threatening to sue the insurer for not protecting her.

Harmon was ready to step in. He and Lisa met on Friday morning.

"I hope you don't have big weekend plans because we need to file some motions on Monday and have some more ready to go on Tuesday."

"Nothing serious."

"Good. I'll handle prep for jury selection. I have some motions in limine that I'd like you to draft. I think we should try to limit the evidence that would hurt Gloria, particularly the state cop's testimony on speed and causation. Remember, this is a small rural area except for the rich enclave in the village. Gloria is an outsider, a Hollywood outsider."

They talked over the case for an hour and identified eight motions seeking to limit the admissible evidence. Lisa would work with the file over the weekend. Harmon made notes he would need to prepare jury questions and the outline of an opening statement and took them home to work over the weekend.

Joan was pissed. She didn't want him running on the weekends and definitely didn't want him working on Saturday or Sunday. "Why do you have to work over the weekend. I bet Rob isn't working."

"First of all, you know Rob works all the time. Second, this is my job. On Tuesday, I have to be in court to try this case with a client I have never met. I need to be prepared. There is a lot of pressure here. I have had this case for exactly one day."

"Why did you even agree to take this case? You're such a pushover."

"I agreed because that's my job. I'm the guy who can take any case and try it. This is what they pay me for and what I'm good at."

There was no accommodation. There would be no peace. Harmon ran in the pre-dawn darkness on Saturday, three miles only. Then he fed the cats, raked the litter box and worked on the case until the house stirred. He did the same on Sunday. There was so much to do, and he was not spending enough time.

He was living under the cloud of a failing marriage.

He told Joan he would have to drive back at dinnertime, rather than 10:00, when everyone was in bed. "I need to get back to the office and spend at least a few hours on this tonight."

"Why? That's stupid."

"You know why. I need to work on this case. I only got it on Thursday. Trial starts in two days. I need more time with the file."

"Nobody can expect you to handle this in the time you were given. That shouldn't be your problem."

"It is definitely my problem. Definitely on me. I have to figure out how to make this case come out the way I want it to. Nobody is going to take care of it for me. This is what my job is."

"So Rob tells you to jump and you just do it. Typical child of an alcoholic. You always seek his approval."

"Child of an alcoholic? My parents weren't . . . That makes no sense."

"COA, COA. That's you to a tee. You should say no. You should quit that job. Move back here."

"That job is what makes the money to pay for this house and everything we have, everything we do."

"I don't care about the house." (She did.) "I don't care about the money." (She absolutely did, spending it faster than he could make it.) "If this job is so important, maybe you should just stay there and work all the time."

"Maybe I should." There would be no resolution. He left as planned and drove back, arrived at the office at 8:00.

The file boxes were in the downstairs small conference room. Lisa was in her office working on the motions. She was on the last one they had discussed on Friday.

"Hey. I'll have the last of the motions we talked about done in a minute. But I think maybe we should do one more. I think we should try to keep out that the car was a rental. That would just confuse the jury and it's prejudicial to us. If she had driven the car 1,000 times and pulled out in front of the pickup, it's still her fault. If she'd driven the car only once, and drove it safely, it's not her fault. The fact that it's a rental car is irrelevant. I'll just do that last motion and then be done for today."

"That's really good. Thanks, Lisa Lisa."

"Do you have to call me that?"

"I think I do." He smirked. "You've done a lot this weekend. I appreciate it. I'll go over everything tonight and we can meet in the morning."

"One other thing, Harmon. I know you looked at the police report. One of the motions is trying to keep most of it out of evidence. But, according to the report, Wilson told the cop he was going 40. According to the report, the speed limit in the area is 35. I pulled the original answer done by Anderson & Hale, and they did allege the standard special defenses, including speed, and including the statute on unreasonable speed. So, I pulled that statute and down the list of things that create a presumption of unreasonable speed is exceeding the posted limit. I know you'll have the jury eating out of your hand. You always do. Maybe you can do something with this. Maybe it's not clear liability."

"Lisa, I think you secretly want to try this case." She shook her head and looked down for a second. "That is great. I was working up my theory of the case completely on damages. I was thinking liability was a throwaway. I appreciate you doing all this work this weekend. I need to look at all this and fine tune my approach. I might have to spend more time with the jurors on liability."

"One other, other thing. Rob was here both days this weekend."

"That doesn't sound good."

"It's not a big deal. But he asked about the case of course. I told him you were already doing an amazing job, that we had met and strategized, had motions lined up. Somewhere in the conversation, I suggested that he had given the case to you because you're the trial guy. He said you would never be the lawyer he is because you're a five-day a week lawyer. I told him you were working at home this weekend and we were going to meet Sunday night to go over the prep. He shook his head and said, 'Lisa, five-day a week lawyer. Five-day a week lawyer.'" She had expertly imitated his voice. Then she rolled her eyes.

Harmon laughed out loud, but a part of him was annoyed. This guy—Rob—had taken on this thankless case in a thankless condition on the very eve of trial. He knew that success would result in money to the firm, but more importantly, more cases from this insurer and a tighter connection with the managers he was bailing out by fixing this problem. And he trusted it all to Harmon, because Harmon was the guy who could pull this off. And he put Lisa on it because Lisa was astute and hardworking and could help Harmon do it. But with all this responsibility he would confer on Harmon, with all that was riding on the case, he couldn't endure a compliment to Harmon. Had to belittle him to Lisa.

This was his life. The main thing right now was the case. The shit all around him would have to wait.

He looked at the police report, the pleadings, the statute. He saw that Lisa was right on target with something he had not really considered. Maybe there was something to an ivy league law school. He changed his jury questioning worksheet to include hypothetical questions on liability and multiple causes of accidents, added questions on the nuances of comparative responsibility and shared fault.

He reviewed the draft motions on his computer, made some minor changes. He would hand-deliver these to court on Monday and fax them to the plaintiff's attorney, Ben Griswold, so that he could request argument on Tuesday morning before jury selection would commence, since some of the motions concerned what facts could be discussed or revealed during jury selection as well as the case itself. After delivering the motions to court, he would meet his client and her personal attorney at her hotel just down the hill from the courthouse. He decided he would bring Lisa with him, if she had time to go.

Before leaving for the night, he wrote a quick update letter to the insurance claims representative on the case. He emphasized that 100% liability on the defendant was almost certain and the case was clearly worth the policy limit and beyond. However, since Attorney Griswold and his client apparently would not accept the policy limit, he would do his best to limit the damages at trial.

It was 1:00 am when he got into his car and went back to his apartment: two rooms in the back of his aunt's farmhouse. He went right to sleep.

He awoke at dawn and ran a quick 3 miles, all the while turning over the case issues in his head, thinking of phrases for the opening statement. He was descending into the tunnel vision of the trial that would consume his next two weeks. He got home for a quick shower and shave and chose his best meet-the-new-client suit and tie from the group of suits all facing the same way, next to the shirts all facing the same way in his closet.

He was at the office by 8:00. He tinkered with the motions a bit and then had his paralegal, Donna, finalize and copy them when she arrived. Donna had worked solely with Harmon the last two years and they had handled 8 trials together. She prided herself at being a part of the trial team. For the next two weeks, she would come in early and leave late and she would handle anything else that might come up on his schedule.

There was a rhythm to trials. She would be in early to review and finalize documents to file in court that day, pack him off to court, take all his calls and handle all urgent business while he was at court, make extensive lists of priorities, talk to him during the court lunch break to deal with issues like subpoenaed witnesses and documents, coordinate work of associates helping on research and memos of law, then wait for him to return after hours to discuss the developments of the day and the issues that would arise the following day. The next morning, she would be there to do it all over again with a smile on her face. She was invaluable.

On this, the day before jury selection, Harmon had the pretrial motions in a folder ready to file. He finalized his jury introduction page and outline of prospective juror questions and placed them in another folder. Then he pulled out the police report and examined it again.

His client had pulled from a side street onto Route 63, a main road, in front of the approaching pickup truck of the plaintiff. She had crossed the shoulder and northbound lane and intended to take a left turn and head south. The pickup was in the southbound lane and it struck the passenger side of his client's rental car just in front of the front door. He did not have photos of the scene, but the report indicated that it had happened mid-afternoon, and the weather was fair, the road dry. The sightline looking right from the stop line of the side street was listed as 650 feet, meaning the contour of the highway was not a factor. The pickup was visible and his client failed to appreciate the risk of pulling out when she did. The speed limit on the main road was 35 in that area, when a southbound driver was just entering the town. From his memory of that road, Harmon knew the speed limit was 55 less than a mile earlier for southbound traffic.

The state police had taken measurements of the roadway because it was an accident with serious injury. From the stop line to the point of impact on the roadway was 30 feet 8 inches. The point of impact was just left of center in the southbound travel lane. The left front bumper and front end of the pickup struck the right front of the rental car 6 inches in front of the front door. The rental car traveled 52 feet south and west after the impact and came to rest on the righthand shoulder and grass to the right of the southbound lane. The pickup went forward 46 feet from the point of impact and came to rest straddling the double yellow centerline.

Gloria Sanns, who was the driver of the rental car and Harmon's future client, walked away from the accident with only minor bumps and bruises. She declined medical treatment at the scene. Bradley Wilson, the driver of the pickup, sustained serious visible injuries and was transported to the local hospital by ambulance.

Both drivers were interviewed by the troopers at the scene. The report paraphrased their responses. Wilson stated that he was headed into town to the hardware store, from his home in the town to the north. He was going about 40 miles per hour. He saw a mid-sized silver car to his left on a side street come to the stop sign and stop. Then, suddenly it pulled in front of him. He jammed on his brakes and struck the car on the front passenger side. He felt serious pain in his right leg and hip and could not walk at the scene. Gloria stated that she was visiting family in town for the weekend. She was driving a Ford rental car. She stopped at the stop sign, saw a truck far down the road to her right and nothing coming from her left and thought it was safe to pull out. She pulled out and was hit on her passenger side. She was shaken up, but thought she was not injured and needed no medical care.

The state police gave Gloria a moving violation for pulling out from a stop sign when a vehicle was approaching on the main road. Wilson was not charged with any violation.

The cryptic statements and diagram told a story to Harmon. Gloria was unsure of herself in a rental car and strange town. She looked both ways several times and pulled out tentatively. Wilson was driving a road he had gone down a thousand times. He had been on the road for at least ten miles through the area where the speed limit was 55, then 45, then 35 just before the accident. When he told the police he was going about 40, that meant more like 50. Harmon would have to tease out the speed issue in front of the jury.

Next Harmon again reviewed the medical records. The ambulance records were unremarkable: 52-year-old white male, oriented times 3, Glasgow Coma Scale of 15, in vehicle, heavy collision, reports severe pain in right upper leg and hip. Stabilized in vehicle, air cast applied to upper leg. Placed supine on stretcher and transported to hospital.

The hospital records picked up at the emergency room. 52-year old Caucasian male arrived by ambulance, oriented times 3, on stretcher, right leg immobilized. Subjective: severe pain upper R leg and hip area. Very tender to palpation. Objective: swelling over hip area. Diagnosis: Rule out dislocated hip, fx femur. Sent to x-ray. The x-ray report showed dislocation of right hip, fracture line on greater trochanter. On-call surgeon from local orthopedic group called in. Surgical report indicated closed reduction of the R hip joint under general anesthesia.

Follow up care indicated that Wilson was immobile for 2 weeks, then went through a course of physical therapy. Because of the healing fracture, he could not bear full weight on the leg and hip for four weeks. During that time, he walked with crutches. The orthopedic surgeon eventually discharged him 11 months post-accident, with a 15% permanent partial impairment of the right lower extremity, full activities as tolerated.

At his deposition taken by the previous firm, Wilson said he could work and get along okay, but the hip throbbed in damp weather and he could no longer walk for exercise with his wife.

Medical bills were $42,745, all paid by Wilson's health insurance, except co-pays of $470.

Not much to work with on the injury side. Serious injury, no excessive treatment. This guy was not a whiner. He hardly complained.

It was 11:30. Harmon had a meeting with Gloria and her personal attorney scheduled for 1:00 at her hotel near the courthouse. Harmon walked down the hall to Lisa's office. Her door was ajar. She was on the phone, but motioned him in. He sat in the arm chair opposite her desk.

She was talking to opposing counsel on one of her cases with that low, smooth voice and light laugh.

"Right. You too." Pause. "Right. I'll keep that in mind. Bye."

She looked up. Light eyelashes, impossibly long. Harmon thought, "Were her eyes always this green?" He said, "Hey, what's up?"

"What's with the old guys? Do you know Doug Willitts?" Harmon did. "We have a case together, and he is kind of all over me. Hand on my shoulder at pretrials and after depositions. Talking low, too intimate. So I asked Con what the deal is with him. He said he's been married like 4 times. Total horndog." She paused, then went on. "Just now, he tells me how nice it is to talk to me, how I should call anytime. Doesn't even have to be about the case. Maybe we should get together for lunch or something. I mean, he's about 50." She was 31. Harmon was 42.

She looked right at him. It must be the green sweater. "So, what can I do for you? Anything. Just say the word."

"Jesus, don't say that to Doug Willits." They both burst into laughter.

"Just you."

"I'm not sure you should say that to me, either."

She smiled, closed-mouthed. "I can handle myself with that. So . . . ?"

"I'm meeting with our esteemed Hollywood casting director at 1:00 at the Northfield Inn. Any interest in coming along?"

"Sure. I can do that."

"We should leave in about 20 minutes."

"I'll come by your office."

The drive up to Northfield, 45 minutes, seemed to take no time, with Harmon and Lisa talking casually about music and concerts they had seen—her love of alternative rock, his penchant for the Grateful Dead. Then she recounted her Grateful Dead camping experience in Wisconsin, the summer after college on a cross-country trip with her hippie cousin. "It was an experience. I felt filthy, camping for three days. But mostly I remember not loving the music."

Harmon gasped in mock horror.

"When you do that, I think you're about to hit a trailer truck or something. It was just the Grateful Dead." He gasped again. "I mean, they would start a song, and it would be great, and everyone was singing along and dancing, and then it would just turn into a jam and the song would be gone, but the jam would go on and on. They just lost me."

"I don't think we can be friends."

"I'm thinking we can get beyond this."

"Well, we'll have to see." They locked eyes for just a moment, as he drove up into the country. She smiled that closed-mouth smile again. He looked away.

* * *

Gloria Sanns greeted them at the entrance to the small conference room at the Northfield Inn. She was about 5'4" and thin, impeccably and expensively dressed. Harmon knew that if he were more in tune with fashion, he would see that her clothes were all designer. Was that a Hermes scarf? He wondered if she would pick up on the cheap suits he bought from the warehouse in Fall River. At least they fit, and he had put on a designer tie for the meeting. When he put his hand out to her, she offered her left hand for that annoying half-shake. Harmon introduced Lisa as his associate there for the meeting. Gloria offered the same left-hand shake, smiled and raised her eyebrows.

Gloria was flanked by her personal attorney, Kaitlin O'Donnell, a former classmate of Harmon. Kaitlin was tall and pretty in an athletic kind of way. She had been very self-assured in law school and all the professors had loved her for her confidence and her good looks. She had landed at the biggest firm in that part of the state, about 60 lawyers. Harmon's most enduring memory of Kaitlin was that as first-year associates, when they had belonged to the same health club, he had followed her around a weight machine circuit and discovered that she pushed heavier weights than he did.

After he introduced himself and Lisa to Gloria and introduced Lisa to Kaitlin, they exchanged pleasantries about Gloria's work. She named two television series and a handful of movies as examples of her work as a casting director.

Then, as usual, Kaitlin tried to take charge. "So, Harmon. Gloria contacted my firm last week and had us look into things. What's this all about? The company won't pay up, huh?"

"Good to see you, as always, Kaitlin. It's more complicated than that. I guess it was a timing thing. Plaintiff's counsel won't take the policy limits anymore."

"Do you know Ben Griswold? He talks a good game, but he's kind of a schlub. He's probably dying to settle."

"Well, we'll see, but he says no right now. I have to assume it's going forward. I'm filing eight motions in limine this afternoon after we meet. Jury selection is tomorrow."

"Okay. You should start preparing Gloria for the trial. But, before I forget, let me give you this." She handed over a two-page letter addressed to Harmon for the benefit of the insurance company: duty to protect . . . failure to settle . . . bad faith . . . expect that any verdict, whether or not within the policy limits will be the responsibility of the insurer.

Harmon handed the letter to Lisa after a cursory skimming of the first page. She had already been taking notes. He turned to Gloria. "Ms. Sanns, I am your attorney, just like Attorney O'Donnell here. I imagine you would like this case to go away, and I will do my best to make that happen and to make sure your insurance company protects you. But for now, we have a trial on our hands, and it's my job to make sure we do our best at trial and you never feel unprepared for your role. I want you to be ready for every question, every situation. Does that work for you?"

"Call me Gloria, please." Her voice was low and smoky, with an aristocratic haughtiness. "I thought you were the attorney from the insurance company. And it's a little late for them to protect me. I think they should have taken care of this three years ago."

"I understand your frustration. You should know that I do not work for the company, even though they pay me to represent you. If it comes down to me protecting you or the insurance company, I protect you."

"What do you need from me?"

They spent an hour going over Harmon's theory of the case and intended themes and what would happen at the trial: jury selection, opening statements, all witnesses, closing arguments, the charge to the jury and deliberations. Harmon explained that a trial was like a play. Her role as defendant in this type of case was to be contrite, but unbowed. She may be asked if the accident was her fault; she should consider that accidents are a combination of factors and that the determination of fault is for the jury. She should answer questions with short decisive responses. Yes, she stopped at the stop sign. Yes, she looked to her left and right before pulling out. No, she was not distracted. Yes, she could see the pickup far up the road. She thought she had plenty of time.

For the last half hour, they did sample q. and a. Gloria was articulate and sharp. Harmon thought they might do okay, except she looked too prosperous and too classy for the people who would likely be on the jury. She smelled of expensive perfume. She had gold jewelry.

As they were finishing the session, Harmon said, “Gloria, I think you’re picking this up very quickly.” She beamed. “But, tomorrow, we’re going to meet the prospective jurors, and I don’t want you to look too glamorous.”

“Harmon. I tend to look glamorous. That I can’t help.”

He smiled. “Maybe a little less jewelry. Conservative outfits. Try to play the role of a regular person.” She started to shake her head. “I know you are far, far from a regular person. Just try to be someone who the good people of this county will like and not want to punish for this accident. I’ll see you at the courthouse tomorrow at 9:00. If there are any developments that you need to hear, I’ll call you at the hotel.”

Back in the car, Lisa turned to him. “How do you get people like that eating out of your hand? I thought right away she was trouble. But she loved you.”

“I think she likes men, especially attention from younger men. She was in her glory when she saw I was focused only on her.”

"You know this case doesn't look good. Hollywood casting agent smashes into local guy and hurts him pretty bad. That has the makings of a big hit. How do you control that?"

"I can only do what I can. Alright, that sounds stupid. I just try to limit the facts the jury hears and focus on the positive. The plaintiff walks and talks, and Gloria seems nice enough."

"Sometimes you seem so in control. So self-possessed."

"Honestly, I find this exciting. It's kind of like being extra alive when the trial is on."

They pulled up to the old stone courthouse that faced the town green and parked on the street. Harmon and Lisa walked up the granite steps and in the front door. The engraved stone arch said 1888. The courthouse was outdated and cramped. For about 15 years the state legislature had been talking about replacing it. But it endured. They went through the metal detectors and down the main hall toward the back of the first floor. On the right was the clerk's office. Harmon entered the room and greeted Bob Dinkle, the assistant clerk, who had been there at least 10 years and probably many more. "Hey, Bob. I have some motions for the Wilson v. Sanns case. Jury selection is tomorrow."

"Judge Lyman already has the file. I'll stamp them and then bring them over to his office."

"Thanks."

Lisa had waited in the hall. Harmon walked out of the clerk's office, motioned for her to follow, and took a right toward the back of the building. They turned left and skirted the stairs to the second floor. On the right was a door. Harmon opened it and they entered the first-floor courtroom, which stood empty. It spanned the back of the first floor, about 30 by 40 feet. There was the bar, the railing that separated the gallery from the counsel tables and jury. The jury box was on the left, cordoned off by another polished wooden railing. There were tables for the parties and of course the judge's raised bench in front, all ancient wood. The gallery looked to be about two dozen mismatched, colonial-style wooden chairs. At the front of the room, two doors were on the wall, one the jury deliberation room and one the judge's chambers.

"This is where all the magic will happen. What do you think?"

"Looks kind of decrepit."

"Because it is. But it's home for the next couple weeks."

Harmon sat for a moment in a chair at the counsel table farther from the jury, the defense table. He sat back, thought of all the activity that would ensue, saw himself talking to the jury, taking evidence, arguing. Lisa sat next to him, said nothing.

Then he got up and walked out of the courtroom door, back into the hall and out the door to his Jetta.

On the ride back, Harmon headed south down Route 63 toward the four corners. Lisa said, "You like to take a different route back to the office?"

"Always, if I can."

"I do that too. It makes a circle."

"Well, it usually makes an irregular trapezoid. It does make the drive nicer though."

Harmon pulled into the lot of the convenience store on the left. Lisa said, "What are you getting here? I think of these places as only having junk food and scratch tickets."

"They're convenient. That's why people like them."

"They're only convenient if you want anything they sell. I don't want anything they sell."

"I'll just be a minute." He walked into the store and emerged two minutes later carrying a 40-ounce fountain drink and a packaged lemon fruit pie.

"Seriously? That's what you get at convenience stores?"

"On my way back from court, I like to get a big soda, about 80% Diet Coke and 20% Dr. Pepper. Tastes good after all the talking I have to do. And I like lemon pies."

"That does not sound appetizing in the least."

"It may just be that convenience stores are not that convenient for you."

"I'm pretty sure they're not."

The rest of the ride back was filled with the same light conversation as the ride up. Lisa's little convertible was in the shop again. Convertibles were like pools, really fun, but only for a few days a year. Harmon's Volkswagen was reliable but boring. Yes, Harmon was still living in the back apartment at his aunt's farmhouse weekdays, and yes, his aunt insisted on making him lunch. Despite his really enjoying Lisa's company and their talk, somewhere along the way, part of Harmon had checked out and was only thinking about the case.

It was streak day 6,188.

* * *

Harmon didn't sleep well and was up before dawn. He had been at the office till 10:00, just going over everything, so he would be ready for any unexpected turn in the case. He ran his three-mile loop, all the time turning phrases over in his head. Catch phrases, for jury selection, for opening statement and again for closing argument. Ways to stitch the case together.

He caught a quick shower and shave and chose another dark suit, white shirt—always white for court—and a trial tie, something classy and not too busy, something to convey poise and power.

He was at the office by 7:45. He sat at his desk to deal with a few things that Donna could tend to while he was at trial. Then he just sat and thought. Donna came in at 8:05 and talked about the case for a minute or two. He was standing organizing documents on the side table next to his desk. Then she hugged him and pressed her body against his. "That's for luck. I know you'll do great."

Harmon was a little stunned. Except for a holiday party kiss and hug, theirs used to be a non-touching relationship, even though they were effectively work spouses. Then about six months ago, the hugs for luck started. Then they got more full-body. "Thanks."

Donna walked out, and he gathered his file materials and put them in his briefcase. Lisa walked in. "So, you think jury selection today and tomorrow, then straight to evidence?"

"You know me, at least two days to pick the jury. Then we'll see when the court has time for us."

She touched his arm. "Good luck. I'm sure you'll do great. Let me know if there's anything I can do for you."

"Anything at all?"

"I already told you that."

“I’ll need jury instructions.”

“Just ask. Anything.”

He exited the back door of his office to the parking lot and was on his way. Generally, on his way to court he would listen to NPR or one of the rock stations, but for trials he liked silence. The threads and phrases rolled through his mind. Jury selection themes, trial themes.

Then his morning invaded his thoughts. What a life. His wife couldn’t stand him. Her disapproval and anger were a constant storm in his mind. His paralegal loved him, or so everyone said, and she had been getting closer, literally. And there was Lisa. What was that? She was 11 years younger, in a different place in her life. Single and very alive. Could she even possibly be interested in him? He was not single, not that alive and had lately started to think that early death (accidental, not intentional, heart attack, most likely) was a viable alternative to his shitty life.

But there was a case to try. It would be starting in an hour and all non-case thoughts would be pushed to the back until it was over.

He parked about 250 yards south of the center of town on Route 63, where he could leave the car all day without a ticket. He took the oversized trial bag from the backseat, checked once more that the folder with the jury selection papers was in there, and walked back to the green. Ice crunched under his cap-toe dress shoes, from a flurry a few days prior.

As he approached the courthouse, he saw Ben Griswold smoking in front. Benedict Griswold III was a legacy in the legal world. His father was Justice Griswold, recently retired from the state supreme court. He was a fixture at this courthouse; Harmon could not remember ever seeing him in another court. He was 45 years old and about 6”1, with a gut that hung over his belt. He had reddish brown hair that was greying at the temples. He had on a dark brown suit over a striped shirt. His tie was green, tied in a crooked half-Windsor. He threw the cigarette down and extended his hand.

"Harmon. I guess you are the hired gun here. Came to beat up the local guy?"

"I don't see much beating up. I've only had this case since Thursday. Seems kind of cut and dried. Why isn't it settled?"

"It's not settled because All-Risk Insurance is a bunch of asses. They sat on my demand for the policy and my offer of judgment for over a year, just trying to hold onto their money. Then last month they say they will pay the $100,000. But the case is worth a lot more and the interest alone would be another $16,000. So, they need to pay $150,000, or we'll see what the jury does with the Hollywood movie personality who hit a local guy."

"I don't know, Ben. You don't think a $100,000 settlement, bird in hand, all that, is a good result? We could go home and do other things today. I'm kinda tired already."

"The case is worth more, six ways to Sunday, and you know it. Christ, he has $42,000 in meds alone. I'm not taking the hundred. And I can tell you: I'm asking for $250,000 from the good ladies and gentlemen of the jury. My guy needs a little justice from his peers."

"Be careful what you ask for. What's that thing old Judge Sherman used to say upstairs? 'Cows and horses eat; pigs get slaughtered.' I never really understood it, but I think it might apply here."

"Let's just do it. Your lady and my guy are already inside."

"You know my client?"

"It's obvious who the Hollywood movie person is."

And it was. Gloria looked resplendent in a black turtleneck and black shin-length wool skirt with a maroon blazer. She had a gold bracelet and a brooch that must have cost more than Harmon's whole outfit, including shoes. "Hello, Harmon," she purred, "this should be quite an experience."

They were standing in the long main hall, which was packed with people, some of them prospective jurors. Harmon's first thought was to get her out of the hall and away from anyone who could be on the jury. He whisked her down the hall, around the corner and into the back of the courtroom. Ben was in there with his client at the counsel table, talking in hushed tones. Wilson was like a local from central casting—big bear of a man, greying dark hair, big bulb of a nose over a small mouth with thin lips. He had on a checked shirt and khakis, but looked like he would be more comfortable in a flannel shirt and jeans.

Ben walked over and Harmon introduced him to Gloria. She said, "Charmed." This was going to be some trial. Harmon could almost see Ben's thoughts on how to use her position and attitude against her.

Harmon instructed Gloria to sit in the back of the room for now, away from Wilson. The last thing he needed was for her to start talking to him. He went to his counsel table and started unloading his briefcase. Ben walked over and said in a low voice, "What the fuck is with all the motions? You think I can't ask her where she's from or what she does for a living? Am I allowed to ask her anything under the law according to Harmon?"

"Why would her residence or job be relevant. The only thing that matters is whether she was negligent."

"Oh, she was negligent. And the motions are bullshit."

"Let's let the judge decide that."

At 9:25, Judge Lyman came out of the Judge's chambers behind the courtroom. He warmly greeted Ben and introduced himself to Harmon, who was starting to feel like an outsider in this provincial judicial district. "So,

Ben, have you had a chance to review all these motions? Are you ready to argue them?"

"Judge, they were faxed to me yesterday morning. I looked at them, but I have not had time to prepare a response."

The Judge turned to Harmon. "Counsel, do you have any issue with these being argued tomorrow at the beginning of court?" (Counsel: judge's term for stranger).

"Your Honor, I have no problem with the Court's schedule for argument. However, the motions seek in part to preclude mention of things that the defense thinks are irrelevant and prejudicial, and that would apply to mentions in jury selection as well. I would prefer to discuss this on the record." This was Harmon's way of saying he wanted to create a record of the motions and rulings for possible appeal, should the Judge make an erroneous ruling.

"Let's discuss them here first. You filed a lot of motions. What are there, eight? And you filed them on the day before jury selection. You're not making things easy."

"Your Honor, I've only had this case, my office has only had this case, since last Thursday. These are motions in limine about facts and evidence to be adduced at trial. They are necessarily filed on the eve of trial. I think they all make sense. I filed them as soon as I could identify them and get them done."

Ben spoke up. "Judge, I don't agree that they make sense. Attorney Willow wants me to tell half the story to the jury. I don't think that's right. But I can make it easy for today. I won't talk about any of the things in jury selection. We can argue these tomorrow."

The Judge turned to Harmon. "Counsel, that seems reasonable. Can we agree on that?"

"Judge. Once again, I'd just like to put it on the record."

"Okay. I think we are in agreement, but we can take it up on the record before we bring out the jury panel."

They made the agreement on the record. Until the motions were decided, Ben wouldn't mention the defendant's hometown or job or the fact that she was driving a rental car.

Harmon prepared for jury selection. Each lawyer would introduce his firm and his witnesses to the jury panel and then the lawyers would question the prospective jurors separately out of the hearing of the rest of the panel. Harmon liked to spend about half an hour with each person they interviewed, so that he could listen to them talk about their understanding of the civil justice system, the burden and standard of proof, the difference between the civil and criminal standards and how they would process evidence. He would use hypotheticals on credulity and credibility. He was looking for people who were skeptical and logical, who would not just accept whatever they were told. He had an outline that he rarely consulted, although he followed the form of it in each interview, so that the jurors would all hear similar things and have a similar experience with him. That way he could revisit themes brought out in the questioning.

The difficulty of being the outsider was evident from the start. Ben introduced himself as a solo practitioner. He gestured toward the front of the courthouse and said, "You may have seen my office across the green, down past the old jailhouse." He introduced his client and noted Wilson's town of residence, just to the north, daring Harmon to say the same for his client.

When Ben sat down Harmon had to introduce himself and his firm. The firm was in a town 45 minutes downstate in the sprawling suburbs. He then had to list all the lawyers and their towns of residence, all in that area, none even from the county in which he now stood. He mentioned the potential witnesses, including Gloria. In the moment, he decided to just mention her town and state of residence, Venice, California. He wanted to act as if this were insignificant. He didn't want it to be dramatically revealed somewhere during the trial. And he was convinced that it would come into the trial in some form, notwithstanding a motion to keep it out.

They brought out the first juror, Nina Paul, from 2 towns away. The attorneys had juror questionnaire sheets with age, town of residence, marital status, occupation, criminal history and whether the prospective juror had any prior jury experience. As he represented the plaintiff, Ben went first.

"Good morning, Mrs. Paul."

"Good morning."

I see you live in Morris, and you teach elementary school."

"Yes, at the Hammarskjold School, right near the center of town."

"And you haven't served on a jury before?"

"No. I was called in but never chosen."

"Do you consider yourself a fair person?"

"Yes."

"You understand, I represent Mr. Wilson here, from Goshen, the guy who brought the lawsuit because he was hurt in a car accident. Can you be fair to him?"

"Yes, of course."

"Can you promise to listen to the Judge's instructions on the law and follow them?"

"Yes. That's my job."

"And if at the end of the case, you think it would be fair to award my client a substantial sum of money for what he has endured, could you do that?"

"Yes. If that's what's fair."

"Thank you. I have no other questions. Attorney Willow may have a few."

Harmon didn't expect this. Even the shortest voir dire questioning was usually ten minutes. He would have to improvise. You can't ask a person questions for a half hour when opposing counsel takes two minutes.

Harmon pared down his usual questioning to ten minutes: starting with a smile and a soft joke about this being the job interview she never asked for, then a history of any claims or suits by the person or someone close, thoughts on the civil justice system, burden of proof and standard of proof and a series of hypothetical questions about liability and damages geared to indoctrinate the prospective juror on the fact that accidents often have more than one cause and a plaintiff may ask for more than the actual fair value of his damages. He paid special attention to the answers on how the person would evaluate a claim for pain and suffering.

Nina Paul was too much of a feeler, too sympathetic for Harmon. He used a preemptory challenge, one of four he was allowed. Zero jurors and three challenges left.

He questioned first with Roger Pickering, a mechanic from the far northwest part of the state. Although his general profile was closer to that of Mr. Wilson, which was a risk, he was more Harmon's kind of guy—mid-40s, very conservative, no history of claims, didn't see why people needed money for pain and suffering, but would consider it if the Judge told him to. "But I ain't giving no one a million dollars." Ben again took two minutes. Harmon accepted Pickering; Ben agreed, and he became juror number one.

Things were moving fast because of Ben Griswold's tactic of asking only a few questions. Harmon couldn't figure out if he was just lazy or if he thought the case was so airtight that any juror would give him the money he wanted. By the lunch break at 1:00 they had five jurors: four men and a woman. They checked in with the Judge, who told them that even if they picked the whole jury, evidence would not start the next day, but on Thursday, as originally planned. "But I want counsel here tomorrow at 9:30 to argue the defendant's motions. And I will need jury instructions, if you feel a need to file them, by the end of the day Thursday."

Although he preferred to be alone with his thoughts during trial, Harmon joined Gloria and her son for lunch at the coffee and sandwich shop on the corner. She insisted.

William Sanns, not Bill or Will, was about 30 years old, six feet tall and thin. He had unkempt brown hair. He was wearing a dark grey sweater over a blue oxford cloth shirt and khakis. He had the studied casual look of a preppie.

After introductions: "So, mother, having fun?"

"William. William. You don't know." Harmon though she might swoon for a moment. She gathered herself and went on. "This parade of jury people. William. All flannel and denim. Hardly a jury of my peers."

"Well, Mother. A little melodramatic, are we?" Then, "Attorney Willow, might some of the people being considered for the jury be lunching here?"

"Call me Harmon. And, yes. They might. We should consider our words."

Gloria looked around in mock horror. "Do you think anyone heard me?"

"I think it's a good idea to be careful what we say in town, in the courthouse and especially in the courtroom. The worst thing that could happen for our case would be for the jury to think you were arrogant or condescending. In fact, don't even think that way. You are contrite, but unbowed."

"Well, I am . . . ."

"Mom! No. Don't say another word. And listen to your attorney."

Gloria ordered a sandwich and herbal tea. She ate less than half the sandwich and never touched the tea.

Back at court, Gloria was subdued. Her lunchtime antics had worn her out. They picked six jurors and two alternates by 3:30, and she never said a word. Harmon made a point of consulting with her on every juror choice, but he was humoring her. The strategy and choices were his alone. Outside the courthouse, he explained that he would be in court arguing motions at 9:30 and would like to meet with her at 12:00 to prepare her testimony. They made a date for the same small conference room at the Inn.

On the way back to the office, Harmon made two calls from his car phone. First, he called the office and talked to Lisa to get her to work on the jury instructions—the defendant's suggestions to the Judge as to how he should instruct the jury on the law after the evidence. He was particularly concerned with the charge on the statute for unreasonable speed, to make sure the court read the full statute, for his defense that the plaintiff was going too fast.

The second call was to Gloria's personal attorney, Kaitlin to tell her about the progress of the case. She would not be joining him for the meeting with Gloria tomorrow, but she was instructed to attend the entire trial and take notes. "I hope you know what you're doing, Harmon. All-Risk is taking a big chance."

“I’m just a soldier. I do what I’m told and try to minimize the hit.”

Back at the office, he met with Donna and told her about the pace of jury selection, the jury make-up and the timing of the trial. He told her that he would be working on his opening statement tonight, getting it to final form, and that she didn’t need to work late for anything. She seemed disappointed.

Harmon walked over to Lisa’s office to discuss the jury instructions. He went over the various instructions and the angle he wanted to take. She knew what he wanted. “I’ll have a draft ready by tomorrow afternoon when you get back to the office. Sure you don’t need anything else?”

“Anything at all? If you keep saying that I might follow you home.”

“I might like that.”

“Be careful what you wish for, Lisa Lisa.”

Harmon retreated to his office and settled in for the night. He finished writing his opening, his direct exam of Gloria and cross exam of Mr. Wilson. He wrote a short report to the insurer on the jury make-up. He walked out of the office at 10:30. When he got home, he ate some cold pasta and went to bed.

The next morning at dawn he was out for the regular three-mile course. Winter was coming; it was about 25 degrees and clear. Harmon wore nylon wind pants and a hoodie, a ski hat and fleece mittens. The run was invigorating, but he switched right into work mode: shower, shave, suit, toast and coffee, work. He walked in at 8:00. Donna was already there.

“I finalized the docs you finished last night. Two copies in the folder. When are you leaving?”

"8:30."

"Anything else you need me to do?"

"No, but we need to have the jury instructions ready for Thursday morning. You can stay tonight or do them in the morning."

"I'll stick around tonight."

"I should be back by about 4:00. I'll see you then."

* * *

At 9:30, Harmon was in court, waiting with Ben. The Judge came out and called them into Chambers.

"I'm not really sure we need to argue these motions. Maybe we can arrive at some agreement. It seems defendant wants to pare the case down to just the tort issues: was the defendant driver negligent in operation of her vehicle? He wants to remove all context: who owned the car, that it was a rental, where she's from, what she does for a living. What are your thoughts counsel?"

Harmon started: "These are my motions, Judge. Your Honor may think I am trying to remove context for the parties, but really I'm just trying to remove things that are immaterial to the issues and prejudicial to the defense. For example, I'm sure Ben would like to have the jury know that my client is not just from California, but she is a Hollywood casting director. He hopes that will influence the jury to award more. But that's not part of the case. She's not a bad driver because of who she is or where she's from. I'm trying to get rid of things like that."

"Ben?"

"Your Honor, I think this is all part of the *res gestae* of the case." (What lawyers say, when they have no arguments, Harmon thought.) "These things tell the jury who she is and what she's doing here."

"Judge, if I may, the only issues in the case are liability and damages. It would be wrong for the jury to award more or less because of who the parties are. Further, revealing that the vehicle was a rental does nothing to say who was at fault, but it will confuse the jury as to why the rental company is not a party and whether it should pay money."

"Ben, can we agree to keep out the casting director part? I don't see how that has anything to do with the case. Where she's from is part of the *res gestae*. (What judges say when they don't understand the evidence and relevance.)

I'm concerned about the rental car situation. That may confuse the jury. Can we agree to keep it out?"

"I think it's in, Judge. We should argue that on the record."

After the argument, the Judge kept out Gloria's occupation, the fact that the car was a rental and the fact that she was given a ticket. Other things were in, making Harmon pleased that he had extracted a promise from each prospective juror that he or she would not allow the decision in the case to be based on who the parties were or where they were from.

Next, he drove to the Inn and met with Gloria. She again looked perfectly dressed and coifed. They spent two hours going over all of Harmon's direct testimony—the questions he would ask her—and the expected cross examination from Ben. Harmon told her the things that would be kept out of the trial and told her not to answer questions on her profession or the rental car. He would object as necessary. He cautioned not to sound dismissive of the claim, but also not to admit fault. Harmon said, "You may be directly asked, 'Didn't you cause this accident?' Just answer obliquely with something like, 'That's what the trial is for: to determine what caused it.'" She was satisfied and seemed very sharp in her understanding of how to respond. Harmon hoped her questioning would be in the morning when she seemed at her best. By the end of the day, she would be worn down and more apt to stumble.

Harmon made his circle, stopped for a big soda and headed back to the office. Lisa was there with a draft of jury instructions: 22 densely written pages of suggested explanation of the law that applies to the case for the judge to read to the jury. Parties in cases had the right to file them and request them, but judges often used their own instructions, refined from years of trials. Harmon and Lisa sat closely in his office going over every instruction to get it to final form for submitting the next day. Donna walked in about three times while they were working, always with some non-crucial thing for Harmon to do.

"Donna seems a little territorial today. Do you think she wants me to leave?"

Harmon laughed. "She just wants to get done the things she wants done by the end of the day and she's very determined."

"Well, we're almost done. Then she can have you all to herself."

He laughed again. Halfheartedly. "Right."

By 5:30 they were done. "Okay, is that all you need me to do for you?"

"I think that's it."

"Well, just call if you need anything else. Do you have my home number?"

"You are just asking for trouble, Lisa."

"Maybe I could use some trouble."

"Suppose I called and Tim answered? That might be awkward?"

"Tim is not going to answer because he doesn't live there anymore. You don't stay up on the office gossip, do you?"

"I guess not."

"Well, if you did you might know we're done."

"Oh. I'm sorry."

"I'm not, Harmon. It's fine."

"He's not good enough for you, anyway." As if Harmon had any idea.

"Funny. Well, not that funny. I don't think he really thought I was good enough for him. Maybe that's not it. But I don't think he ever pictured himself with me long-term."

"Okay. That's crazy. He should think he died and went to heaven."

"Well, things don't always work out."

"Don't I know it." The flirting all of a sudden seemed a lot more real. The thought passed his mind again: could she really be interested in him? There seemed to be an answer from the void. "No."

As soon as Lisa left, with Harmon still musing about their flirting, Donna sped into the office. "Man, I'm glad she's gone. She's like second-hand smoke. The silent killer. She hangs around and keeps us from getting work done."

Harmon wondered: where did that come from? "Actually, we were finishing up the jury instructions that she drafted. I needed to have them done so you could finalize them for court tomorrow."

"Yeah, well you seem to work better without distractions."

She finished the jury instructions and packed 3 copies in a folder in his briefcase. Then she was on her way out. She brushed his arm. "I'm just trying to take care of my man, making sure you get everything done so you can be your best at trial." Her man.

Then Harmon was on his own for the evening to get ready for trial. He stood, buttoned his jacket, and recited his opening statement four times through, as close as possible to what he intended to say to the jury the next morning. He paid particular attention to the questions he would ask the jury to consider. "While you're listening to the evidence, Ladies and Gentlemen, consider three questions that will help you arrive at the decision in the case. First, how fast was the plaintiff going and what was the speed limit? Second, how far was the stop sign from the point of impact on Route 63, and how long would it reasonably take Ms. Sanns to get there? Lastly, is there anything the plaintiff could do before the accident that he can't do now, in work, in life? Consider the evidence and think of these questions."

Harmon went over his cross exam of the plaintiff, his treating doctor and the State Police officer who was at the scene. With the plaintiff, he would emphasize speed and strong recovery. With the doctor, he would emphasize the excellent work he and his practice did and the strong recovery of the plaintiff with no work restrictions or life restrictions after discharge. With the state trooper, he needed to discuss the measurements, the 30 feet six inches from the stop line to the point of impact, and the plaintiff's own admission that he was going 40 in a 35 before the accident. Under the court's rulings, the police report would be given to the jury heavily redacted. The jury would not know that Wilson had admitted to speeding. Harmon would have to get this through the testimony of the trooper. It would come into evidence as the admission of a party, an exception to the hearsay rule.

By 10:00 Harmon was headed home. His aunt had left him an eggplant parmigiana sub for dinner. He ate and went to bed. There was no room in his head to contemplate his increasingly strange life. Everything was the trial.

He awoke before dawn and went on another 3-miler. Breathing the cold morning air was bracing, but he was just treading water with running this week. He had a trial.

Back at the apartment, he showered, shaved, chose a dark grey suit, white shirt and conservative maroon tie. He tied the black cap-toes and felt ready.

He was only in the office for 10 minutes before heading up to court. Donna came into his office and closed the door. She wished him luck "But you don't need it" in a low voice. Then she hugged him again for luck and kissed him right on the lips, startling him. "Sorry, I just want you to know I'm here for you. Just let me know and I'll take care of anything I can. Have a great day and then come back and tell me everything."

Harmon exited the back door and drove to court. He was there by 9:00. He placed his briefcase and folders on his counsel table and walked back to the front of the old building to wait for Gloria. Several jurors walked in and said hi. Harmon smiled and nodded, but never said a word. He never talked to jurors during a trial. It was the rule. Gloria arrived full of energy and condescension. "This town is ridiculous. I couldn't even get a good cup of tea this morning. I can't wait to get out of here."

He shushed her gently and reminded her that jurors would be right in the same hall. "Think humble. Think regular."

"It's no use Harmon. You know me by now. That's not who I am."

Gently, but firmly: "Then act it. Just till the trial is over."

They walked into the courtroom and he held her chair for her. First, she warmly greeted Ben and Wilson, while Harmon frowned.

Then the trial was on. Kaitlin walked in and sat in the gallery. The jury was seated and the judge gave them introductory remarks. Harmon looked over and had that feeling all trial lawyers do when the jury is seated. "I picked these people?"

Then Ben rose to give an opening. It would be short. After introductions, he said, "This case will be short, but not because it's unimportant. It's very important. It will be short because it is painfully obvious what happened on Route 63 three years ago. The defendant (he pointed) pulled out from a stop sign and caused a heavy accident. My client (he touched Wilson's shoulder), his life was changed forever in a moment. Changed forever. My client was seriously injured and will never be the same. At the end of the case I will suggest a reasonable award, but I can tell you, it's a lot of money because this was a serious accident, with serious consequences. Thank you."

Harmon was getting used to Ben's short form of trial work. He had a truncated opening of his own, but he nailed the three questions. He was going to push the comparative fault even in a stop sign case, and he was going to harp on the fact that Wilson was released to full duty work with no restrictions per his treating orthopedist.

He sat and got ready for the evidence. Ten minutes later, he got an idea of how the trial would go. Ben asked a question that called for a hearsay answer, asked something that Wilson had said to the doctor. Harmon rose and objected. "Objection. Hearsay." The judge looked a little flustered and sent the jury out. He then asked each lawyer his view on the propriety of the question.

Harmon said, "Your Honor, it's classic hearsay. An out of court statement offered for the truth of the statement."

Ben: "Judge, he's a party and it's his own prior statement for the purpose of medical treatment. Not hearsay."

"Doesn't matter, Your Honor. Hearsay can be prior statements of the person on the stand."

The Judge hesitated. He called a recess. He called counsel into his chambers and tried to broker some compromise. Harmon was frustrated. He wanted the Judge to sustain the objection, but most of all he wanted the trial to flow. A judge who can't make a decision on the fly is not a good trial judge. Ben eventually withdrew the question, but Harmon went back with the knowledge that any objection could occasion at half hour delay in the evidence. For this one, the jury would probably blame him because he had objected.

Back in the courtroom, Ben resumed with Wilson. Twenty minutes later, Harmon objected again, again for hearsay, as to a doctor's advice. The Judge hesitated, and Ben looked pained. "I'll withdraw the question Your Honor." The trial would be bumpy.

Wilson testified for two hours on direct. Harmon wanted only about 20 minutes of cross exam, so he was brief and to the point.

"You drove down Route 63 for 10 miles before the accident."

"Right."

"You went through the part where the speed limit was 55."

"Right."

"Now, where the accident occurred had a 35-miles per hour speed limit for you."

"That's right."

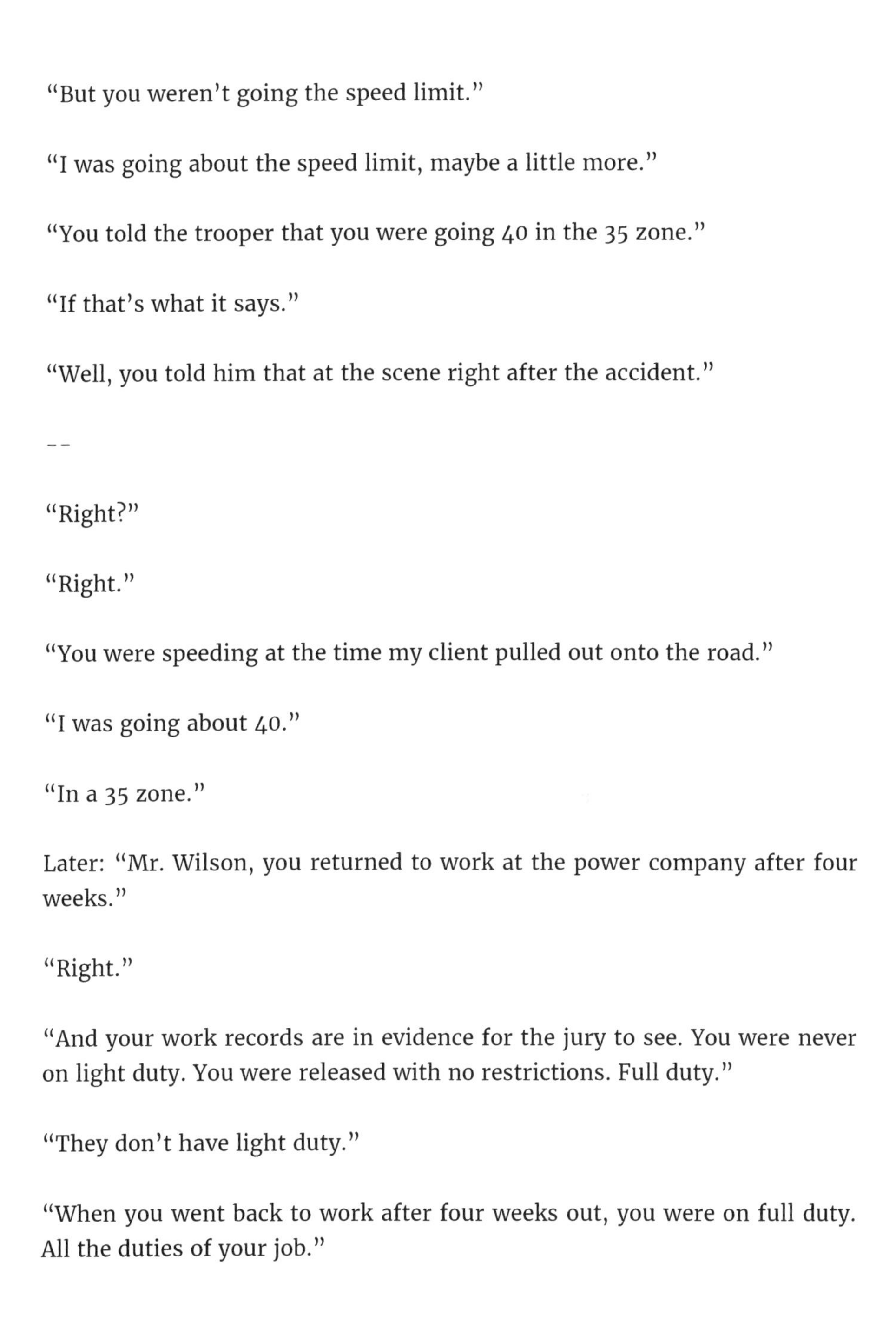

"But you weren't going the speed limit."

"I was going about the speed limit, maybe a little more."

"You told the trooper that you were going 40 in the 35 zone."

"If that's what it says."

"Well, you told him that at the scene right after the accident."

- -

"Right?"

"Right."

"You were speeding at the time my client pulled out onto the road."

"I was going about 40."

"In a 35 zone."

Later: "Mr. Wilson, you returned to work at the power company after four weeks."

"Right."

"And your work records are in evidence for the jury to see. You were never on light duty. You were released with no restrictions. Full duty."

"They don't have light duty."

"When you went back to work after four weeks out, you were on full duty. All the duties of your job."

"Yeah."

Later still: "Mr. Wilson. I have this stack of medical records from the hospital and from your doctor and from the physical therapy. Can we agree that nowhere in here, nowhere in this stack of records does a doctor say there is anything that you could do before the accident that you cannot do now."

"I don't know."

"Well, here are the records. You are welcome to review them to see, because I couldn't find any doctor putting any restrictions on any of your activities."

"I guess you're right."

"Do you want to read through them while we wait?"

"No. I guess not."

"So, no restrictions at work. No restrictions at home."

"Right."

Harmon sat down, satisfied that he had made the points he had.

After the lunch break, Ben called the trooper. He recounted the severity of the collision and that Wilson was not able to get out of the pickup or walk due to his injuries and had to be transported by ambulance with a serious leg injury.

On cross exam, Harmon asked about the 40 miles per hour. The trooper consulted his own copy of the police report and recalled that Wilson had indeed said that. Harmon asked, "In your 26 years as a trooper, have you found that drivers are always honest about their speed?" The trooper laughed, as did the jury.

Ben stood up and objected. Harmon withdrew the question. The Judge instructed the jury to disregard it.

Later, Harmon asked about the measurements. "So, the Ford had to travel over 30 feet from a stop to where the accident happened. In that time, the pickup stayed right in its lane. Didn't swerve or leave skid marks."

"That's what we found."

Not perfect. But it showed Wilson had taken no evasive action.

The first day of evidence was done. The Judge met with the lawyers and talked about the pace of the trial. At Ben's request, he decided to have the jury report at 11:00 the next day because he had been informed that Dr. Silverman was available at that time after morning rounds at Mercy Hospital. Then Ben would call the plaintiff's wife in the afternoon and the plaintiff would rest. The defendant's case would go forward Tuesday morning and closing arguments and deliberations would be on Wednesday, no matter when court finished on Tuesday. Counsel and the Judge would meet Tuesday afternoon to discuss the requests to charge and the charge on the law that the Judge proposed to read to the jury.

Harmon kept to the same routine. He stayed late at the office to prepare the next day's testimony. The women who were making his life interesting both made appearances and both left, to Harmon's relief and disappointment. He liked Donna's devotion and attention, and he found he really wanted to spend more time with Lisa—to strategize the case or just to talk about anything.

He went home at 10:00 and ate quickly, before falling into bed. Then he was up before dawn for the too-short three-mile loop and another full day in court in a dark suit, white shirt and conservative tie.

On day two of evidence, Ben called the doctor. He made a point of going over all of his credentials and board certifications. Harmon stood up at the beginning and offered to stipulate that the doctor was qualified to testify as an expert, to no avail. Harmon was waiting for Ben to mention Dr. Silverman's middle school drama award or something similar. Finally, Silverman got to what he was paid for. He talked about the dislocation, extreme discomfort. The closed reduction under general anesthesia because of the severe discomfort, the difficult therapy and the permanent partial impairment. "Will he ever be back to the condition he was in before the accident?"

"No. He is permanently impaired, with a 15% impairment of the right lower extremity."

From cross exam by Harmon: "Doctor, you did a great job here, right?"

"I believe the records say there was a good result."

"Well, you were able to reduce the joint with no complications, correct."

"Right."

"You had good placement. Yes?"

"Yes."

"Mr. Wilson was out of the hospital in two days, right?"

"Yes."

"And you wouldn't have sent him home if he wasn't ready, correct?"

"That's correct."

"And he was on crutches for only four weeks, right?"

"Right."

"Then he was able to bear weight on the leg."

"Yes."

"And at that time, he went back to his usual employment?"

"Yes."

"Full duty. No restrictions."

"Well, I would advise a patient to take it easy at first."

"Hmm, I'm just going by your records. It says here, 'Doing well. Back to work no restrictions.' You would agree with your own record, right?"

"Yes."

"And this impairment rating, the 15%. That's not part of your medical treatment, right?"

"What do you mean? He has the impairment according to the American Medical Association guidelines."

"Right Doctor, but you wouldn't make this opinion unless there was a legal case, a claim for money? You don't give ratings to patients who are not making personal injury claims, right?"

"No, that is part of the guidelines for orthopedic injuries used for claims."

“Right, for claims. Now, Doctor, when you discharged Mr. Wilson from your care, you did not put any restriction on his personal activities. You didn’t tell him that anything was off limits, right?”

“We discussed his activities and I told him to use his good sense.”

“Right. But the records. They would say no restrictions. Can we agree on that?”

“Yes.”

“One last thing, Doctor. You’re not here out of the kindness of your heart, right?”

“What?”

“You’re here testifying on behalf of Mr. Wilson because you are being paid for this testimony.”

“I’m being paid for my time, not the testimony.”

“Really. But it’s a flat fee for you being here today, isn’t that right?”

“What do you mean?”

“You’re being paid $3,000 for these few hours in court, right?”

“Yes. That’s my usual charge for my time testifying.”

“And you’ve already been paid, haven’t you? You were paid for your testimony before you took the witness stand?”

“For my time.”

"Right. Before you'd spent any time, and before you knew how much time this would take. Thank you, doctor. No more questions."

There was some redirect by Ben, trying to emphasize the serious injury and pain and permanent injury. There was some re-cross by Harmon trying to re-emphasize his points.

When it was over and Harmon sat down, he felt pretty good. He had clouded the testimony of the serious injury with his two main points that the healing was good enough that Wilson had no restrictions at work or in his leisure life, and that Silverman was bought and paid for.

It was a little past time for the lunch break.

Harmon walked to a different sandwich shop with Gloria and Kaitlin. Gloria was beaming. "Wow, so this is what you do. You take a case and chop it to pieces. It's like an elaborate play."

"Let's not get ahead of ourselves, Gloria. I'm just trying to plant a little doubt. Trying to score a few points for our team."

"Nicely done, Harmon," said Kaitlin. Harmon thought this was probably the first time she had ever complimented him for anything.

After a few minutes, he left them to eat and went back to his car to go over notes for the afternoon. He didn't need to go over notes. He just wanted his private down time.

For the afternoon session, Mrs. Cynthia Wilson testified. She was a stocky, buxom, white-haired woman in her mid-fifties. She wore a plain conservative dress and a cardigan sweater. Like her husband Brad, her testimony tended to be understated. Brad didn't complain. He did move a little slower. He had a bit of a limp. His shoes wore down more on the right heel. She worried about him.

There was little for Harmon to do on cross examination. He decided to ask only three leading questions.

"Mrs. Wilson, the plaintiff, the person here asking for money, the guy sitting over here. That's your husband, right?"

"Yes. Brad is my husband."

"And you would like him to do well in this trial?"

"I don't know what you mean."

"If he gets more money, that's more money for you too."

"Well, I guess so. I don't think of it that way."

"Mm hmm. No further questions."

When Mrs. Wilson was done, the plaintiff rested, meaning he had completed his part of the evidence. It was up to Harmon to call any witnesses for the defense. He only planned to call one: Gloria. But he wanted her testimony to be on Tuesday, the next jury trial day in that courthouse.

It was 3:00 on Friday afternoon, and the jury was released for the day with the usual caution not to discuss the case with anyone, including other jurors. The Judge called the lawyers into his chambers to discuss the rest of the trial. Before going in, Harmon said goodbye to Gloria for the weekend. They would meet again Monday afternoon for final preparation of her testimony.

The Judge wanted to map out the rest of the trial. No trial Monday. Tuesday, testimony of Gloria, then defendant rests. Tuesday afternoon charge conference where the Judge would explain his proposed jury charge.

Wednesday morning closing arguments. Then the charge to the jury, then deliberations and verdict.

By 3:45, Harmon was in the car. After he got a big soda and a lemon pie, he called the office from the car and spoke to Donna. They went over the day's events at trial and anything important at the office. Donna had handled everything. There was no need to go back to the office; he could go straight home. He asked to be transferred to Lisa. There was a pause.

"Why?"

"Because I want to talk to her about the trial."

"You just talked to me about it."

"Because she's helping me with things. On the trial."

"Have a nice weekend." The line clicked and Lisa's line was ringing. It went to voicemail.

"Hey, Lisa. It's me. I'm on the way home. I'll be in the car for a while if you want to call and hear all the important news from the trial. Or not . . . So, have a nice weekend." He felt like a dope.

Five minutes later his car phone rang.

"Hello."

"Hey. Sorry I didn't get your call. I didn't know who it was. I hate just answering the phone."

"Well, it was just me."

"So, what happened?"

"Nothing of importance. The doctor went really well, the wife not as great."

They talked for about ten minutes about the day's trial. Then weekend plans. Harmon would be at home. Lisa was going to a winter vacation house with her parents. Harmon was running out of things to say.

"Well, have a great weekend. See you Monday."

"You don't need me to do anything this weekend, do you?"

"No, everything's done. We just have to finish the trial next week."

"Well, if anything comes up, call me at home. I'll be back late Sunday afternoon."

"Okay. Have fun."

"You already said that. You must want me to have extra fun."

"I do. Well, bye."

"Bye."

* * *

Two hours later he got off exit 19A and drove through his little shore line town to his house. Joan's car was not there, which was a relief. He didn't have the energy for more drama tonight. His mother-in-law was home with the kids and he took over. They went for a walk around the village and he made them dinner back at home. Iris was in first grade and told him all about her week. Harmon was four and in preschool. Although they talked on the phone every night, it was great to see them and spend time. After dinner, they sat on the couch and watched Aladdin on video. He gave them baths and put them to bed.

The house was quiet. His mother in law's tv droned in her room upstairs. He sat back on the couch and thought for the thousandth time about his failing marriage. His connection to this house, this town and those two beautiful kids was all wrapped up in the marriage. His parents had chosen to split up, but he could see how people stayed together "for the sake of the children." In reality, society pushed people to stay married even if miserable. Divorce meant more acrimony, less access to your children, more guilt over the effects of the split on the kids. But Harmon knew that if they stayed together, the kids would also see that Mom and Dad just didn't get along. He knew from his earliest memories that his parents didn't like each other. He had no memories of them having fun or being gentle with one another. A cloud of doom swirled around his head. It seemed there were no good answers.

He thought of his own overwhelming unhappiness. He again entertained the fantasy of having a heart attack and dying young. But he also knew how wrong it was that he should abandon hope of a happy life at 42. There had to be time to make something more positive.

He went to bed at 10:30. Joan arrived home at 11:00, and there was some argument about something, but he refused to put up a fight and went to sleep. He got up early the next morning and ran 5 miles before anyone stirred. The rest of the weekend was uneventful and followed the usual pattern. He walked with the kids to see Santa and get hot chocolate at the wharf on Saturday afternoon. On Sunday, he again got up at dawn and ran 5 miles, then took the kids to the little local zoo, where Iris liked to ride the pony. His sister Hope came over for pasta on Sunday night, to the delight of Iris and Harmon (Joan didn't like her). He left at 10:00 to drive back since there was no court on Monday.

For two hours in the car, the same issues kept rolling over in his mind. In one way, he felt resigned; in another he thought his life could not go on this way. Somewhere along the way, he started to think he and Joan had to split up, but he also thought that she wasn't so much a villain as someone who just wanted what she wanted. It was more a matter of compatibility than good and evil or right and wrong. He didn't care who was right. He wanted to be happy, wanted to value life again.

When he got back to the apartment, he brushed his teeth and looked in the mirror. A paunchy, balding, haggard middle-aged man stared back, but his internal malaise was more serious. He shut off the light and climbed into his single bed.

* * *

Monday morning, he ran the three-mile loop with less urgency since he did not have to hurry off to court. He made it to the office by 8:15 and caught up on some work he had been neglecting while in court. Donna had a long list of things for them to go over.

Next, he again looked at his direct examination notes for Gloria. He changed a few things, but he wanted to keep it simple and as brief as possible. Lawyers often have problems with direct examination. They have to ask open-ended questions and let the witness form the sentences and testimony. The lawyer lacks control over the situation, as clients often answer in unpredictable ways and phrase answers in ways that counter the lawyer's themes of the case. He trusted Gloria's intelligence, but not her attention to the details of his case. He wanted her to sound clear and thoughtful. He wanted her to convey in clean, complete sentences that she was leaving her son's house and headed for the hotel where she was staying. She stopped at the stop sign of the intersection. She knew that traffic on Route 63 had the right of way. She looked left and right. Saw a pickup approaching from her right a long way up the road. Saw that it was safe to go, pulled out deliberately and carefully and was smashed by the pickup at least three seconds later in the travel lane, much to her surprise. She did not hear squealing tires.

For the third meeting at the Inn, it was just Harmon and Gloria. He told her she was doing great and that the trial would wrap up no later than Thursday morning. She was interested in the drama of the trial, but she was just as anxious to get back to California. They went over all the points of the testimony. Harmon asked every question he would ask her, suggested rephrasing some answers, talked about how to convey her points. Then he asked her the questions he anticipated for cross examination. He finished by reminding her of the areas of questioning that were off limits based on motions in limine. He left after about 90 minutes.

After an uneventful night at the office and another predawn run, he found himself sitting at the counsel table in the courtroom, ready for the defense part of the case. When the jury was seated and the Judge asked if he was ready to call his first witness, he called Gloria Sanns to the stand. He went through the questions in the same phrasing and same order as practiced. And she did a great job: explaining her side of the story, how she stopped and looked and proceeded carefully, not blaming Wilson, but not admitting that it was her fault.

Then it was time for cross examination, and it went about as expected. Ben was aggressive and tried to get her to admit that the accident was entirely her fault. She smiled sweetly and said, "I thought that's what the trial was for."

He seemed annoyed and a bit flustered and then he asked a forbidden question out of frustration: "You were driving a rental car, not your own car."

Time seemed to slow down, but really, Harmon had to gauge the proper response in less than a second. He could object, because the issue of the rental car had been precluded based on the pretrial motions and rulings. But making an objection, even when successful, highlights the question and suggests to a jury that there was something of significance there. No matter what happened, Harmon did not want the jury to think that the rental issue mattered to him. He sat still and hoped for the best.

And Gloria came through. She paused as she had been instructed to do in the event of an improper question area. When Harmon didn't object, she smiled and said, "I'm not sure that I was." And the moment passed. The Judge was glaring at Ben and he did not dare to ask a follow up on the issue.

Then Gloria was off the stand, and the defense rested. The evidence portion of the trial was complete. The jury was dismissed for the day and told they were to return the next day at 9:00, court to start promptly at 9:30 for final arguments, the jury charge and deliberations. The Judge then ordered counsel to return at 2:00 to discuss the charge to the jury.

At 2:00 both lawyers were seated in chambers, and the Judge went over the entire charge to the jury to see if the lawyers approved. As the Judge did not want any objections if possible, he wanted agreement of the lawyers that they would accept the proposed charge. Neither agreed. They both said they would have to hear the charge and may object if it sounded wrong in the courtroom. The Judge was not pleased.

Harmon drove to four corners for his soda and returned to the office. He filled Donna in on the events of the day and she left at 5:00. Harmon was working on the final touches of his closing. Lisa came by and he tested some of the closing argument on her. She seemed underwhelmed, and he decided to keep working. At 10:00, he drove home, grabbed some pasta and went to bed.

He barely slept and got up before dawn. He bundled up for the 3-mile loop, showered, shaved and dressed. He wore his best-fitting, dark blue suit, a white button-down oxford cloth shirt and a red Tommy Hilfiger tie with blue checks, cordovan wing tips. He looked in the mirror and thought, "I look like a lawyer."

He stopped at the office for only a few minutes. Donna gave him another tight hug for luck. Lisa said she would drive up and watch.

And then it was 9:30, and he was sitting at counsel table as the Judge explained to the jury that it was time for the lawyers to give their closing arguments. He told the jury that because the plaintiff had the burden of proving the case, the plaintiff's attorney would go first and last. He would give a closing argument; then the defendant would go. Then the plaintiff would do a rebuttal of the defendant's argument. Kaitlin was there; Lisa was there.

Ben stood up and kept it short and simple. Harmon took notes because he wanted to use some of Ben's phrases in his closing. He went over the evidence briefly and said that the defendant was trying to get out of responsibility, but the evidence was clear and simple. She had a stop sign. She pulled out; she caused the accident. She caused his severe and permanent injury. He would never be the same again. He had $42,745 of medical bills. He had $4,240 of lost wages. He had pain and suffering every day. His case was worth $250,000. He had talked for 25 minutes of the allotted hour. He sat down.

Harmon rose and went over his take on the evidence, the speed, the distances. He went over the three questions. "(1) The plaintiff was going over the speed limit, by his own admission. (2) The point of impact was just over 30 feet from the stop line, a long way. (3) Ms. Sanns testified that it took all of three seconds to pull out and cross the road to where the accident happened." Then Harmon went over the actual feet per second of a vehicle at 40 miles per hour. "40 times 5,280, divided by 3,600, the number of seconds in an hour." He held his calculator and entered the numbers. "That comes out to 58 feet eight inches every second at 40 miles per hour. You heard Ms. Sanns say she pulled out and took about three seconds to go from a stop across the shoulder and northbound travel lane to the point of the accident. In three seconds that is 176 feet. All while Mr. Wilson is barreling down on Ms. Sanns. This isn't magic; you can use simple arithmetic to get to these figures. Going faster than the posted speed makes a difference."

He continued his closing, going over the injuries and the fine doctor's work and good results for the plaintiff—back to work with no restrictions, and no restrictions in his non-work activities.

When he got to the end of the nuts and bolts of the evidence, he launched into a story. "Ladies and gentlemen, sometimes we're presented with issues and people tell us they're cut and dried. Plain as can be. But are they? Ladies and gentlemen, when I was a boy around eight or nine, my two best friends were twins, Greg and Tommie. I used to play at their house after school and used to eat dinner over there all the time. To get there from my house, I had to walk through a section of woods. At this time of year, when the days were short, I would be walking home in the dark, really running home in the dark. And for an eight or nine-year old, it was a little scary. One night, I was running home through the dark woods and I froze. I saw a man standing up ahead and next to him a huge dog. My heart was beating so fast. I had no idea what to do and I just stood perfectly still. And something happened. My eyes adjusted to the darkness and I could see. What I thought was a man was a small tree. The dog was a big rock. It wasn't what I thought it was. All I had to do was take a closer look, let my eyes adjust.

"And ladies and gentlemen, that's what this case is like. Attorney Griswold says things are simple and plain as can be: stop sign, injured hip. But then you take a closer look and you see his client, Mr. Wilson was going too fast. You see how far Ms. Sanns pulled out to get to the point of the accident. You see the injury, but you also see the great doctor work, the strong recovery and the future with no restrictions. All you have to do is take a closer look and let your eyes see all the evidence."

Then Harmon went to an easel and flipped to a page that had the same blanks as the verdict form. "Now, I'm not going to say Ms. Sanns had nothing to do with this accident. But I am going to say the evidence shows that both sides contributed to it. And this is what I think you should put on that form. The medical bills and lost wages on the economic damages line. For noneconomic damages, the same number, $46,985. Then I will leave the comparative fault of the plaintiff up to you. Just to say he has some fault. He was going faster than the speed limit. And when the Judge instructs you on the law, he will say that exceeding the posted limit is an element of going too fast for conditions under the laws of our state. So, something needs to go on that line.

"One last thing, Attorney Griswold has the last word. I've done a few trials and sometimes attorneys act mad or indignant, sometimes they shout or bang things. But nothing he says can change the evidence. Nothing can change the real view of what happened and what the fair result would be. Thank you."

Ben stood and spent five minutes on rebuttal, mostly reiterating his points. Harmon had found that when you mention that the other lawyer might act mad or shout, he or she rarely did.

The Judge called a 15-minute recess. Gloria was beaming, holding him by the arm. "Wow, Harmon, that was inspired. I loved it."

Kaitlin walked up. "Nice going. Now, let's see what the jury does with it. I'm going back to my office. Call me when the verdict comes in."

Harmon walked to the back of the room. To Lisa: "Better than yesterday?"

"Better. Much better. It was really good. I have to get back to the office."

"I'll walk you out." And he did. "We may have a verdict by today."

"Does that mean drinks? Either way? Celebrate or drown our sorrows?"

"I guess. But only if it's over."

She touched his arm and turned to walk to her car. He called out, "You know, you could stay, wait for the verdict." He wasn't sure where that came from.

She stopped, turned, and gave him that close-mouthed smile.

"I have to call in to the office, but I can probably stay." They walked down the street together breathing the cool air of the quaint New England town. After going around the block, they returned, making small talk about anything but the trial.

Back in court, the Judge read the charge to the jury. It was painfully slow and long, and Harmon could barely follow all of it. He wondered what the jury would be able to make of it. He listened with particular care to the charge on statutory unreasonable speed, a written law that was long and hard to read or make sense of. The key for Harmon's purposes was that the Judge would read the part that said that exceeding the posted speed was evidence of unreasonable speed. He read part of the statute, but not the key part.

After the entire charge, the Judge asked if there were any exceptions. Harmon spoke up and noted that he had not read the part of the statute that he had mentioned to the jury and that the judge said he intended to read. The Judge took a recess and called counsel to his chambers. He was flustered. Harmon wasn't going to give in on this point. "Your Honor I just said in closing argument that the court would tell them when the Judge explained the law that going over the posted speed is evidence of traveling unreasonably fast. You didn't read that part of the statute."

"Do you want me to call them back out and read it?"

"Yes. That's the only fair thing to do."

Ben spoke up: "Judge, that is completely unfair to my client. It just highlights Harmon's defense."

After about twenty minutes of haggling, the Judge said, "Harmon has a point and he's entitled to have the whole statute read. I am going to call them back out and say I neglected to read one of the laws in its entirety and just read the whole thing without additional comment. Any objection."

Harmon: "No, Your Honor."

Ben: "I guess not."

As they walked out of chambers, Ben said under his breath, "This is a bag job."

The Judge read the additional charge and dismissed the jury for lunch. They were to start deliberations at 2:00.

Now that all of the trial pressure was over, Harmon ate lunch with Gloria and Lisa. Gloria was in good spirits; she actually ate half her lunch sandwich. Harmon just had a cup of coffee and cheese sandwich. Gloria was animated, talking about her work in Hollywood, how it was not really that glamorous, although it sounded that way.

At 2:00, they were back in the courtroom, as the Judge ordered the jury in and made a show of telling them that now was the time to deliberate and consider the evidence that the clerk would deliver to them: the redacted police report, medical records and photos of the vehicles. Then the jury was sent to the deliberation room, and court recessed. Counsel was supposed to stay on premises for the expected verdict, but could walk about the courthouse. Ben wandered out to smoke. Harmon explained to Gloria that the jury would take at least an hour and he had seen deliberations go on for several days if there were disagreements. He told her that she should stay in the building.

He walked back and sat with Lisa, made small talk about music and concerts. She said she had seen Dylan with her friend Mandy. "It was one of his tours where all the songs sounded the same. He'd be mumbling, then you would hear a line and say, 'Okay, that is Tangled up in Blue.' Then another song that sounded exactly the same, and you're like, 'I think that's Like a Rolling Stone.' The whole show was like that. Not what I expected."

"I've seen him twice and he was good, but I've heard what you're talking about. That would be so disappointing. When I was in high school, I loved his early music, memorized it all."

The afternoon wore away. At one point, Harmon and Lisa walked outside and around the Town Green. The sun was weak and the air sharp. Ben had gone across to his office, telling the clerk to call him when the verdict came in. Wilson was still in the courthouse as was Gloria.

Harmon and Lisa walked back in at about 4:00. Still no verdict. They walked into the courtroom and Gloria was talking to Wilson. They seemed to be getting along great. Harmon and Lisa sat in the back of the gallery. After a minute, Gloria walked up to them. "What a nice man. I of course wished him well. That's okay with you, right?"

"It's fine. The evidence is over. I just didn't want you to be talking about the case with him while the trial was going on. That has a way of working against you."

At 4:25, Ben walked in. "The clerk called me. The Judge wants to talk to us."

They knocked and entered the Judge's chambers. "Okay, if there's no verdict by 4:40, I'm going to call them in and release them for the day. We can pick it up tomorrow at 9:30."

The clerk knocked and entered. "I think there's a verdict, Your Honor."

"Even better. Tom, get the court reporter. We'll go on the record as soon as she's ready."

Ben and Harmon shuffled out and went to their counsel tables. Harmon patted Gloria's hand. "There's a verdict. They're going to read it in a few minutes."

"What is it? Is there a problem?"

"We don't know anything until the clerk reads the verdict. We get no preview."

The court reporter entered and set up quickly. The Judge knocked at his door to signal his entrance and he took the bench as the judicial marshal opened court. "It appears that we have a verdict. Mr. Clerk, please call the jury in."

Everything seemed extra formal. There wasn't enough oxygen in the room. Out of habit, Harmon had a single legal pad and pen on his table, with which he would record the time of events and the verdict. He wrote, "4:32 court in session for verdict." The six members of the jury entered and sat. Harmon and Gloria stood when they entered, sat when they sat. Seated closest to the Judge was one of the two women, a high school science teacher from Warren. She was holding the verdict form, meaning she was the foreperson. Harmon was trying to remember what it was he liked about her as a prospective juror last week.

The Judge turned to the jury. "Have you reached a verdict?"

The foreperson said, "We have." The others nodded. None of them seemed particularly focused on either party.

"Madame foreperson, please hand the verdict form to the clerk." The clerk took the form and passed it to the Judge. He looked at it for a moment and handed it back to the clerk. "You may read the verdict."

Harmon wrote: "4:36 reading the verdict."

"In the matter of docket number CV 960400321, Bradley Wilson v. Gloria Sanns. Verdict form. Plaintiff's verdict." (This was expected.) "We, the jury, find for the plaintiff as follows: Economic damages: $46,985." (All the economic damages as expected. Harmon wrote down the figure and held his breath. The clerk seemed to be reading in slow motion.) "Noneconomic damages: $65,000. Subtotal: $111,985. Percentage of fault attributable to the plaintiff: 20%. Final verdict: $89,588."

Gloria put her hand over Harmon's and squeezed.

"Thank you, Mr. Clerk. The verdict is accepted and may be recorded."

The clerk read the entire form into the record again.

"Counsel. Any motions before I release the jury?" Neither Ben nor Harmon spoke.

"Ladies and gentlemen of the jury, I would like to thank you for your service. Your job is now complete. All of the cautions and prohibitions are now over. You are free to talk to the lawyers or anyone else or just keep your experience to yourself."

It was over. Harmon was standing, and Gloria was hugging him. Ben shook his hand formally. He shook Wilson's hand and wished him the very best in the future. Lisa walked up with the beautiful close-mouthed smile. She locked her eyes on him and didn't speak right away. Gloria turned to her and said, "I don't know the terms of your relationship, but you should stick with this guy. He's something special."

With no hesitation, Lisa replied, "I intend to." She smiled again, inscrutably.

Lisa walked out of the courtroom, while Harmon spoke to Gloria about what was to come. The verdict was within her coverage. All her worries about the insurance company and a verdict over the coverage were over. He would deal with the company and tell Kaitlin.

"Harmon. Thank you so much. I was worried about everything. Now it looks like it will all work out. You worked a miracle here. I really appreciate everything. You know, what you do here is not that different from my business. You are basically putting on a drama. I'm glad this one had a happy ending."

"Gloria. You were a great client. I'm glad this worked out. You just never know what a jury will do. But this was really good."

They walked out of the courthouse together. She gave him her business card, made him promise to look her up if he was ever in Southern California. She hugged him hard, her skinny body against his, whispered in his ear, "Thank you." Then she was gone, walking down the street to her car. Harmon knew he would never see her again.

He turned and saw Lisa in front of the courthouse. He walked up to her and they walked together to their cars parked one in front of the other just down the road from the green where all-day parking was allowed. "I called the office. Everybody is meeting at the bar at Yesterday's. Time to celebrate. See you there." She touched his arm and was gone.

Harmon stowed his briefcase on the back seat of the Jetta and got in slowly. He had an out-of-body feeling, like he had just finished a great race, but was empty just the same, tired, mind wandering. He drove to four corners and got a big soda. He didn't feel like going out, but it had to be done. He drove back to the office to put the file away before heading to the bar.

The office was quiet at 6:00; everyone was at the happy hour to celebrate the successful trial. The fluorescent lights were on in the main room where the paralegals and assistants sat. His office door was ajar, and his light was off. He walked into the office and left it dark. A shaft of light from the main room gave it a twilight quality. He put the briefcase down next to the desk.

He sat in his chair, put his head back and closed his eyes. The high from the trial was fading and life was leaking, even rushing, back.

He could weave these effective trial themes. Prevail in difficult cases. Gain the respect of colleagues, opponents, judges. But he was a failure as a husband; he just could not make his marriage work. Where there had been something like love, there was now only contempt coming from Joan, and withdrawal and silence from him. He knew it was ending. He would be alone. He would have to figure out how to be a good dad, under the worst circumstances. There used to be much joy in life. He used to love running, now just did the morning run out of habit and obsession. He felt fat and slow and out of shape. And so old. Where the hell was life headed? Lyrics from a favorite song, Runaway Train, ran through his mind: "How on earth did I get so jaded? Life's mystery seems so faded." Ten minutes passed, then twenty. He just sat there.

He heard movement in the main room, thought it might be the cleaning crew. Then a figure in the doorway: it was Donna. "Hey trial man. Nice work today. Why aren't we at the happy hour?"

"Just feeling the weight of life. Not really in the happy hour mood at this moment."

"Harmon, you're really good at what you do. But it doesn't fix the rest of your life. It's still there when the trial's over."

"Don't I know it."

She moved closer. "Well, the whole office is over at Yesterday's for drinks, even Con and Rob. So, let's go."

He rose. She moved closer. Then her body was against him. "Sometimes, I think I could make you happy. We work so well together."

He said nothing. She kissed him quick and hard, still pressed against him. He could feel why the young associates called her Donna D-cup. It felt nice. He could smell her make-up, mousse, a tinge of body odor after a long day. It was intoxicating being this close to a voluptuous woman. But she wasn't the one, even if she was his work wife.

"Okay, off to Yesterday's." He disengaged gently, put his hand on her arm. "I don't know where I'd be without you. You're the best." They walked out together, and each drove to the bar.

* * *

He walked into the back room of Yesterday's to cheers and a smattering of applause. The party was in full swing. Of the 55 employees of the firm, about 30 were there, although some were already edging toward the door. There were pitchers of beer, mixed drinks and shot glasses on the tables. Most people were standing and mingling. Rob came up and shook his hand. "Great result. I knew that was the perfect case for you." (Was he complimenting Harmon or himself? Probably a little of both.)

Lisa was in a group of young lawyers, holding a beer glass. John Fletcher, one of the senior associates, walked over with a beer. John had proclaimed at other firm events that he was clearly the smartest and most cultured person at the firm. He had gone to University of Virginia Law and worked at a big firm for 5 years before coming over, probably because he had gotten "the talk," meaning he was told he was not partnership material. "This is for you, buddy. You probably think you're something special right now. It'll pass when you talk to Rob."

Harmon took the beer and said, "He does have a way of bringing you down."

"Way down."

Luke Rinaldi walked over, coke in hand. He never drank at firm parties. Rob liked to talk about everyone rowing in one direction and how bad negativity was for the firm. Luke was the hub of organizational negativity, finding and reveling in the gallows humor and cynicism in every situation. "Hey, nice result. You're great. Get the bill out, Harmie. Get the bill out (imitating Rob's voice)."

Harmon moved to a group of paralegals and admin assistants. The conversation was lively. They looked halfway to tipsy. Donna was in the group and she seemed well on her way too. A waitress appeared with a tray packed with shot glasses. They cheered. "Have a shot, Harmon." It was Joyce, Donna's friend and the den mother of the paras.

Rob strode over and grabbed a shot. "Kamikaze shooters. Just discovered these with my kids." Then he raised his voice. "Everyone. Let's all raise a glass to Harmon, who got a great verdict today. Way to go, Harmon. But, you know what's most important, right?"

"That I get the bill out."

"Get the bill out, while they still love you. It's all fine to do good lawyering. But it's better to get paid for it." He raised his glass.

"Hear, hear!"

Harmon poured down the shot; it tasted like something for high schoolers.

An hour and four shots later, the group had thinned, and the conversation was looser. Con was making off-color references about Donna's chest. She giggled. Lisa was debating two other associates on presidential politics and sex acts in the White House.

Rob walked up and grabbed Harmon by the shoulder in an annoying but superficially brotherly way. He was buzzed. "Harmie . . . Harmie." (This was going to be good.) "You know . . . You know, when I was in school, I always hated people like you. I studied. I worked hard and got C's. You were the guy who got the girl and got A's without even working. I hated that, hated people like you."

"What do you mean, Rob?"

"You know what I mean. Donna loves you. Look at how she looks at you. Loves you. Lisa loves you. She can't say enough about you. She's looking over here right now. Katrina loves you. She asked me if she could work with you more."

"They're all really nice."

"Eh, you don't get it. They love you. I would go with Donna. She is dedicated, man. She would love you forever."

"I don't really know what to say."

"That's why I always hated guys like you." Con walked over. "I always hated guys like this guy. The guys who got the girls and the grades."
"What?"

"Get the bill out, Harmie. While the good feelings are still there." He sidled away, soon to leave.

Then it was just five or six of them. Donna left, giving him a big, boozy hug and kiss on the way out. 30 minutes later, everyone was gone. Except Lisa. Harmon had a smooth beer and kamikaze buzz. He was tired, ready to go back to the apartment and fall into bed. He and Lisa walked out together.

The night had turned colder and a breeze flapped the tails of Harmon's overcoat as he walked through the parking lot with Lisa. They stood too long in the lot, wasting time, talking about nothing. Harmon made some joke and Lisa laughed. Then Lisa looked up at him, her hand on his arm, "Do you have a brother at home or anything?"

He laughed, looked past her. "Just me."

"Mmm. Just you."

Then the moment passed. Harmon was heading back to the apartment, the moments of the night rolling over in his head. (He hates me? Hates people like me? They all love me?) But those last five minutes played over in his head 10,000 times. (A brother? Like, she likes me? Could something be there?)

It was running streak day 6,197.

* * *

Wilson v. Sanns was the last trial of the year. Harmon cleaned up his other work and tried to placate Joan for the holidays. Rob came through with a decent year-end bonus, which Joan promptly spent on a new rug and couch. She followed up with contempt for his job, his earnings, running, everything that was in his daily life. One theme was that he should give up running every day, since he was fat and slow anyway. What was the point with his little obsessive thing? Had to have his little thing to feel special.

The days flowed by, and one year moved to the next.

Then, he was out of the house. One Sunday afternoon, as he was packing up for the week, Joan got mad about something, then madder, then told him to get out. Permanently. "Please don't say that, unless you mean it. If you are really throwing me out, after all we've gone through, if you want me out, I'm not coming back. You can't bring this back to what you want if you change your mind." There were other things said, less thoughtful and logical on both sides.

Then: "Get . . . the . . . fuck . . . out! I hate you!"

He got out.

He drove back to the apartment. He called Hope from his car and told her he would need a favor. Could she make room in her tiny house for him and the kids on the weekends? "Are you okay, baby brother? Because, sure, we can do anything. But are you okay?"

"Yeah. I'm okay. Time to change things. I feel half dead, but not even half alive."

"Maybe you need to learn how to live."

"Maybe. Maybe, I don't know how."

It was running streak day 6,256.

BOOK THREE

Finding it Again

CHAPTER ELEVEN

If you lose the love of running, when you get it back, it's true love all over again. It's even better the second time. There is nothing more beautiful than getting your sorry ass back in shape. You know you need it.

Underground Runner's Guide

Harmon poured himself into his work, staying even later and working harder, except for weekends, which were reserved for Iris and young Harmon. In March, he handled an appeal before the state supreme court. In April, another trial. He felt so in-control at work, so at sea otherwise. In May, Joan ordered him to return home, after twelve weekends at Hope's. They stood face to face, in front of the lighthouse on the edge of town. He declined; he told her this wasn't coming back together, that it had been falling apart for years and they both knew it. She reached out and dug her nails into his arm and slapped him hard, making an animal growl that he had never heard before. He didn't react, figured he had earned this for his role in the failure of their marriage. Maybe he had earned more.

He tried to move on and make a life. He spent every weekend at Hope's. He bought a bunkbed for the kids and painted a room for them. He had them every Friday night and on Saturday too every other weekend. Hope doted on the kids, as she had none of her own; she loved their time together. On weekends, he would run at dawn, no more than five miles, so he was always there when the kids woke up. The weekends started to fall into a rhythm. He made them pancakes for breakfast. He took them to movies and zoos. They hung out at the house together.

He took Panda and Stripey to the apartment, where his Aunt spoiled them. They were lazy old housecats and she let them have the run of the house when he was at work. She started planning an elevated screened porch for them.

He bought a digital scale from a mail order place and put it in his bathroom. The next morning, he hopped on and it read 208. 208. He knew he had gained weight, even while running over 20 miles a week. He knew his pants were tighter and it was more of an effort to hook the button on his jacket as he rose to speak to the jury. One of his older suits had just disintegrated in the crotch due to wear. But 208? He was not a whippet, was never going to be 150 at six feet tall, but 180, maybe 175. Not 208. Time to make an effort. He wasn't going to be that middle-aged fat guy racing toward death. Wasn't that what he was trying to avoid?

As the weather turned, he started running a five-mile loop in the mornings. Then he started running four miles in the evening from work, before coming back and working on into the night. That, too, became a rhythm, and he started back to real fitness, crossing the 200-pound mark in May. The first weekend in June, Joan had the kids on Sunday and he ran a 5-mile road race, his first since the previous year. His mind wrote checks that his body could not cash. He wanted to go out at 6 flat, remembering the fast days. He went out at 6:45 under great effort. From there, he just tried to hang on and stay with his group. He faded the last mile and finished at 35:47. It felt good to go all-out again, even if he had lost his speed. That metallic taste in the back of his mouth and spittle on his chin as he sprinted for the finish made him feel young for a moment.

He noticed a few things. There weren't as many young guys as he had remembered 15 or more years ago. And there weren't as many fast guys. His time placed him in the top 15%. Back in his first year of running every day, he would have been in the middle of the pack. Harmon knew that at 42 his fastest days were behind him, but he wanted to see what he had left. He pushed his training a little harder.

At work, the word that he was separated and getting divorced filtered through the firm and became general knowledge. The flirtation with Lisa or even Donna was attenuated, now that it was potentially real. Katrina did in fact start to work with him and spent too much time in his office and worked too late. Although she was closer to his age, she pursued him in a quirky, indirect way. She told him one night over Diet Cokes that she never had a real boyfriend. She was tall and pretty with dark wavy hair halfway down her back. She was clearly interested. He liked her but did not have any romantic interest in her.

With Donna, the trial hugs and kisses became the rule. She was a good friend and confidant, there for him through this period of him being untethered and rudderless. She listened; she offered advice. But at some point, he realized her preferred solution might involve him and her together. That just wasn't his future. He wasn't sure why, but it wasn't.

At a happy hour after the April trial, Rob pulled him aside and tried to give him love-life advice. "Harmie, how you doin'? Are you hanging in there?"

"I'm okay. It's mostly work and weekends with the kids."

"Stick with it. Kids are everything. They know if you're making the effort."

"Well, I am. I will."

"Harmie. Donna's interested. You see the way she looks at you. She loves you, man. She's a good person. She would stick with you forever. You could not go wrong with that choice."

"I don't know, Rob. I'm just feeling my way here."

"You would not go wrong. You should think about it."

Donna was not the right person. She was dedicated. She was a great friend and co-worker. She had been an integral part of the trial successes. He loved her—like a sister. Closer than a sister, but not like a wife. They were so close and shared everything, almost. She knew about his failing and then failed marriage before anyone. He knew about her comically bad string of blind dates and boyfriend failures. She didn't know, had no idea, that he already had a crush, one that may be entirely frivolous. That was his one secret from her.

Then there was Lisa. Tim was out of the picture, but then she was dating a chiropractor, a firefighter, a drummer in a local cover band. She and Harmon were friends and still put their heads together as happy hours grew late and people went home to families. Harmon knew too much of her love life, even gave her advice in juggling her several love interests. She still looked at him that way that made him feel like there was something, maybe a really good thing, but neither made a move. It seemed less and less likely as time went on.

Then something happened. The firm had another appeal headed to the state supreme court. This was on underinsured motorist insurance coverage, a narrow and arcane area of the law that Harmon knew better than anyone at the firm. He was sure Rob would give it to him and he was looking forward to arguing another case there. Rob assigned it to Lisa, but he also assigned Harmon to help her on the brief and help her prepare for the argument.

For two weeks in June they worked late every night together on the brief. They dug through dozens of cases on the issue. They debated the various arguments. The case was intuitively difficult but legally strong. It appeared that the plaintiff was getting screwed, but it was also according to the letter of the insurance policy he had purchased, and the letter of the law.

On Tuesday night at about 7:00, the brief was complete. Harmon was going to hand-deliver it to the printer the next morning.

"This is good stuff, Lisa. You know the court will do what it wants, but we're right on the law. This brief is a winner."

"You think? I'm a little worried."

"I don't blame you. We could easily lose if the court decides to take care of the plaintiff. But this is our best argument and it will win if they want to follow the law." He paused. Time seemed to stop. "Do you want to grab dinner?"

Split second of hesitation. "Umm. Sure."

"Place?"

"How about La Riviera?" A place in the city much closer to her condo than his apartment.

"I would love that." He would love that.

Then it was 9:00 and she had finished about half of her linguine with white clam sauce, while he had scarfed down all of the eggplant parmigiana. They had split two carafes of red wine. They had talked about everything, the conversation flowing easily among close friends.

She looked directly at him with those big green eyes. Blond hair framed her thin face. She smiled, close-mouthed. "Do you want to come back to the condo for a drink? You've never seen it."

He melted. The oxygen went out of the room, but he played it cool and didn't gulp for air or pitch onto the floor. He just looked back, non-descript brown eyes, dark, greying hair, handsome, too-round face. "Sure."

"Follow me. When we get to the complex, park in a space marked V for visitor."

Then he was sitting on her couch drinking gin on the rocks (there really wasn't much to drink in the condo), flanked by two cats, Pen and Bobbie, and the conversation was still flowing, almost dancing around what was happening and Harmon was still too cool, but was terrified, stomach knotted. They were listening to a classic rock station on Lisa's stereo. Zeppelin played, then AC-DC, then Moondance came on.

"I love this song," she said. "Let's dance."

They stood in the living room, a little buzzed, and danced. Harmon worried that his hands would be sweaty, but it was nice and natural and then it ended and she kept his hand and led him upstairs, past the guest bedroom, past the bathroom to the master bedroom, to her bed. And they stood there and kissed. Really kissed for the first time after all that flirting. Her lips were warm and wet and he never wanted to stop. Then she started to unbutton his work shirt and he took off her blouse and bra and then they were kissing again naked to the waist and he was so excited. And she took off his pants and boxers and he her skirt and pantyhose. And now they kissed naked, him pressed to her. They lay on the bed and touched each other, caressed each other. He found her and she him. He kissed her breasts and caressed her arms and legs and was between her legs and touching her and she was dripping and then they were together and it was so good and he was on top and then she was on top and he whispered, "What can I do for you?" and she replied, "Next time." And he was falling. Falling. Really falling. This woman he had known. Had known for over 6 years. This friend.

He was falling. He realized he had been falling all along. Few people get to fall like that. Few get it once and fewer get it twice. And here he was. It was exhilarating and terrifying. And nothing else mattered right then.

And then they were lying impossibly close under the covers. “I was supposed to go out for dinner with Mike tonight.” The firefighter. “I cancelled.”

He was still falling, could barely breathe. “I’m glad. Really glad.”

“Me too. If you have to get back to your Aunt’s house, that’s okay.”

“At some point. But not yet.” He was caressing her hair, her shoulder and side as they spooned. “I think we have some unfinished work here.” He burrowed under the covers and finished things. And then for good measure they did it all again.

He had climbed a thousand mountains that night, had swum an ocean. Had died a thousand deaths. Had launched into space. He was perfectly spooning with her smooth skin.

It was running streak day 6,375.

* * *

The next morning he arose at 5:30 in full June sunlight. He fed the cats and ran the new five-mile loop, then added a mile. He was floating. He drove into work and picked up the brief and delivered it to the printer. They would print 25 copies, put the proper cover on it and deliver it to the supreme court clerk’s office.

He was back in the office by 9:15. He went straight to Lisa’s office. She was on the phone and motioned him in. He shut the door behind him. She hung up right away.

“Yes?”

“I delivered the brief.” He could not stop smiling.

“I figured. And . . . ?”

“And I thought we might talk.” Still smiling. He was fucking elated. Brilliant and stupid and crazy.

“You were going to say that what happened was a long time coming, and we both deserve it?”

“That.”

“And we’re really good together, maybe even great?”

“And that.”

“And we owe it to ourselves to see where this will go?”

“Definitely that. Listen, seriously . . . .”

“I’m being serious. That’s what I would say.”

“My turn to say serious stuff. Look, you have a life, and a lot of people who want to go out with you. I’m not saying you have to throw that all away because we finally got together.”

“Do you want me to throw it away? Not like I’m Miss Popular. But do you want us to be exclusive?”

“Truth? Absolutely. Already. Right now.”

“Good. Me too. What are you smiling at?”

“This. This is good.”

She flashed her green eyes. She gave that closed-mouth smile, her long blond hair cascading past the thin face. She looked gorgeous. “I like that.”

"So . . . you want to get dinner tonight?"

She laughed out loud. "I have a feeling we're going to get a lot of dinner."

"Oh god, I hope so."

They got a lot of dinner.

He realized that he really knew little about lovemaking. Lisa seemed to know it. He decided he would learn everything. So, he practiced whenever he could.

* * *

Summer came and Harmon ran long and spent as much time with Lisa as possible. Work suffered in the sense that he didn't stay till 10 o'clock every night. He and Lisa went to the condo and took long walks and listened to music and hung out and made love.

They had started as colleagues, then grew into friends. They shared, they flirted and finally loved. They came into the relationship knowing each other as close friends. Soon they forged an overwhelming dedication to each other, each to the other's loves and interests.

Harmon kept the weekend schedule. His son Matthew contacted him, and he started seeing him on some weekday evenings and then brought him up to spend weekends with Hope, Iris and Harmon. He spent all his other time with Lisa. Except running.

Harmon's other love was running; he genuinely loved the act of getting up and running every day. Rather than try to tame or minimize this, rather than shame Harmon and call him aberrant, Lisa urged him to embrace it and find whatever he wanted in running. Harmon didn't know what he wanted at that point, but he wanted something. He continued to add in the miles and tried to get back some of the fitness he had enjoyed all those years ago.

In July, he ran the 4th of July race for the 17th time, this time with daughter Iris, running and walking next to him, not yet 7 years old. They finished in 1:10. After the race, he ran a quick three miles, while Hope hung out with the kids.

On Labor Day, he ran the New Haven 20k again, coming back to the site of his first-ever race 21 years earlier. He stood in a group of 3,000 runners in front of the old courthouse on the green and soaked up the festive, late-summer atmosphere in the morning shadows. The gun went off and a mass of runners headed west past the Yale dorms and off into the neighborhoods. He held a 7-minute mile as long as he could. By the time he reached the harbor and turned north toward east rock, he was flagging. The shadows were gone, and the day had turned warm. With 5 miles to go, he was hanging on the best he could, as runners started passing him. By the time he reached Whitney Avenue and turned back toward the green for the last mile, he had nothing left. He picked up the pace by sheer will and stayed with the cluster around him, pounding down the flat, wide avenue. He finished in 1:32, red-faced and panting. It felt good to stretch out the pace and distance a little, but he didn't really have the stamina to keep a steady 7-minute mile. He decided to wait till the following fall to go back to the marathon distance and concentrate on training longer and racing shorter in the interim.

In October, Lisa argued before the state supreme court with Harmon sitting by her side. She was excellent, handling all the expected questions on what was the correct result under the law versus the appearance of fairness to an insurance policyholder. And she fielded a couple of unfair hypotheticals coming down gracefully on the side of consistent interpretation of the statutory scheme. In truth, Harmon thought she did at least as well as he could have done, maybe better. And though he was a little envious of her getting this rare opportunity instead of him, it was only fair, as he had argued similar cases before the court on six prior occasions.

After the argument, they ate lunch at a brew pub in the city. Harmon got a veggie burger and Lisa a cheeseburger. She was aglow with the excitement of the experience—facing five intimidating judges, any of whom could ask any type of question to trip you up.

"That was pretty cool."

"You were great. That last question, the hypothetical, you killed them with coolness. I couldn't have answered that one as well as you did."

"What do you think? Can they rule for us?"

"I think that was a winning argument. If the real thinkers on the court have anything to do with it, they'll rule in our favor."

After lunch, the raw excitement of the experience still in the air, they skipped the afternoon at work, went to the condo and made love.

In December, Harmon had another trial, this one a slip and fall accident on metal back stairs at an apartment building. There was expert testimony on both sides on the safety of the stairs—two engineers explaining drag sleds and the coefficient of friction of wet metal stairs. In the end, Harmon got the jury to accept that the plaintiff shouldn't have been using the stairs at all. It was supposed to be an emergency exit. The jury was out for 45 minutes before finding in his favor.

By year's end, Harmon had run 2,051 miles, his best year in the last nine. As the year ended it was running streak day number 6,576. He was slowly getting in shape and still shedding the middle-age fat he had accumulated. He was adept at his job. He was in love. But something was not right.

He celebrated New Years with Lisa and knew he wanted to spend the rest of his life with her. But something was still not right. And it wasn't her. He had done nothing to move his life along. He was separated and never getting back together with Joan, but he was not divorced. Each day passed, and he failed to move ahead. He had gotten to the point of declaring his marriage over and splitting up for good; he just couldn't clean up the residue. It involved confronting the failure and contemplating whether he was really marriage material. And the failure loomed.

Lisa was patient, more than patient. She knew that Harmon loved her and wanted to spend his life with her. She knew intuitively that Harmon was wrestling with the failure of his marriage, his feelings of unlovable-ness and the difficulty of moving on, and that it would take time. Eventually, she said something. He assured her that he would get things done, but they languished. He had talked to a lawyer. Joan had as well. But still nothing happened.

Finally, a collaborative divorce agreement was reached. Harmon, for all his competitiveness in running and his control in the courtroom, always had feet of clay in his personal life. He vowed never to judge people with whacky marriage situations—separated for decades, but not divorced, living together and "engaged" for decades—it all made more sense to him after his experience.

When it was over, he thought, "Why didn't I just do that right away? Right, because I am I."

And when it was finally resolved, the floodgates of life opened and Harmon and Lisa got married, on the beach, standing next to each other. And they would have two kids: Emmi and then Richie. But first, there were races to run.

He ran some summer races with Iris and Harmon. He ran the Labor Day 20k again, and he was signed up for the Hartford Marathon in the fall. Because he couldn't really run long on weekends, except the Sundays Joan had Iris and Harmon, he started running two longer runs on Wednesdays when he didn't have court all day. He was trying to get the minimum mileage in to feel comfortable at the marathon. He did about 60 miles a week, sometimes with no single run over 7 or 8 miles.

Marathon day, in mid-October, dawned cool and clear. It was going up to 70, so it would feel warm by the end. Harmon had no real expectations, but he knew the Boston qualifying time for a masters runner was 3:20. A perfect race on paper would have him hitting 20 miles at about 2:30 (a 7:30 pace) and doing the last 10k in about 50 minutes (just over an 8 minute pace), for a qualifier. This was the A-goal; Boston was always the A-goal.

And so, he found himself with 2,000 other runners in the early morning shadows, crossing the Connecticut River and heading up into South Windsor on a perfectly flat road. He was clicking off miles at about 7:25 to give himself that chance at a Boston qualifier. The half-marathon runners peeled off, and the crowd thinned a bit. He was running in a small group. He was taking in water and Gatorade and nothing else and felt fine. At 10 miles, he was right on 1:14 flat as the course wound around and back toward Hartford. He was just starting to feel the pace and effort. By 15 miles, he was struggling to maintain, and it was a losing battle. The sun was up and the miles longer and harder. He passed the start-finish area just before mile 20, heading out for the final 10k in the hills of the west end of the city. At 20 miles, the digital display read 2:40:22. He was 10 minutes off his goal pace and felt gassed, and he was heading up Asylum hill, the first hill of many. The sure, steady pace of the first miles had deteriorated to a shambling jog. He just wanted to finish as soon as possible, so he could stop. But the miles grew longer still. He finally came back down the hill and into the park to finish at 3:48:25, missing the Boston qualifier by about half an hour. He was wiped, but at least he was back running races for fun. It was his first marathon in a decade. It was running streak day number 6,794.

Running every day and marathon training were not the same thing. He had gotten back to 192 pounds, but he had a long way to go. He knew logically that, at 43, the sub-40 10k was probably gone forever, but there was no reason he couldn't run a respectable half marathon or marathon. He would just have to train harder and get in better shape.

That winter, he concentrated on not gaining holiday pounds, so he could get to a good marathon weight for the next season. As the weather warmed, he ate less and trained more. Both he and Lisa lost weight. That summer, in the evening, they regularly walked a three-mile loop or ran it together. Harmon again ran summer races with the kids and ran long, whenever he had a chance. He ran the Labor Day 20k again and held a 7:15 pace on a cool drizzly day, finishing just over 1:30. He was entered in the Hudson-Mohawk Marathon in upstate New York in October. Lisa was driving up with him. Hope was running it too. Harmon was concerned that he did not have enough long-run miles, but he was thin again, and that made him feel faster—or at least less slow.

He was 44 and would be 45 the following spring, so his Boston qualifier time was 3:25. As always, as it had been for 19 years, that was his A-goal.

On Sunday morning, he stood in a plaza in Albany. The finish line was already set up. He and Hope were waiting to board school buses to ride to the start. Harmon was wearing a sleeveless tee, nylon shorts with inner liner and a pair of Asics Gel DS racers over thin polypropylene socks. He had a long sleeve tee shirt on over the sleeveless and a small backpack. It was his plan to stow the long sleeve in the backpack and pick it up at the finish. He also had a quart of a new electrolyte mixture—with protein!—that promised to deliver energy for the long run. Hope was also wearing a long sleeve tee that she would stow in Harmon's pack.

They got on the bus and Harmon took out the plastic bottle of the mixture. He gestured to Hope.

"Oh god, no. That looks awful." (It was lime green, thick and opaque.)

"Suit yourself. This is my latest magic elixir."

"Right. Well, good luck with that, baby brother."

Between the bus ride and the wait at the starting line, he downed the quart of mix. It was sweet with a vague taste of citrus, not that bad. The protein was a little chalky.

Then in a park in Schenectady, a race official said a few words about the course along the Mohawk River bike path, then through a town, then the Hudson River bike path. Then they played the national anthem through speakers and called the runners to the starting line. The gun went off and about 400 runners headed down the road to the bike path. He could run at full speed right from the start. And he did. He clicked off the early miles at 7:10. The morning was cool and the course flat and fast. The narrow, paved bike path gave the feeling of moving fast. At about the halfway point, he was still running 7:15 miles, and he felt fine. The race official at the half-marathon shouted out 1:33:15 as he cruised by. They came off the bike path along the Mohawk River and went through a small town on the roads. It was partly cloudy and starting to warm up, heading toward 70. They went up a hill and the pace held. The race felt right. They dipped onto the bike path along the Hudson and the miles climbed higher into the teens, and he was still around 7:15 a mile. Harmon was now running alone. He could see two runners at least a minute ahead, but no one close by. He passed 20 miles in 2:25:30, felt no let-up and ran on. As he got closer to the finish and the magnitude of the effort started to weigh on him, Harmon ran judiciously. This was that perfect day, and he wanted to honor it, but at the same time, he didn't want to blow up and ruin it. He slowed to 7:30 and closed in on the City of Albany and the finish. Then he was off the bike path on a city street and could hear the crowd. A runner passed him, said something about following him for five miles. Harmon didn't care. He was only focused on the finish.

Then he came around a corner and up a small rise and could see the digital clock. It read 3:16:32. He saw Lisa on the right near the finish, with a camera. He did his best imitation of a finishing sprint and crossed the line right at 3:16:50. He went through the chute and they announced he was

42nd. He was tired, but elated. As he walked through the chute, his mind was a jumble. All those years. Every time he was on the starting line since his second marathon 19 years earlier, he had been aware of the Boston qualifying time. Every time he had missed—missed badly. Here he was, with the Boston qualifier—by over eight minutes! He hugged Lisa. She was excited.

"Was that a Boston qualifying time?"

"Yeah. We did it. We're going to Boston in the spring!" He was stunned; he never expected this. He had come to accept that he would never qualify for Boston. It seemed just beyond his grasp. And here he was.

He retrieved the backpack from the bus, put on the long sleeve shirt and waited for Hope. She finished in 4:22:09, delighted with her time and the experience. They hung out at the finish for a while, and then Hope said she had to head back home because she had to teach tomorrow (she was an art teacher). Harmon and Lisa would have brunch before heading home.

Later at an outdoor brunch in the afternoon sun, Lisa said, "That was great. I can't believe you did it."

"I know. It's something I have been chasing for almost 20 years. 20 years."

"Well you got it."

"Hunny."

"Yes?"

"What if this is as good as it gets? What if this is it. It never gets better?"

"Why even wonder? And if this is the best, it's good. So, you shouldn't worry about it."

"You're right. But everything just went right today. I've never felt that before. I don't think this will ever happen again."

"Maybe you're thinking about it wrong. Maybe you should be really happy that it happened. That it happened at all."

"I know you're right. It's just a weird feeling. Like you're on a mountain and it heads down in every direction."

"Maybe you need another beer." Man, he loved this woman; he had clearly met his match. It was running streak day number 7,159.

* * *

The following April 15th, early on a cloudy morning, he waited in a crowd on Boston Common. He had run a not-too-hard 20-miler in 2:42 two weeks earlier and felt ready for this. He boarded a school bus and went for a 50-minute ride. It delivered him to the high school in Hopkinton, where he walked over and stood under a huge party tent—one of three on the school grounds—and ate a bagel. The place was teeming with runners: behind him in one corner were about ten men in red and white speaking Polish. Farther along was a group speaking French. Still farther, were two runners in matching Union Jack singlets. He sat in a corner, his back to a tent pole and soaked in the international atmosphere. The Boston Marathon was different from anything he had seen.

The mass of people started to move off the school grounds and down the road. It was cool and cloudy. Buses were lined up along the road with open windows and bib number ranges on them. Harmon pushed his running bag through the window corresponding to his bib number and walked to the starting line of the most famous marathon in the world. Boston. He was in corral number 6, crammed in with hundreds of people. From there he couldn't see the starting line, although he knew it was over the hill by the

Town Green. It could have been worse. A mass of tightly packed runners stretched down the hill behind him and around the corner.

At noon, the race started. Somewhere a gun went off, but he never heard it. Instead, people just started moving forward, and it took him over three minutes to make it to the starting line by the green. By then he could run a bit and the course dipped downhill and the runners thinned out. In the early going, the sides of the road were empty, except at cross roads where race fans were standing. By Framingham at mile six, there were fans behind barriers and thousands of children's hands extended onto the course. Harmon tried to slap them all. Another five miles along, in Natick, there were more crowds and more hands to slap. Harmon touched a thousand hands that day. Then on up a hill and a left fork in the road. Harmon could hear a steady shrieking. He came over the top of the hill to more barriers and the women of Wellesley College on the right, making so much noise it was frightening. He slapped more hands and hugged co-eds and moved along. At 16 miles, he turned right at the Newton Corners Firehouse and onto Commonwealth Avenue. The race was like a dream. He knew he was cruising along under 8 minutes a mile, but was unsure just how he was doing. He crested the series of hills called heartbreak and charged down to Cleveland Circle. Then he ran along the "T" line, past Fenway park, over the overpass, past the Citgo sign and into the downtown. Then a left turn and the sprint to the finish. He was floating. This was the fucking Boston Marathon, the race he had been chasing all these years, the race everyone asked him if he had run. Now, the answer was yes. He crossed the line in 3:27:52, net time of 3:24:10. He had qualified for the next year as well.

He retrieved his running bag from the bus and walked up the finish area gauntlet to the end, where Lisa was waiting. She looked beautiful in the afternoon sun. They hugged. Lisa's belly was rounded; she was pregnant with Emmi. They had lunch in Boston and then drove home. Both had court the next day. It was running streak day number 7,412.

Harmon had reached his personal mountaintop of marathoning. He had run Boston. He would run it twice more, but it was never like the first time. He ran other marathons as well, but found himself two years later, at age 47, wondering if there was more to the running life.

CHAPTER TWELVE

When you have run your best 10k and your best marathon, when you think you still have more to accomplish in this sport, and you still want to push yourself, consider going to the dark side. Read Fixx's book, chapter 24. You probably didn't know it was there. There is life beyond the marathon. Way beyond. Go find it.

Underground Runner's Guide

One day in late June, Harmon was eating breakfast with Lisa and reading the paper. "Hunny, I remember watching the Wide World of Sports back in the 80's, and they had a segment on this 100-mile race in California. Like, you start early in the morning and you can run all day and all night. It says here that some guy named Jurek just won it for the sixth straight time. And a woman named Anne Trason has won the woman's race 14 times."

"Are you saying you want to do something like that? Sounds a little crazy. Think how you feel after a marathon. Could you run 74 more miles?"

"No. That's too far. That's hard to even drive."

She smiled that closed-mouth smile. Did she know something he didn't?

She did.

He started to feel the pull of a new challenge in the sport he already loved. He read about it and thought about it. What if the marathon distance wasn't the end. What if it was just the beginning. He felt like he could keep going, maybe do something special in longer distance races. He was already going about 3,000 miles a year. He just kept up the base mileage and worked on weekend long runs to be ready to go beyond the marathon.

* * *

Through the harder running, he was still the lead trial lawyer for his firm. He was still putting in long hours, but there were fewer hours for everything. He was traveling to see Iris and Harmon every weekend. He and Lisa bought a house less than a mile from the firm, narrowing the commute to three minutes. They had Emmi and Richie and left them in home daycare close to work and home. But it was still too much demand and not enough capacity.

One evening, Lisa started the conversation. "Hunny, I think something has to give. I want you to see your kids grow up. I want us to be able to do what we want to do in life. I want you to have time for Harmon and Iris. I want us to feel good about our jobs and our lives."

"So, what are you saying?"

"What if we just planned an exit, got away from the stress of our jobs and started our own firm? Got away from Rob and Con and that feeling that nothing will ever be enough for them? What if we worked for ourselves?"

Just like that. "Okay, I'm in. But you know I will have to count on your planning and organization . . . And, just so you know, I'm terrified."

So, they did it. One morning in January, they delivered resignation letters and left (on running streak day 8,424). Con decided Harmon should work another month on two files that were coming to trial, but finally they were on their own. They brought no work with them; they trusted their reputations to bring in business.

And with Lisa's planning, it came together; they found work. It was lower volume, higher sophistication. They represented mostly lawyers and accountants. The levels of insulation between Harmon and his clients—associate, paralegal, administrative assistant—were stripped away. Work was more direct and hands-on. Trials still required nights and weekends, but otherwise the work took on a rhythm that allowed them both to feel more connected to the world. And allowed Harmon to run. Run ultra.

CHAPTER THIRTEEN

You're going to run your first ultra, and you probably think you're different. That all the training, all the long steady miles will allow you to keep that near-marathon pace on indefinitely. Maybe you're built differently and you won't fatigue as the miles add up. Right. You're a fool.

Underground Runner's Guide

He entered a 24-hour race, around a lake in Massachusetts. Each lap around the lake was about 5k. The race ran from 7:00 pm Friday night to Saturday night. Harmon and Lisa arrived with the whole family. Matt, now 17, planned to ride his bike along the course through the overnight as a guide, as recommended in the race materials. Harmon missed much of the race briefing, because he was holding a boisterous three-year old Emmi, but he heard enough. Run around the lake and keep going. Try to have a bike escort for the overnight, because there is no one on the course to make sure you're safe.

At 7:00 pm, with little fanfare, about 75 runners eased off into the warm evening. Harmon immediately fell into a slightly slower than marathon pace, which put him in the top half of the group. He generally ran alone, not knowing anyone and not knowing anything about the ultra culture. He expected he would see Lisa and the kids after 3 or 4 laps, but nothing. He was turning laps in about 28 minutes. After the 5th lap, he steered into the host hotel just off the course near the start-finish and knocked on the room door. Nothing. He was concerned and distracted, but he realized he had no way of contacting anyone and would just have to wait. After the 6th lap, he tried again. Nothing. He was more concerned, but he turned another lap. Again he tried, again nothing. Then as he swung around after the eighth lap, Lisa was out there. She explained that she had been at the emergency room of the closest hospital because Emmi had managed to put pebbles in her ear, and they were stuck. Lisa had brought the whole troupe with her, and they had waited for hours.

Harmon was relieved. He just wanted to end the race and stay with the family, but Lisa urged him to continue. So, he did. Matt came out after the tenth lap and rode his bike around with Harmon overnight. It was slow going, but Matt was a great help. He kept the mood light and had energy befitting his age.

Harmon had fantasized that he would keep a 4:30 marathon pace for the duration. He knew he was in good shape and he thought maybe he would be able to extend his pace through a 24-hour race. On paper, 100 miles seemed pretty easy, and a good first-time goal. Even with his stops to look for Lisa and the kids, Harmon had gone through the 9th lap in 4:45. The tenth lap didn't feel that bad—about 31 miles in—but then things deteriorated. Harmon started walking parts of the course and the running got slower and slower as the night wore on. As dawn broke, Harmon was dragging. Matt urged him on and he was just over 50 miles in 11:45. He was tired and ready to pack it in. Matt suggested one more lap to get to the double marathon distance. He reached that in about 12:30 on the race clock, and he was done. It was 7:30 in the morning and they were on their way up to visit his mom in Maine that weekend, and he decided he needed to get going—a rookie ultrarunner rationalization. Must leave, family waiting, things to do.

And that was it. He had gone 53.4 miles and was officially an ultrarunner. By the next day, he felt empty for having given up. He thought he could have gotten to at least about 80 miles, and that would have been infinitely more honorable than quitting in the morning. But it was over, and he was looking ahead. He limped around Maine complaining of leg soreness, but really had no serious consequences. He ran 2-3 miles a day and went hiking with the family.

* * *

Ultra still fascinated him. He decided he wanted to try a fixed distance race, thinking maybe he would fare better with a finish line to run to. He entered a 50-miler on dirt roads in Pennsylvania. He still knew nothing about ultras. Lisa crewed him, but he had no idea what he wanted to eat or drink or how he would feel. The course started on a paved road and then went up a killer hill with switchbacks right on the road, steep and relentless for at least half a mile. He just ran up the hill, reaching the top winded and with jelly legs. Then there was a nice steady soft downhill and he got his legs back. He was caught by a guy who looked to be about his age and build. They made small talk. His name was Ed. It was his first 50 miler too. He had run 50 miles in training just to prove he could. Harmon had not.

Ed looked over at him, and said, "You don't look like a distance runner. You look more like a linebacker."

"I'm taking that as a compliment."

"Just an observation."

They ran together and chatted about life and careers. They caught up to a third runner and the three of them continued together for miles. When they reached another series of up-hills on a dirt road, Mike, the third guy, said, "In ultras, you walk hills like this. You run the flats and downhills." Harmon had never heard this.

"That first hill?"

"Definitely walk," said Mike.

"I didn't get that memo. I ran it." Mike shook his head.

And so, the morning wore into afternoon and the three stayed together up to about the 35-mile point. They were climbing what seemed like an endless hill in a series of step-ups, and Mike just pulled ahead on a flatter part. Harmon was wearing a single bottle waist pack that he had read about and just had to buy from some mail-order house. Now it was bothering his stomach, and he was not running much of the hill, even the flatter parts. Ed was right with him.

When they crested the hill, at an aid station, there was a left turn to an out-and-back. It went over a little rise and down a fairly steep hill before turning around. They saw Mike on the way back a full ten minutes ahead, moving well. The downhill at mile 42 was a new experience for Harmon. With every step, his quads ached, really burned, so much so that he slowed down to minimize the pounding. He felt better when they reached the turn and started up again. Harmon was amazed that running uphill could feel better than downhill. All part of his ultra-education.

Ed and Harmon went back through the aid station and started the last four miles to the finish. It was a gentle downhill, then flat. The downhill tweaked the aching quads, but then they were running on the flat and finished together in 9:52. The cutoff was eleven hours, but there were not many people left on the course. As they finished, there was a worker on a ladder taking down the finish line banner. There were about five cars left in the once-full parking lot.

Harmon shook hands with Ed, gave him a manly hug. They met each other's wives. They said goodbyes. Lisa drove him home. Harmon's legs were shot. He swore off ultras, told her not to let him enter another one. Ever.

* * *

By two weeks later he started to think: maybe 100 miles. Maybe that was the distance that would draw out his inner endurance star. Maybe he would just run it to the end. The longer the better. It made so much sense. On paper. In race reports from the ultrarunning veterans, who seemed to laugh at difficulty and fatigue, 100 miles seemed like the distance of truth. So, 100 miles it would be.

* * *

After two races, Harmon Willow thought he knew something about ultrarunning, but he was definitely full of shit. It was 3:30 am in mid-July, and he was standing in a field in the middle of nowhere Vermont. He was wearing short racing shorts over compression shorts, over running briefs. He had a hat from a mail order outfitter and a preposterously large hard-plastic water bottle from Target. He was wearing his Asics road shoes, his Timex stopwatch. He had read up on the race and on 100 milers in general. He read that he should train like he would for a marathon only longer, so he did train for a marathon and ran a 3:27 10 weeks before Vermont. He felt good and strong. He thought 24 hours was a good goal, maybe a little faster.

He had read that he should try running overnight, so he did a run from sundown to sunup at the shore, 40 flat miles, on Memorial Day weekend. He was tired at the finish, but hardly felt tested. He had read that he should taper, so he eased off to just a few miles a day after the 4th of July 5-miler. He had read that he needed to take salt capsules and eat real food, but he wasn't sure how. He had no well of experience, had no idea what it would really take to complete a 100 miler on his 49-year old legs.

Despite the hour, it was not cold, not even cool, about 65 and humid. There was light ground fog in the hollow down the hill. Lisa was there. She kissed him and wished him well and said she would see him at the aid station at 18 miles. She walked off to the car and he ventured under the huge party tent, got a half-cup of coffee, ate a piece of bagel. As the time neared, he moved toward the starting line, his shoes getting wet in the dewy grass.

At 4:00, they were off, 250 runners jogging down the hill, headlamps bobbing, heading for the fork and left turn on the hard dirt road. They went about a mile down the road, and then the course veered off onto a trail. It was damp and rocky and looked like it had been a wagon road two hundred years ago. It delivered them onto another dirt road, something that would be repeated 50 or more times. Harmon was mid-pack, trying to stay in line and see the rocks and hazards on the course with his new on-line purchased headlamp. By 5:00, it was light, and Harmon could switch off the headlamp. He ran down some dirt and then paved roads and crossed a main road and onto a covered bridge. On the far side, he climbed more hills and moved along to the first aid station with crew access at 18 miles. He felt good and was moving along at what felt like a forever pace. He hoped it was a forever pace.

At the aid station, he saw Lisa and she said he was doing great and he moved along. She would see him again at 30 miles. He went over more hills, and then climbed a long and huge hill. At the top, there were views in every direction. People were taking photos. Harmon ran along in the still-damp grass. His heels had blisters, but they were not that bad. He came down off the big hill, and it was impossibly steep in places, so steep he thought he might slip and fall in the grass. His toes were jammed to the front of his shoes. His quads felt the downhill stress. Then he was back on a flat and heading for the 30-mile aid station.

He saw Lisa and there were dozens of cars at the aid station and she said he looked great, and they were doing this. He was concerned about his quads, but said nothing. What good would it do to voice it?

He left the aid station and trotted down the road, following the race signs. They directed him right into a driveway, behind a barn and up a steep, long grassy hill. He would later learn this was a ski hill. He power-walked in a group up the hill, into the woods at the top and up and up, to a short trail that delivered him to another driveway and then a dirt road. It was getting hot. Harmon was in a tech fabric singlet, and was sweating hard. He came to an unmanned, water-only aid, and filled his big water bottle from a plastic water bladder lying in the sun. When he drank as he pulled away, the taste was pure plastic, causing him to spit the water. The sun was up and beating on him and it was three miles to the next aid. He drank and spit several times along the way. He just couldn't swallow the plastic water.

He came down the hill, and across a road to an aid station, dumped the bad water and refilled. He ate some peanut butter and jelly and fruit and moved along. He was talking to a tall, thin man from Canada, Dave. Then Dave moved ahead. Then, a mile or so later, he saw Dave, bent and retching on the roadside. Harmon asked if he needed help. Dave waved him away. "I'll be fine." Harmon moved on. He came down another hill to a turn onto a main road and to another aid station that had popsicles. They tasted great. He took two and ate both. Then he turned left across another covered bridge and along the river on a smaller road. He worked his way along on a combination of dirt and paved roads and connecting trails, finally arriving at the biggest aid station, Camp 10-Bear. He was at about mile 48. There were cars lining the sides of the dirt road for a quarter mile before the aid station. The place was packed with runners, and the race officials were weighing and checking the runners. Harmon was the same weight that he had started at. The official who weighed him asked if he had taken any salt capsules. He responded that he had taken over 10, but he wasn't sure exactly how many. The official suggested taking it easy, as it was common to lose a few pounds on a hot day. Harmon saw Lisa again. She told him he was doing great and that it was 90 degrees. He changed his shoes and socks (he had read you should) and moved along out of the zoo that was 10-Bear.

He walked up the dirt-road hill and ran down the back side and then turned left at the T intersection onto the 20-mile circuit that would take him back to 10-Bear. He ran along some pretty fields before turning into the woods on more hilly, dirt wagon roads. It was now over 90 and humid and the air in the woods was stifling. He passed a small sign that said 50 miles. He was just at 12 hours. Although 24 hours was always the goal, he was not getting there today. The B-goal was to finish his first 100 miler. He had 18 more hours to do it.

He came to some places in the dirt road that were big puddles, spanning the width of the road. Harmon had read that he did not want to get his feet wet, so he slowed and took great pains to avoid the puddles, walking on stone walls along the edge of the roadway. Another runner he had met ran right through and disappeared ahead.

He arrived at an aid station at a lovely country farmhouse. The table was covered with homemade baked goods, like lemon squares and cookies. Harmon ate several. Then a few more. From there, the course turned right across a big field. It started to drizzle in the humid afternoon. The field was boggy, and his feet got muddy and wet. He moved through the woods on a trail and onto another road to the next crew aid at Tracer Brook, really just a parking area along a turn on the road. Harmon took off the wet shoes and changed socks and forged on up a long series of hills to Margaritaville, the most famous aid station. Harmon was getting blisters on the bottoms of his feet, on the foot-pads, and he was moving slower. He saw Lisa again at Margaritaville and told her he was getting tired and his feet hurt. It was about to get dark. He would see her again at 10-Bear in 8 miles, maybe two hours or a little less.

He was walking with a young woman from Washington and another guy, also young. Dave from Canada went by, looking really good, despite his earlier pukefest. Harmon and the other two moved slower and slower. As the gloom of twilight fell, they turned onto another wagon road, that looked like a little used and rocky trail, with water running down it. The pace slowed yet again as they picked their way down this hilly trail by headlamp. Finally, they were on another dirt road, and it was dark. Dark-dark. Like no ambient light at all in the woods, with no houses nearby. The young woman, Abby, moved ahead, as Harmon was limping because of underfoot blisters on both feet. Twenty minutes later, he saw a head lamp coming toward him. It was Abby; she had lost her direction and way in the dark. She was unsure which way to go. Harmon assured her that he may be faltering and he may just suck at ultrarunning, but he was going in the right direction. And he was.

They stayed together toward 10-Bear. They talked of dropping at that point, knowing that their pace of less than 3 miles an hour wouldn't give them time to finish within the 30-hour limit. It was a conspiracy of negativity and failure.

Finally, they arrived at the left turn back to the hill and Camp 10-Bear on the other side. They staggered into camp at 11:00, a full three-hours after they left Margaritaville. They weighed Harmon and he was declared good to go, but he wanted some help for blisters. Abby said goodbye. She had wanted to drop, but she had a pacer at 10-Bear, a pacer who would not take no and implored her to move along.

Harmon sat and took off his shoes and socks. He had a half-dollar sized blister on the bottom of each foot. Both had torn and leaked fluid into his socks, which had in-turn dried to a crusty hardness and irritated the feet more. A podiatrist declared that he could help. He lanced and drained the rest of the fluid. He injected something into the blisters to fuse the skin to the foot. It felt . . . awful. Like his feet were on fire.

It was still excruciating five minutes later when he limped down the road to his car and dropped. Lisa was consoling. "You did great, hunny. 68 miles is really good. That's the farthest you've ever run. Don't worry about it."

Harmon appreciated all her efforts and told her so. But he felt like shit and told her that too. This was his first ever dnf. He had run marathons and the 50 miler and had never quit a race before the finish, no matter how bad he felt. They went back to the bed and breakfast and went to bed. In the morning he ran 2 miles on still-burning feet and drove home brooding. It was running streak day number 8,963.

* * *

Over the next several weeks, he came to understand that he really didn't know shit about ultrarunning. Despite his fantasies of being an ace at longer distances, despite thinking maybe he was special, he was really a wimp. Running 100 miles took a certain grit, a determination that he lacked in his first try. Could he learn it? Was there any point? Should he be content to run marathons or 50 milers? They were fine. They were challenging. That could easily be his running life. Besides, 100 miles was such a random distance. It had no intrinsic value.

Who was he kidding? He would try again.

He trained harder after his feet healed, and he ran a 50 miler on the road in Rhode Island that fall in 8:50. 100 miles should be a breeze; 24 hours should be so doable. The race on paper again started to take over. Fantasy loomed larger than reality.

As part of his gearing up mileage in the winter, Harmon appeared on the beach at Cape Cod in January for the first Frozen Fatass 50k, all sand and rocks on the beach and roads along the tidal ponds. It was freezing and grueling, and he loved it. The RD was a great guy, and he and Harmon became friends.

He entered a race in North Carolina in April: the Umstead 100. He trained like he was trying to run a fast marathon, with 20-mile weekend runs and 7 or 8 a day during the week. He tapered for two weeks. He and Lisa drove down to Raleigh and made a romantic long weekend of it. They stopped at Lisa's sister's house at the shore on Thursday night and walked to the beach. A stinging breeze came off the water. Most of the houses were dark this time of year. In the morning, they headed to a local breakfast place, Prince Coffee, for giant lattes and cinnamon rolls before heading south to Raleigh.

Harmon had no idea what to expect at Umstead. What he found was an enthusiastic group that felt like an extended family. He met some people who were friends on line, runners he had never met, but heard of or corresponded with on the ultralist, the internet forum that served the ultra community. The race briefing was like a revival meeting, with the participants dedicated to ultra. The Race Director specifically said the race catered to first-timers. He asked for a show of hands of all the first time 100 milers. He talked about them finishing and reminded them to respect the distance and obey three tenets: drink before you're thirsty, eat before you're hungry, walk before you're tired. Harmon looked around the room at veterans and newbies alike, looking interested and ready. He felt that these were his people. He was at home.

He and Lisa ate at the pre-race pasta dinner at the race headquarters just after the briefing. They talked to nervous new runners and calm vets. The atmosphere was almost festive.

Harmon drove back to the hotel, set his alarm for 4:15 am, spooned with Lisa and tried to sleep, knowing that tomorrow was a chance to redeem himself at the 100-mile distance.

At exactly 6:00 am, the race started. 260 runners moseyed down a gravel road onto Umstead's 8-loop course of smooth crushed stone roads. Harmon still knew next to nothing about ultra. He was dressed in his running hat, a long-sleeved tech top over a singlet in the cool morning darkness, compression shorts under running shorts, Asics road shoes with expensive tech fabric socks and gaiters he had bought on-line to keep pebbles out of his shoes, because he had read that's what you are supposed to do.

The morning was cool, but it promised to heat up, might reach the high 70s. Harmon was scared. He was 0 for 1 in 100 milers. It seemed doable, really doable, but he had never done it. Lisa would stay there the entire time to crew and support him. She would sleep in the driver's seat of their little Subaru to be there for him.

The Umstead course made a big loop of 12.5 miles with 1000 feet of elevation gain and loss each loop. The course bent back on itself in a few places, and people could greet one another. It left from the start-finish on the access road only for the start. It went a little more than a half mile, then turned right at a T intersection for the airport spur, an out-and-back of about a mile each way. On the way back from the airport spur, you continued straight, and went along a series of small rises and dips to the serpentine downhill that started just before mile 4 and continued to about 4.5. Each mile of the loop was marked with a sign. At the bottom of the serpentine, you crossed a bridge and went up a long but gentle hill, past the 5-mile sign to about 5.3, where the course turned left. It then was relatively flat or downhill, past the 6-mile sign and then downhill to the back aid station at 6.85. From there the course went into the saw-tooth section, a series of shorter, steep up-and-down hills. There was a long downhill at the 9-mile mark then an uphill to another T intersection and a left turn. From there the course was level and then downhill past the 10-mile sign, along the powerlines, across another bridge and up a long hill, where the course joined the outbound course at a T at which you turned right and passed people outbound at about mile 3.3. Then you retraced your steps up to the right turn for the start-finish and ran down through a parking area and then up railroad tie stairs to the start-finish. Voila, one complete lap.

The first two loops were fine. Umstead was far from flat, but very far from other hilly or mountainous 100s. The day grew warm and Harmon was down to his singlet. He had swapped out hats because the first one was sweat-soaked. He was carrying a 20 oz. handheld water bottle. He had read that that was the preferable way to hydrate in an ultra. On the third loop he started to feel it. Out from the start-finish, he walked up the hill and slow-jogged the level to the right turn of the airport spur out-and-back, past the turnaround cone at about 1.5 miles of the loop and back past the cutoff to the start-finish. Then on down the crushed stone road past the 3-mile mark and down the big serpentine hill to the bridge with the wooden deck. He walked from the bridge all the way up the hill to the left turn, then slow-jogged to the back aid. Just after the aid station, by 32 miles, he was feeling like he hit a wall. He couldn't imagine going another 68 miles. It just seemed so far. But he kept going down the path, finished the loop.

Back at the start-finish headquarters, he felt a little better and made the turnaround a quick one. Halfway out on loop four, he faltered again. He walked most of the hilly second half of the loop after the back aid station. A few people he knew moved by: the race director from Connecticut at whose race Harmon had volunteered, a runner from the Cape, a couple years older, very tough guy, who had run the Boston Marathon 25 straight years. Harmon hooked on with this group and finished the loop just behind them in 11:07. He was tired; his legs felt shot, but there was no reason he couldn't continue. He changed shoes and socks, because he had read it was advisable at 50 miles. He wasted 20 minutes, then got back on the course, with his headlamp at the ready. It got dark on the back half of loop 5, and he slowed in the night. He was having trouble breathing and used his inhaler. At times, he couldn't stop coughing. (He later learned that the yellowish powder on the trail was tree pollen.) He finished the 6th loop a few minutes before 1:00. He swung around the start-finish aid and drank some soda. None of the food looked good. He walked back to the car, just off the course down from the start-finish. Lisa had been napping in the car, but she awoke to talk to him. He leaned on the car and said he was beat. He couldn't imagine doing another 25 miles. It was deep night and getting colder. She got him a can of Starbuck's double-shot espresso, and she urged him to just walk on up the trail and onto the airport spur. And he did. He walked all the way to the turnaround and tried to jog back down past the cut-off. He couldn't get a rhythm going and walked most of the loop. At the back aid station, he drank an iced ginger ale and ate some ginger cookies. They calmed his stomach, and he moved on through the hilly back part. Finally, he was back in the start-finish area, just before dawn, almost 24 hours into this race, with one lap to go. He ate some peanut butter and jelly sandwich squares and some salted baked potatoes. He drank some Pepsi. He walked back down the course to the car and told Lisa he was ready to do that last loop, although he still felt wiped. He had no energy for running or even fast walking. Her sleepy advice was the same: just get out there and keep moving. It would come.

About 3 miles into the loop, dawn came. He turned off his headlamp and could see the road and the woods around him. He felt energy return to his

legs. He jogged down the serpentine hill at 4 miles. He shuffled in a slow jog up the gentle hills after the bridge and all the way down to the back aid station. He drank another ginger ale over ice, ate more cookies, thanked the aid station workers, and forged on to the hills. At about the 9 mile mark his energy surged. He could picture and feel the finish and he ran parts of the course he had walked since the first loop. He passed several groups of runners and pacers, never staying with any group. He took the right turn to the start-finish area and passed the 12-mile maker for the loop, half a mile to go. All running with increasing speed from this point, down to the fork, down through the parking lots, onto the soft path with the railroad tie steps and up to the finish tent. 26:50, his first 100-mile finish! He was elated. Lisa was there snapping pictures. The race official shook his hand and handed him a bronze belt buckle, his first. He was all smiles, even in his fatigue.
He and Lisa walked into the race headquarters cabin, where they had eaten dinner on a Friday night that seemed like a week ago. Harmon sat at a table, while Lisa grabbed him a breakfast of a cheese omelet and toast, with water and juice. Harmon slumped on the table, head in his hands. He was aware that the room was full of people, some who had finished and were full of the post-race glow, some waiting for their runners out there on the course, some walking wounded, who had faltered and dropped.

Across the way, a smallish, balding, thin runner was holding court, telling a story of seeing a fox cross the course in the night. He had a strong southern accent, voice like molasses. "Well, let me tell you: I've run a bit in these woods. I cain't even remember seein' a fox out there. You know, then I thought, I just never looked for one, either. So, either that was a fox, or I was worse off than I thought. I guess it could have been a runner. Short guy; red hair." He was engaging. The people around him nodded and laughed and commented and were into the tale. Harmon was just too tired to get in on this.

Someone walked into the building and called out: "What'd you finish in, Ben?" (pronounced Be-in)

The small runner replied: "22:15."

"Fuck," thought Harmon. "I have a long way to go." Then he thought, "I may never get there."

Harmon looked around. The room was full of runners. Among them was another shorter guy, with glasses. He was sitting at one of the tables with his crew member, fingering a bronze buckle like the one Harmon was holding. Farther back from the door was a table of people Harmon recognized from races up north. Sitting with them was a big guy he had never seen before. Harmon could tell he was a big guy when he was seated. Then he stood up and towered over the ultra crowd that tended toward the smallish. He was about 6'6" and not thin, big feet, thick calves, thick thighs, solid through the abdomen, huge head with wiry red hair.

A minute later they were both in the kitchen getting more breakfast. Harmon spoke first: "Hey."

"Hey," the big guy replied. He held out his hand. "Rufus."

Rufus's hand engulfed Harmon's. "Harmon. Did you do the 100?"

"No, just the 50. I'm working up to the 100."

"I think a place like this is the only place people would say, 'Just 50.'" They both chuckled. "I mean just the sound of it. 'Yeah, I only ran 50 miles in the last day.'"

"How about you?" Rufus inquired.

"First 100 finish, like 20 minutes ago."

"Nice."

"Yeah, I'm pretty psyched. But, I'm kinda tired." They both laughed again. "In fact, I need to get my wife to drive me back to the hotel before I pass out."

They shook hands again. "I'll see you down the road, Rufus."

"Yup. See ya."

Harmon walked over to Lisa, sitting alone at a table. "Had enough ultra talk?"

"Yeah. I'm beat."

"You can stay as long as you want to soak up the feeling."

"Nah. I'm done now. I'm so tired, I could sleep on my feet."
He gathered his things, while she pulled the car up to the front of the cabin. He staggered out stiff-legged, and she drove him back to the hotel. By that time, he was teetering. Everything was sore and every step an adventure.

Once in the room, he wanted to lie down, but knew he needed to shower away the grime before he slept. After a long, warm shower, he toweled off and climbed into bed next to Lisa. She had had a fitful sleep herself, seat reclined in the car, being interrupted every lap. It was about 10:00 am.

Harmon felt both elated and exhausted. He caressed Lisa's shoulder.

She said, "Hunny, you need to sleep."

"I need to sleep . . . in about 30 minutes." He winked.

They went to sleep in about 30 minutes, slept the morning away in the cool hotel room, drapes pulled, air conditioning unit thrumming softly.

When he woke up mid-afternoon, everything was sore and stiff, but he was still elated. He and Lisa got dressed and walked over to the Irish pub at the far end of the shopping center next to the hotel. A few beers and an order of fries went down real easy. He didn't feel so stiff after all.

They walked back to the hotel and spent some time in the lobby talking to other runners hanging around. At dinnertime, they walked to the Greek restaurant at the near end of the shopping center and had a leisurely dinner. They shared a bottle of wine. Harmon tried to articulate his feelings. "I don't know; I feel like I can accomplish anything, like obstacles are nothing."

"Like you've really been changed by this."

"Yeah, that's how it feels. Like I'll go back to work and be better. Get more things done."

She took a sip of wine, smiled the closed-mouth smile.
They walked back to the room, watched a pay-per-view movie. Afterward, though it was early, it was time to catch up on sleep.

Harmon: "Before we go to sleep, I think we should . . . ."

"Again?"

"Hunny, I've changed. I am decisive. I can get more things done."

She laughed. He turned off the lights, found her in the dark. They got things done.

Life was perfect. It was running streak day number 9,224.

The next day, running was tough. He had built up to the training and determination necessary to complete a 100 miler. But no one had ever counseled him on how to run the next day. He awoke Monday morning in a hotel room in Raleigh, barely able to walk to the bathroom. But he got dressed in a tee shirt and shorts, groaning as he bent to lace his shoes. He got himself down the elevator and out the door to run and headed into the shopping center and beyond on a beat-up sidewalk then the side of the highway for a few hundred yards before he found a right turn into a small subdivision. It was a beautiful sunny morning about 60 degrees and he was running, really slow-jogging, down a short hill past closely spaced ranch style houses shaded by pines and oaks. The subdivision went down through a glade of tall pines and around a circle. Harmon did the circle a few times to make the run 35 minutes, figuring that even at his slow-jog pace, he would be over two miles in that time. As hard as it had been to get started, the run loosened him up. He could hardly lift his feet; his hamstrings were dead. With each downhill step, he felt a stabbing pain in his quads. But it eased as the run went on, and he embraced the exquisite pain of the post-ultra, recovery run. He got back to the hotel, nodded to other runners in the lobby and waited for the elevator.

He got back to the room, showered and went down to the free continental breakfast with Lisa. He stuffed himself without guilt before starting the all-day drive home. On the way, they stopped for biscuits at Bojangles. There wasn't enough food to satisfy him that day.

* * *

It turned out Harmon wasn't changed in other aspects of his life. He was still good at procrastinating, hated mowing the lawn. Work was the same. Life was generally the same. He was, however, a better runner. He had broken through the ultra-wall. He had stayed with it when he wanted to quit. Finishing a 100 miler had taught him one useful thing. When you feel like shit, just keep going down the road or trail. You'll probably finish.

His other life change was that he was starting to get to know other people in ultrarunning. He looked up the results for Umstead, saw that Ben who was sub-24 was Ben Jarvis from Virginia. There was only one Rufus: Rufus Saletti, from suburban New York.

Two weeks after Umstead, he ran the Boston Marathon for the third time, this time with Hope. They had both qualified the previous spring in the redwoods in Northern California. Boston was an extravaganza; Hope was thrilled to finally be running the most famous marathon. They had a great time in Boston, but Harmon thought he would probably not be back. Something about ultras was sucking him in deeper.

He volunteered at an ultra in Connecticut in late April for the second straight year to get volunteer hours for another try at Vermont. Many of the faces looked familiar, circling a lake in the northwest hills. Harmon handed out aid, cheered on the runners, passed out medals to finishers. The volunteers were bundled up, the weak spring sunshine being no match for the biting breeze off the lake. Many of the runners were in tights and long sleeves, some even in windbreakers. Rufus came around the start-finish area in shorts and a tee shirt, sweating like it was summer. He filled his handheld water bottle, but refused food each time around. At the finish, Harmon handed him a medal.

"Hey, Harmon."

"Rufus, nice job."

"My best 50k, by half an hour."

"So, no food?"

"Yeah, that. I'm trying to work on fat adaptation. Using fat as primary fuel. I've got plenty of it."

Harmon said nothing. He looked up at Rufus. Man, he was a big fucker, a very big fucker. Like NFL nose-tackle big.

"I'm just fucking with you. Everyone has enough fat on board to run an ultra, even a 100 miler."

They both laughed. Then made ultrarunner small talk. Rufus was from New York, commuted into the City for work, married with children, in his 30s. Ran every day starting a year ago over the Christmas holiday. “Underneath it all, I might be a lazy ass. Running every day is a brute force way to hold myself accountable. Don’t worry about whether you’re doing it or not doing it today. Just commit to every day, and forget about it.”

Later: “Yeah, Rufus. My father’s favorite name. I’m guessing you never met a Rufus. Definitely not a white guy named Rufus.” Harmon shook his head. “But, it means red-haired in Latin, so it works.”

Later still: “6’6”, 290. My life goal is to be the fattest person to complete a 100 miler under 24 hours.” Harmon raised his eyebrows. “Really, my goal is to lose about 100 pounds and look like that fucker.” He pointed to a tall, really-thin runner passing by in the 50-miler. “Then I’ll run 100 in about 18 hours. Now, that’s a goal.”

“Everyone needs a dream.”

They both laughed again. All this time, Harmon was handing out medals, congratulating runners.

Then Rufus had to get home. “See you at the next one, Harmon.”

“See you down the road. Be good.”

* * *

He was putting in good mileage preparing for Vermont. He would not falter this time. It had only worked once, and in an easier 100, but Harmon thought he at least knew the key: don’t quit. Keep moving. Want it. Show some grit. Show a lot of grit.

As always, he ran the 4th of July 5-miler, this time with young Harmon. Iris had bowed out when she reached her teen years. It would be so embarrassing to be seen running the race with her family. He and Harmon went fast, finishing in 37:20. He had to really push it to keep up. The race was fun, but the next day, his right knee was clearly messed up. He could barely run; he managed two painful miles.

The next week was really no better. He kept mileage under 5 a day between the race and Vermont. He bought a cheap knee brace, and that made things a little better, but he didn't have high hopes for his chances. He had waited a year to make up for his dnf, and now this. But he was already entered in the race and they had a reservation in Woodstock, so he decided to at least start and see how it went.

So, he found himself in Silver Hill Meadow again in the middle of the night with a group of nervous runners. This time, he knew a few of them and exchanged quick greetings. It was cooler and less humid than the previous year. He was wearing the over-the-counter knee brace right from the start. A few people remarked and asked what was wrong. He underplayed it. The knee didn't feel great even just walking around on the uneven ground of the field before the start. Then the race started and hundreds of lights bounced down the dirt road. Harmon had lined up near the back and he stayed near the back, letting the front-runners, and mid-packers and even slower runners move off ahead. Harmon found himself running alone within the first three miles. Dawn came and the weather warmed but stayed in the 70s. Harmon had arranged with Lisa to first meet at the 30-mile aid station so she could get some morning sleep. He knew he would be slow to get there, maybe even drop right there. He got to the first big aid at 18 miles, and it was closing up and nearly deserted. Picked over fruit was left on the table, and Harmon filled his handheld water bottle. A race volunteer questioned him as to whether there was anyone behind him. He had no idea, but there was certainly no one around. He headed on down the course alone. He went over the big hill with the panoramic view, all without seeing another runner. He reached Stage Road, the 30-mile aid, and it was empty. There were about three cars: two for volunteers and Lisa. He refilled water and said he would keep going up the ski hill and over to the next crew aid station. Once there, he said he would continue again. He was running all this alone, and he was close to cutoffs, but still within them. He pushed on to Camp 10-Bear, arriving 10 minutes before the cutoff. He was weighed and took off, feeling okay, if not great. His feet, in Asics road shoes as usual, were killing him, but he dare not stop because of cutoffs.

At Tracer Brook, at 55 miles, he saw Lisa again, still within the last 3 in the race and still struggling. She said, "You're going to do this, aren't you?"

"I don't know. I'm just going aid station to aid station. Can you get me two Advil?" He had never taken ibuprofen in a race before. He took two and moved on. At Margaritaville, it was closing, and the volunteers told him that he was last. Maybe he wanted to drop? He declined. He was still within the cutoff, had actually gained 10 minutes. While waiting for him, Lisa had overheard a runner saying she had a pacer waiting at 10-Bear, but she was going to drop and needed to get word to him. Lisa told Harmon she was going to 10-Bear to find that pacer and secure him for Harmon. Harmon was reluctant, he never thought of himself as needing a pacer, but he relented, since he was right on the edge and was afraid he would miss a cutoff. At the next aid up the hill, everything was closed down. There was a bowl of gummy bears left. He took a handful, even though he didn't like them, just to eat something. Then he was back at 10-Bear, still alone, as he had been for almost the entire 68 miles. It was 12:45 am; the cutoff was 1:00. He met Helmut, his assigned pacer, a German guy living in Burlington. Helmut was considering running a 100 and wanted to pace to see what it was about. Harmon told him that he was suffering but was just trying to beat each cutoff. Off they went into the darkness, Helmut ahead, with Harmon following. They introduced themselves and made small talk as they walked the hilly trail section. The initial going in the woods was tough on the knee and they were not making good time. They got to the spirit of '76 aid just at the 3:00 cutoff. Harmon never even paused, just slogged right through onto the dirt road and better footing. Helmut got some food and he caught up a few minutes later. Harmon was trying to run the levels and downhills on the road, but the knee really hurt on the downhills, and he moaned audibly with each step. At 82 miles, he got 2 more Advil to try to ease the pain. The rest of the night and early morning were the same, moaning on the downhills, slow jogging the flats, trying to fast walk up the hills. They started catching the back of the pack and passing it. At each aid station, there were people lying around like an infirmary. Harmon never sat. He just kept thinking of the finish. His feet were messed up, but that actually attenuated the knee pain. Then they were near the end, and he could hear cheers at the finish line and he was in the woods and emerging at the line. 29:35. Less than 25 minutes to spare. Only 11 people came in after him. But he had done it. Finished Vermont after last year's dnf. Helmut shook his hand. They hugged briefly. From the finish line, he could barely walk to the big tent across the field. It was almost time for brunch. He and Lisa sat with Helmut for a bit. Harmon apologized for moaning in pain on the downhills. In a thick German accent, Helmut said, "It was like listening to porno." They all laughed. Helmut said his goodbyes and moved through the crowd.

Later, at the motel, Harmon took off his shoes and noted that his feet were seriously fucked. Although he had been wearing toe-socks he had read about on line that "guaranteed" no blisters, four of his toenails were floating on big toe-end blisters. In addition, both big toes were blistered on the sides and under the toenails. He also had blistered around his heels. He showered and he and Lisa went to bed, going to sleep . . . about 30 minutes later.

After the race, his knee was worse than ever. He ran just a few miles a day for weeks, including the comically painful day-after run, in which he stagger-jogged down the sidewalks of Woodstock like a running zombie.

Slowly, over the late fall and winter, the knee started hurting less and feeling like whatever was wrong was healing. He ran a slow 50k in January and a marathon in February, both on Cape Cod, just trying to get some miles in for Umstead in April. By March, he was able get back to 10 miles a day. He ditched the brace.

The first weekend of April, he and Lisa were in North Carolina again for Umstead. They went to the race briefing and dinner and saw what were now familiar faces, including Ben and Rufus and a few other running friends Harmon had met at other races.

Saturday morning at about 5:30, the race headquarters cabin was bustling with 250 runners and crews nervously milling and exchanging greetings. Harmon said good luck to many familiar faces. The rookies were there looking nervous, not quite knowing what to expect. Harmon thought, "That was me last year."

He saw Rufus across the room standing a head taller than the people around him. He edged through the crowd and said hi and good luck. Rufus said, "I went over 100 miles in a 48-hour over the New Years, but this is my first real try at 100."

Harmon's sage advice in reply: "Just keep moving. Don't quit." (Like he knew anything.)

Harmon had a plan for the race that he hadn't shared with anyone: he wanted to go harder from the start, reach 50 miles in 10 hours or less, so he could have a decent chance of going sub-24 hours. With that in mind, when the race started just before dawn, he pushed the first four laps. The weather was cool and cloudy and running was easy. His inner message was to run all the runnable parts and only walk the steep uphills. As long as he never found himself trudging along a level or downhill part of the course, he was confident he could approach his goal. He had to push though the first wall at about 32 miles, that feeling that he had so much more to go and so little energy to get him there. He came in at the 50-mile mark at the end of lap four in just under 10 hours, feeling okay. Lisa encouraged him and sent him right back out—no more wasting time or shoe changes. She did have him bring his headlamp, although she said he might not even need it.

He didn't. When he got back to the start-finish with 5 laps down, it was just after 7:15. It was getting dark and the weather was gloomier. A soft drizzle began. Lisa rigged him up with an iPod, the first time he had used music in a 100-miler. As dark gathered and the rain intensified, a mixture of classic rock and 1990s alt rock kept him company, and his spirits were fine through lap 6, even as his pace deteriorated. He got back in, drank a Starbuck's double-shot and left the iPod to be charged while he did the seventh loop. He went back out at about 10:45. About three hours later he was back and a little bedraggled: wet and tired and worn. He got the music set up again, drank another double-shot and went back out for the last lap. The music perked him up, as did the knowledge he was finishing up. In the rain and ground fog, his headlamp illuminated a small circle and the rest was darkness. He shrank into his own little world of music and running. Certain songs made him pick up the pace: Machinehead, Running Down a Dream, Statesboro Blues, Truckin', Monkey Wrench. Love songs made him almost weepy; his emotions were so raw. He was pushing hard, knowing sub-24 was there, thinking sub-23 was even possible. He passed a few runners with pacers on the back, hilly part of the course. Then he made the left turn at the top of the hill to head to the 10-mile sign on the lap on the powerline downhill. He gained momentum and plunged down the powerlines in a steady rain, holding the run over the bridge and up the beginning of the long hill before the right turn. Then he had less than two miles to go, and he could feel the finish, envision a sub-23. He never let up, running almost everything, powerwalking cemetery hill, then running the rain-slick final mile, sprinting through the muddy parking lots to the railroad tie stairs and up to the finish area. 22:56, and total elation in the darkness and rain. The race official handed him the silver buckle for sub-24. He was all smiles in photos taken by Lisa.

He was done! It was still night, just shy of 5:00 am. How cool was that! They went into the cabin and had some breakfast and Harmon talked to some of the runners and crews. Showed off his silver buckle, accepted praise. Ben was there, having come in a few minutes earlier. They exchanged pleasantries, and he congratulated Harmon on the sub-24 and the silver buckle.

By the time there were streaks of light in the sky, Harmon had played out his euphoria, and they were ready to leave. Lisa drove him back to the hotel, and they followed last year's routine.

They were up in the early afternoon and went down to the lobby. Several runners were there talking about the race. Harmon saw Rufus reclined in a chair at the far end of the lobby, feet up on a hassock. Harmon walked over. Before he could ask, Rufus said "I did it! 28:25. I fucking did it. I feel great!"

"Nice! Way to go."

"Thanks. You know, it wasn't as bad as I expected. I mean it was hard. But, 30 hours is plenty of time to go 100 miles on foot. You keep going and you get it done."

"Hey, Lisa and I are going over to the Irish pub for beers. Do you and your wife want to go?"

"Man, I haven't slept yet. Or showered or done anything. Kathy is getting stuff out of the car and then we're going up for a nap."
"Alright, don't say I didn't invite you. See you around later, maybe. Way to get it done out there."

"Take it easy."

Harmon and Lisa walked across the shopping center to the Irish pub and had a late lunch and beers. It was even better than last year. Another 100 finish. Sub-24. A delicious black and tan in the afternoon. Then another. And a third.

The post-race morning run wasn't even as hard. A light rain was falling, and Harmon ran the same route through the subdivision. The din of commuter traffic gave way to the quiet seclusion of the subdivision. In the rain, sound was muted, but color seemed more vivid. The azaleas and flowering fruit trees on manicured lawns stood out in red and pink and purple. He was at peace for those minutes before packing for the long drive back.

* * *

Recovery from this third 100-miler also didn't seem as hard. Harmon thought maybe he was figuring things out. He was embracing the 100-mile distance: it allowed for highs and lows and required stamina and perseverance through the night for an average runner like Harmon. He came to like having to face the doubt and difficulty late into the night, running alone in the gloom.

He felt he was ready for a bigger challenge, so he entered the Headlands 100 in August and got his first look at West Coast ultras. The course was relentless, climbing on smooth trails, then plunging back down to sea level in one 50-mile loop, followed by two 25-mile loops. He traversed iconic trails of the Marin Headlands, just north of the Golden Gate Bridge, running the Miwok trail and along Pirates Cove. He ran up through the coastal redwood groves and past fragrant eucalyptus trees. In his exuberance, he passed 50 miles right at 12 hours, but he had used well over half his energy. The next 25-mile loop took him nearly nine hours, run all alone through the cooling night, with a big moon hanging over the Pacific as he labored up out of Pirates Cove across Coyote Ridge around midnight. The ground fog was so heavy it made his headlamp useless. He took it off and carried it in his hand so the rebound light from the fog wasn't right in his face. He felt like he was floating, like his feet weren't touching the ground. It was hard to make out the trail. He felt almost disembodied. He stopped and turned back, looked at the ocean and the moon reflecting a sparkled line in the water. Higher in the sky, he saw a long shooting star, bright, almost orange, then yellow and flaring out. He turned and continued up the hill, finally arriving at the start-finish at 4:30 am, when he had wanted to come in about 1:00. Another 25-mile loop with sister Hope, and he finished mid-afternoon in 30:58. Exhausted. Lisa hugged him. Hope hugged him. Then he got a hug from the indefatigable race director, who had seemingly been at every aid station all day and night and was still full of energy long into the next day. It was the beginning of a friendship. He would be back to run several other races she put on.

He was so slow that the finish line was pretty quiet, although he did meet some ultra celebrities. After a few minutes and some serious snacking, he and Lisa made for the rental car and drove back into San Francisco, where the plan was to go to Chinatown for dinner with friends. Harmon just had time for an hour nap and then it was time to walk a mile to the restaurant. Harmon hobbled, while Lisa waited. Patiently.

The next morning, the day-after run was more challenging. He was worn from the race and lack of sleep and hobbled by blisters. He ran while Lisa fast-walked next to him. She had no problem keeping up with his pace as he shuffled along the waterfront. It was a painful 45 minutes.

They flew home that day, and Harmon could only think that he could have done so much better, and that there was a whole other world of ultras out west. The Bay Area alone seemed to have an ultra of some distance every weekend. His mind reeled with the possibilities, but mostly he thought, "If only I were 10 years younger when I started this."

Following the Headlands 100, Harmon for the first time encountered an ultra overuse injury. He did his usual ramp-up of the mileage from the painfully slow couple of miles in San Francisco. He climbed Mount Katahdin with Matt, Iris and Harmon on the annual Maine vacation. He ran about 50 miles a week through the late summer and fall, but his right hamstring never came back. It felt ragged even as the year came to a close, as if it wanted to shorten, diminishing his already poor front bending ability. He researched the issue and concluded that he had a hamstring tendon problem. He stretched the leg several times a day, but it persisted. Driving was especially painful, with the pain going from the buttocks to the back of the knee. He started driving rolling a tennis ball under his right upper leg. He wondered, "Is this how it ends? You get an overuse injury and it just gets worse till you can't run?" He pushed through. Each day he would run 5 or 7 or 10 slow miles, and then suffer sitting at work or driving to court or a deposition.

The holidays came and went and the leg still hurt. He ran the 50k on the beach in late January and was an hour slower than the previous year. He still was focused on Umstead, but had no expectations.

The first week of April he and Lisa were driving down to North Carolina for their third Umstead. For the first time they brought Emmi and Rich. They would stay at the race overnight with everyone sleeping in the new SUV. The drive down was excruciating, Harmon changing positions every few minutes and rolling the tennis ball to try to ease the stabbing pain in his leg. By the time they got to the park for the race briefing and spaghetti dinner, Harmon was exhausted. He went to bed early and got a ride to the race in the morning so that Lisa and the kids could sleep.

So, for the third time, he stood on the steps of the start-finish headquarters cabin looking out over the sea of lights as the time counted down to the start. He had no expectations for this day, just to finish and not have too much leg pain. The day promised to be warmer with no rain. He said hi to Ben and Rufus and some others he recognized from up north.

As the race got going, Harmon's leg felt surprisingly good. He tried not to think about it or channel any of the pain he had had while driving. He was careful not to run too fast, but tried to run more of the course slow enough that it didn't overstress his leg. He passed 50 miles in just over 10 hours and was still moving well. There were friends spread all over the course, but he knew Ben was ahead and Rufus behind. Ben was far enough up ahead that Harmon was not passing him where the course had runners going in both directions. He was a fast little fucker. Rufus was coming up to the mile 11 mark of the 12.5-mile loop, while Harmon was at mile 3 on the 5th loop. Harmon felt like he was doing well, within striking distance of a sub-24. Rufus was pretty close behind, only 4.5 miles back. Night was falling and it was time to hold on to form and keep running when he could.

The next two lap times crept over 3 hours, but he was still on an under 24-hour pace, as he finished the 6th loop at about 11:00. He put on music and sank into his own world for the long lonely night. The key was the 7th loop. It was late and quiet. He was exhausted, but he knew he was not coming to the end and would have to do this exact terrain another lap. Lisa had given him a new mix of upbeat alternative rock and it helped him stay alert for the loop, even as his energy ebbed. Finally, he was back at the start-finish, drinking coffee and excited that he was on the final loop. He took off at 2:00 a.m., knowing that he just had to keep steady to go sub-24. By the back aid station, he knew he had it, but could he beat last year's time? He mixed running and walking through the saw tooth section and then bombed down the power lines one more time, over the bridge and as far up the hill as he could before walking. He turned right and started a slow jog. He walked up cemetery hill and felt it slipping away. He made the best time he could down the main roadway and then right for the last half mile to the finish line. He gathered speed as he ran down the road and then down the hill into the two parking areas. He pushed the last bit of trail with the railroad tie stairs to the finish line. 23:05. After 100 miles, 9 minutes slower than last year. But another sub-24.

Ben was already in, of course. Rufus was still out there, and he was holding up well. Harmon, Lisa and the kids left the headquarters cabin about an hour after his finish, while Rufus was on the last lap. Harmon never saw him after his finish, but the website said 26:25.

All four of them napped at the hotel, then Harmon slept another hour as Lisa and the kids watched tv in the room. Then, after he was up, they walked across to the Irish pub and the kids had a late lunch while Harmon and Lisa ate fries and drank beer. They walked around the shopping center, spent time back in the lobby and the room and then went out to dinner, before Harmon fell asleep watching a movie with the family in the room.

The next morning, he was up at sunrise to do his short run through the subdivision. It seemed even easier this year and Harmon did an extra loop of the neighborhood before heading back. Another Umstead in the books. Another sub-24, after being humbled by the grueling hills of the Marin Headlands, and after suffering with the sore hamstring all winter.

The leg was still compromised, but Harmon recovered quickly from his third Umstead. Within 10 days, he felt like he was back to where he had been: able to run a slow 5-10 miles on any given day.

And then the days clicked up to a milestone, and on May 16th, he clocked his 10,000th consecutive day running at least 2 miles. It was a nice Saturday morning and he ran an easy 7 miles. There was no fanfare, and Harmon thought of the moment. The run had been no more momentous or life-changing than the run the day before. And he planned to run the day after, so the number would continue to click ahead with each passing day. He called Hope to say he did it because over 26 years earlier he had said that he wanted to run 10,000 days in a row and now it was here. They laughed about how silly that boast seemed then and now.

And then it was gone, and it was day 10,001. And so it went. The days and the weeks and months. Harmon ran the 4th of July race again. Young Harmon kicked his ass, running with friends from the high school cross country team. Harmon's goal for the summer was to beat the constant nagging soreness at the top of the hamstring. He stretched every day after running. He ran slowly. He cut down his mileage for two months. He changed shoes. He tried to alter his running stride to land less on his heels. Nothing worked a magic cure. Finally, in the fall, he started to feel it ease slightly. The key was time, over a year of time, and a lot of slow running. And then the fall turned to winter and another year of running ended, with Harmon getting just over 3,000 miles.

He was 10 pounds too heavy. He hadn't run fast (for him) since 4th of July. He still felt soreness when he drove. But he was optimistic that the coming year would be better. He would put the hamstring issue behind him and get his ultra fitness back before Umstead.

CHAPTER FOURTEEN

Some days are bad days. You can have them in a 10k and your time will be off by 2 minutes. But in a 100-miler—you can lose hours. Few things suck more than walking 40 miles through the woods at night. Just because you suck. You'll see. If you toe the line enough, you'll see.

Underground Runner's Guide

January was cold and snowy, and the miles were slow and slower, and hard to come by. Harmon ran most of the month in his screw shoes—an old pair of running shoes with about ten 3/8 inch hex-head screws in the sole of each shoe for traction. He managed to avoid falling on the snow and ice, but he wasn't really getting solid training in. The first week of February, he ran the 50k on the beach at the Cape and was slower than ever, over 7:30. As winter waned, the weather eased and he did some good long weekend runs, but he was still behind in his training when it was time to drive to North Carolina. The miles that had seemed to click off at 9:30 the previous year were now over 10 minutes.

The whole family went down to Umstead again, but the plan was for Lisa and the kids to spend Saturday night at the hotel, instead of the car. The Umstead ritual started again. Drive to the shore Thursday. Drive long to Raleigh Friday. Greet old friends, check in, go to race briefing and stand in the back. Then pasta dinner and cake, then back to the hotel to lay out the running man on the floor (all his clothes for tomorrow laid out like a flat runner—which always made the kids giggle), then pack the gear bag for tomorrow, then put the foot taping kit in the bathroom, then off to bed. Up at 4:00: tape feet, put on running clothes, grab gear bag, go to lobby for ride to race. At the headquarters, greet all the old friends, wish everyone luck and a great day of running, drink a coffee, eat a bagel. And wait. Until everyone shuffles out of the headquarters cabin to the roadway for the start.

This year, it was cold, colder than it had been the previous three. The forecast was for highs in the 50s, going down to 20s at night, with a breeze. The crowd in the lights outside the cabin was bouncing around to stay warm and Harmon could see everyone's breath. The race started and he found himself walking in the crowd next to a friend he had met at many ultras, who had been running ultras for decades and was well known in the community. He was in short sleeves, but it seemed too cold for that. Then Harmon found himself next to Rufus, also in short sleeves, going on about how he loved this weather and hated the previous years in the 70s.

Rufus looked . . . really tall. But he announced something else: "I lost 20 pounds for this race. Race weight is my best predictor of results."

And he did seem to be moving well. They ran together to the turnaround on the airport spur, then ran the straightaway back past the start-finish cutoff and along the main roadway, down cemetery hill and off to where the back end of the course came in at mile 11 of the loop. Then a right turn along a flat stretch to the first long, serpentine downhill. Rufus announced, "Last year, a local kid paced me for the last lap. He runs cross country for his high school, and he told me all the hills have names." They started down the twisting hill toward the four-mile marker. "This one's called Snake." And it was snakelike; Harmon had already been calling it serpentine. They crossed the first bridge and went up the hill toward the five-mile marker, and Rufus was still there, walking with impossibly long ground-eating strides. Still chatting away. They passed the back aid station at 6.85 and went on to the saw-tooth section on the back side. Harmon feeling okay, Rufus talking up a storm of enthusiasm. They came to the longest, steepest

hill in the saw-tooth section. Rufus happily: "They call this one Despair. Good name. Let's run it." So they did, arriving panting at the top.
They finished the first loop, grabbed something at the aid table at the start-finish and took off down the railroad ties, up through the parking lots and out to the road. Still together. Rufus still happy and enthusiastic, Harmon, not feeling great, but not willing to admit it. Surely, he could stay with this big fucker. He was all of 90 pounds lighter. They chatted idly. Rufus had his friend Missy down from Pennsylvania to pace him the last three loops. They ran and walked together out to the airport turnaround, past the cutoff, down to the right turn and down, down, down Snake. Across the bridge up the long gentle hill to the left turn after the 5-mile marker. Together. Down to the back aid station. Together. Through the saw-tooth section and another breathless run up Despair. Together. Up to the left turn and down powerlines. Together. And across the bridge and up to the right turn on the main road. At cemetery hill, they started to separate. But it was Rufus who pulled steadily ahead walking so fast up that hill and then running again when he reached the top.

Rufus was just pulling out of the start-finish aid station when Harmon arrived. And Harmon could have run right through. This was only mile 25. There was nothing he really needed. But he didn't want to. He didn't feel like it. Rufus's pace was just not his pace for some reason, and he wasn't feeling sharp and he was not going to push it 25 miles into the race. He was cold and the wind bothered him, and it was just a bad day. So, he let Rufus go ahead and settled into a pace of his own. But that deteriorated too. Third loop of eight and he hit the first wall and felt lightheaded and so slow. As he was finishing that loop, Rufus was coming down from the airport spur already almost 3 miles ahead of him. They greeted warmly, but Harmon felt a stab of despair. Not because the big fucker was beating him. (Well, mostly not.) But because he still had 63 miles left, and he couldn't find a smooth pace and wasn't comfortable. Not at all. He got back to the start-finish aid station and wasted a few minutes trying to find some food or drink that would make him feel better, maybe give him some energy. He had a cup of Mountain Dew for sugar and caffeine, a cup of ginger ale to calm his stomach. He ate a quarter pb&j and some grapes. He took a handful of pretzel sticks and refilled his water. He walked out of the aid station wondering if he could even do it this year. And, as he got up the hill and on the access road, he found a rhythm, a slow pathetic rhythm, but something. He walked a steady walk and punctuated that with short slow jogs as he headed toward the turnaround on the airport spur. He was violating the rule he had adhered to so well the last two years of running all the runnable parts. Here he was walking on the flat, even a slight downhill as he headed to the turnaround. But he got the fourth loop done in this fashion and did the fifth as well.

He shuffled in from the fifth loop at about 9:30 p.m., at least two hours slower than last year. 24 hours was gone. Rufus was long gone. He was alone in the cold windy night to try to force himself to do 37.5 more miles. He set out on the sixth loop with music and tried to use it to pick up his pace, but his attempts were laughable. He would run a maximum of 100 steps before slowing to a shuffle, then walk. He got to the back aid station and stopped, looking for another magic bullet. He had a veggie burger with ketchup and mustard, so he could eat something that would stimulate his taste buds. He drank more ginger ale, left with a baggie-full of Oreos. He stuffed them in his pocket and never ate them. He walked the whole saw tooth section feeling sorry for himself. Trudging up Despair, he felt like the run up the hill with Rufus must have been years ago, not just this morning. He made a half-hearted slog down the powerlines and started the walk before the bridge.

Finally, at 1:30 a.m. he was back at the start-finish with two loops to go and over 10 hours to get it done. This was his fourth Umstead. He knew how to do this: you grab a bite or two and get going down the trail. There was plenty of time to walk it in if necessary. But he was so tired, so drained. Conventional wisdom told him, shouted to him to just keep moving. But it was so cold and he was so slow. He grabbed a pair of running pants from the plastic gear bag near the steps to the cabin. Conventional wisdom told him, screamed at him to never, never ever, go into the headquarters cabin during the race. It was the kiss of death, the smart people would tell him. He walked up the stairs and never hesitated.

He walked through the double doors into the big room with benches and picnic tables and people strewn about in various states of mental and physical decomposition. On the far wall, about 60 feet away was a roaring fire, around which were about a dozen people, some standing, most in chairs. Even by the doors, the room was at least 30 degrees warmer than the outside air. Harmon sat on a bench just inside the door. He dare not go near the fire, but here he was in the cabin, going against everything he had ever been told about how to run a 100 miler. He pulled on the pants, struggling in his fatigue to pull the stretchy material over his shoes. He bowed his head and spaced out for 20 minutes. Then, with effort, he stood. He felt lightheaded, but shook it off and went through the door back into the cold. From the porch, he saw Rufus come up the path and circle around the start-finish headed to the aid table with his pacer, a young woman with long brown hair, running strong. He'd been lapped. Rufus was 12.5 miles ahead of him and on a sub-24 pace. For a fleeting moment, Harmon thought of trying to pace with him for his last lap. But that was silly. Rufus was flying high; Harmon was demoralized. Harmon waited till Rufus started down the path and then went over to the aid station table and grabbed more pretzels, had a cup of ginger ale. He took his time. He looked at the coffee, but his stomach said no. Off into the darkness he went at about 2:15 a.m., putting the music back on. 25 cold and lonely miles and he could rest.

Loop seven was more of the same. Too much walking and not enough running. And the walking even seemed slower. He passed Rufus heading in the opposite direction on the airport spur, but in the dark, there was no greeting. Harmon sank into his music and tried to run when he could. The loop dragged, and there were streaks of light in the sky when he got back. This time he made a quick turn and went back out to get it done. He knew this would be his worst Umstead, but he could finish and try to keep it under 28 hours. He did almost the whole loop in full light, but the morning did not inspire or charge him up. He was way beyond that. He just kept moving. The music started to annoy him, but when he shut it off, he was so exhausted, he could hardly keep moving. So, he marched on. He swore that he would run the powerlines one last time, and he managed a staggering jog that he thought of as a jagger (could have been a stog). He throttled back to a trudging walk before the bridge again. But he could feel the end coming. The morning was cold and clear. Birds were singing in the trees and he had two miles left. He climbed the hill and turned right. The mile 11 sign seemed farther than he had remembered. Cemetery hill steeper and longer. Then he was over the top and he could see he would have to hurry to break 28 hours. He pushed the last mile, and came in at 27:58. Lisa and the kids were there. Lisa looked concerned.

"Are you okay?"

"Yeah. I'm cold. I suck, and I'm really tired. But I'm fine."

They went back to the room, and he had one of those showers where it took ten minutes just to feel warm again. He got out and slipped right into bed for three hours. Then they followed the Sunday ritual of the pub, the Greek restaurant and a movie in-room. It was running streak day number 10,316.

The next morning the subdivision run was not fun or inspiring. The weather was fine, a nice 55-degree morning, but he still felt spent. He did his two miles and got back to the hotel for breakfast and the drive back.

CHAPTER FIFTEEN

When you have a bad ultra, and you will, the best cure is another ultra. Get back out there, fool. You know you want to anyway.

Underground Runner's Guide

In the week that followed, Harmon felt fine. He came back strong, as if he hadn't run that hard at Umstead. Because he hadn't; he'd just slogged through a bad day. He needed to get the feeling of that terrible race out of his head, and he was happy that he had another ultra 7 weeks later. Something entirely different. A 72-hour fixed time race. Three days at the fair.

Harmon had run two 24 hour races, but had never ventured into multiday running. The fairgrounds had a .85-mile loop, and the idea was to run as many miles as possible within the time limitation. Harmon had no idea what to expect. Lisa, as always, had questions. "Do you have to start with a 72-hour? What about a 48?"

Harmon assured her that 72 was the place to start multiday running. It just felt right. Besides, it was the longest timed race available at the fair. And so he found himself buying a four-person tent to pitch at the fairgrounds and packing a cooler filled with soda and chocolate almond milk and V-8. He went alone on Wednesday night for the race that would start Thursday morning. Lisa would get a ride with her parents and arrive Friday night to visit and then come back Saturday morning to stay over to the finish. But Harmon didn't really need much help. The aid station was set up at the start-finish and he would pass it every 10-15 minutes. Bathrooms were also right on the loop.

At 9:00 a.m., Thursday morning the race started. There were about 40 runners in the 72 hour, with the 48 starting Friday morning and the 24 Saturday morning. Harmon had been in contact with Rufus and knew he would be in the 48, as would Missy his pacer from Umstead. Ben was in the 72, as was the short guy with glasses Harmon had seen the day he finished his first 100 at Umstead, Jaime Everett. Jaime had driven down with his friend Jim Fisher, who had a pop-up camper. Jim was in the 48, but he informed Harmon that he was mostly there to walk. His knee was bone-on-bone, not good for running. There were other people Harmon knew from ultras: Mary, a woman from Pennsylvania, Billie, the guy from the Cape, the race director of the Connecticut race where Harmon volunteered every year.

This race was easy on paper: 200 miles were right there in front of him. He planned 80-65-60, for the three 24-hour periods, giving himself a nice 5-mile cushion.

Harmon stayed on pace the first day and night. He was out on the course until about 3:30 a.m., when, at 75 miles in, he was really tired and started to feel cold in the dewy darkness. He retreated to his tent and found his sleeping bag felt damp, as if the dew had gone right through the barn tent roof onto his bedding. Nonetheless, he was bushed and slept till 7:15 in the clammy embrace of the bag. Rising was inefficient. It took him 20 minutes to get out the door of the tent dressed to run and another 15 on the course to warm up at all in the morning sun. He passed 80 miles just before the start of the 48, at about 8:50 a.m. The second day everything slowed down. He felt his ambition, goal of 200 and legs fading. He found himself walking a lot that day and socializing. Ben told great stories, about races, about his work, about anything. He seemed to know all the ultrarunners. When he found out Harmon was a lawyer, he told him a long tale about serving on a jury. Great story and about 4 laps of the course. Then there was Jaime, from Pennsylvania, another talkative friendly guy. Jaime talked of his family and life, but mostly he tried to calculate the miles from the .85-mile course. Where he was at any given time and where he would be at any time in the future. Then he and Ben talked speed, time and mileage, and it became inscrutable. At this point, Harmon was second male. A woman from the Canadian national team was in first overall and the first male was a tall thin guy from the Midwest, Ken Kennet. Harmon turned some walking and slow jogging miles with Ken. Ken wanted to win—well, be first male—and there was no reason he shouldn't. He was a stronger runner than any other guy in the 72-hour. Ken had a simple mantra: "Think like a dog." No past, no future, just the here and now. Just this stretch of pavement, this loop. It worked for him.

Later Harmon met and walked with Mark Taylor, an experienced multiday runner. They found themselves talking about family and divorce and kids. The miles slowly clicked off. Harmon started thinking of Lisa arriving that evening with a veggie sub, and he realized he hadn't even passed 100 miles yet, even though he had been at it for 31 hours. He tried to run a few laps, but his legs were leaden. Then he was walking again, with Mark, with Ken, with Jaime, with Ben. Rufus joined in, even though he was on his first day and fresher. Missy was walking with Rufus. Harmon had met her but never really looked at her. She was tall with square shoulders, long brown hair and very blue eyes. As the afternoon wore on, Harmon noted that Missy was a positive force. She joked; she told stories. She seemed to know a lot of the other runners. She and Rufus were apparently good friends and had run and rode bikes many times. Her presence in the group lightened the load of slogging ever forward for mileage.

When Lisa arrived with her parents and the kids at 7:30, Harmon was at 105 miles in 34:30, hardly a blistering pace. But he was having a great time. He was always conscious of the competition; it was a race, after all. But he loved the mid-race social component, something he had never experienced during the numerous ultras he had done. Through over 10,000 running days, Harmon had thought of running as solitary—him pushing alone against something, in hopes of finding something. Here he was running, a race, no less. But running with others and forging friendships.

Lisa cleaned up the tent and gave him a kiss for good luck. Harmon moved on, walking and running with the new crew. He slept about 3 hours and in the morning was invited to have some good coffee at Jim and Jaime's camper. He sat in the misty morning light, with Jim, Jaime, Rufus, Missy, Ken, Mark and Ben. Others came by and took part. It was a coffee party in the middle of a race with the clock running all the time. And it was great.

The 48-hour mark passed, and Harmon was at 125, meaning he had covered only 45 miles in the previous 24 hours. He was at peace with it; he was even happy. The ever-changing crew made its way around the course, now with the addition of fresh 24-hour runners. Running and walking, together and separately. Encouraging those who were passed or who passed them. And the miles clicked along. In the late afternoon, the weather turned. A cool breeze blew out of the northeast and a drizzle coated the course. People took breaks and the festive daytime atmosphere faded as night fell. There was a formal (unrelated) party in a large building adjacent to the start-finish area. When the party ended around 11:00, the building stayed open. After midnight, as the drizzle continued, the guys took refuge, sitting around the banquet tables, listening to the rain drumming on the metal roof. Ken had a lead of about 8 miles. Jaime had moved safely into second. Mark was holding third and Harmon fourth. Ben was just behind Harmon. He was three laps ahead before he had taken a nap in the early evening. It was apparent to Harmon in his fatigue that he would not catch Mark. He was content to turn a few miles, then sit again with the other guys, stay in fourth place. People were telling ultra stories and just resting easy in their chairs. Ben's stories of ultras and ultrarunners went back decades. Jaime excused himself to go to the bathroom. When he didn't return for 20 minutes, Ken went out on the course and found that Jaime had turned a lap and was on a second lap, trying to sneak up on Ken. There would be no catching Ken, as he was matching every move and was not going to sleep till after the race.

A grey dawn broke, and Harmon and the other guys got back to the course for the final hours. Harmon had his sights on 180 miles and fourth male. He was only 5 miles behind Mark, but he had no way to make up those miles, as Mark was too savvy to rest in these final hours. The rain stopped and the morning wore on. At 8:00 everyone started running again fueled by the certainty that they could stop in one hour. Harmon was two laps ahead of Ben, but Ben had been a track runner in college with a best 10k of 32 minutes. As the clock wound toward 8:30, he cranked it up. His last 5 laps were sub-7 minute pace, and he blew right by Harmon to take fourth. The competitive part of Harmon was a little annoyed being caught at the end, but his overall feeling was elation. The 72-hour was a great race and great time. In those three days, ultra acquaintances had become friends.

Harmon wrote a race report and published it to the ultralist two days later:

Race Report – Three Days at the Fair.

Think of your life as traveling a road through space and time. People meet; their roads intersect. Or they live or work together, and their roads run along parallel for a time. Then they diverge. Your old college buddy or best work friend, whose road ran steady and next to yours for all those years, may now be on a faraway path, one that intersects yours only on rare occasions. And as we age, our roads seem more and more solitary. Sure, we have a spouse, significant other, children, family, something. We are not alone or lonely, but the days where it seemed like there were many roads next to ours have faded.

Last Thursday my road led to western New Jersey to the Sussex County Fairgrounds for a 72-hour race. I went to challenge myself at the longest fixed time race I had ever tried. I went with the expectation that I would get drained, find the bottom of the energy cup, learn something about myself. It was all personal, solitary, in my mind, my expectation. I found something completely different.

Coming in, I knew a few of the people in the various races: Billy, the godfather of ultrarunning on Cape Cod, a friend and inspiration, John from Maine, a veteran of the 6-day race in Queens, Sheila, Stacy, Dan, Rufus, a few others. I expected the typical hellos and the "way to go," or "good job" during the race, but I was thinking this was a solo effort for three days. I had in my mind, as did most of us if we tell the truth, that I could get to about 200 miles. I hoped to go about 80 miles the first day, then 65, then about 60, for 205.

I spent the first day running and walking mostly alone, in typical fashion. Monique, the Canadian National Team runner was way ahead. It was warm and very sunny. I wasn't really paying attention to the other runners, just trying to get to my mileage, and eat and drink enough. I talked to a few of the other runners, but briefly. I went to bed about 4:30 a.m. Friday, with about 75 miles, and got up in time to be at just about 80 miles by 9:00 a.m. At that point I was second male, behind Ken. The other guys with about the same mileage: Mark, Ben and Jaime. And here's what happened. The five of us, Ken, Mark, Ben, Jaime and I covered a lot of laps together the next two days. A lot. All at a conversational pace, and we conversed about everything: other races and experiences, other sports, work, family, everything, from the most superficial to the most personal.

And the days passed. Mark pressed ahead of me when my late-night walk on the second night was slower than on night one. I couldn't catch him. Ben got closer. Jaime, who turned a few laps with us, surged the third day and kind of challenged Ken.

And then there we were at about 3:00 a.m. Sunday morning, wet, but smart enough to ride out some of the heavier showers sitting in a large building that had housed a party earlier in the night. We sat in metal folding chairs at long tables with paper table cloths. Ken had to go back out in the rain to protect his lead. Jaime was in second and was pushing him. Mark and I started to doze off. As dawn neared, Ben went out for some laps. I was 8 behind Mark at that point and Ben was 3 behind me. Then I went out too. It was a misty drizzle and dawn came under a heavy sky. My mind sensed the impending finish, and all of a sudden I could run again. I turned a few steady jogging laps, then a few more. The last hour came. I came up on Ken walking and walked with him. Then Mark was with us and we three walked a few last laps. Meanwhile Ben, with a PR sub-33:00 10k from the depths of history, cranked up a blistering last hour. He had said to Ken sometime much earlier that he wanted to really run the last hour to squeeze all the juice out of the orange. He did. He fired off about 4 or 5 sub-6-minute laps as the clock wound down to finish 2 laps ahead of me. He was wiped, but really charged up at the finish.

I finished with Mark and Ken about 7 minutes before the end. Final total 212 laps, 181 point something miles, 6th place overall, 5th male, a lot learned. What I really felt, though, was that I had made some friends, not something that happens every day to me. It was really a pleasure to turn laps with Ken, Mark, Rufus, Jaime, Missy and Ben, to share three days of friendly competition and the common purpose of chasing our goals on this course. And so the roads of our lives ran next to each other for 72 hours in New Jersey and then diverged—back to the Midwest, West, South and Northeast. I may never see these guys again, will probably never see them all in one place again, but they are friends nonetheless, and they made the three days at the fair more than just another race for me.

A Few Other Thoughts:

My wife, Lisa, arrived on Friday night and again Saturday morning and crewed me through the rest of the race. That was great. It is so helpful to have someone who thinks intelligently on your behalf when you get stupid.

Among the subjects covered in some of the many social laps was the allure of the Volstate race. Billie used the term "romance" to describe it. I think that's about right. That's a race I have to do if I can figure out the start date.

It does hurt the feet to spend most of 72 hours running or walking on pavement. By the third day, I had to stop about every 3-4 hours to take my shoes and socks off and put my feet up for about a half hour. It helped. The day following the race my ankles and knees were swollen, and it felt like someone had beaten my feet with a hammer.

For those of you who think that ultrarunning is necessarily on a trail or a mountain or point-to-point course, who find yourselves mentioning hamster wheels and assuming it must be boring to run a fixed time race on a short loop course, I urge you to try it before you criticize it. Trails and hills and mountain 100s are great, but what if you removed all the obstacles and tried to run for 72 hours? It's a substantial mental and physical challenge (and it's not boring).

Harmon's father-in-law drove the family home Sunday night as Harmon was in no shape to drive even after a three-hour nap. He was bushed, but smiling. He had found another something in this ultra journey. It was running streak day number 10,365.

He slept fitfully Sunday night, feet throbbing under the sheet with each heartbeat, calves twitching as if they would cramp. He took an aspirin at 3:00 a.m.

And then Monday morning came, and he ran a slow 2 miles. His feet were so tender and swollen. He could barely get the shoes on. By the end of the first mile, his muscles were sore but okay. But the feet. The feet. Not blisters. Tenderness and swelling.

As the days rolled on, the swelling ebbed as did the pain. On Thursday, Harmon peed about 10 times as his body let go of the extra water from his inflamed legs and feet. By the weekend, he was running an easy 5 miles, and he pronounced himself to Lisa 80% back. He continued to raise the mileage over the summer, going over 300 miles for June through October, before easing off as winter came. Just the same, most of his miles were slow and easy, and he ran no ultras the rest of the year.

In December, he passed the 29-year mark. And it passed like everything else. The days led up to it, and then it was there. He noted it, toasted to it with a beer, thought of the past and the future. But there was always the present. Always today's run. The days led away into the following year. Each day with a run. Some as short as 5 miles. Some several times longer. But each day a run. Or two.

He had big plans for the new year: the 50k frozen fat ass on the beach on Cape Cod, Umstead number 5 and some redemption after last year's debacle, and another 72 hours at the fair. He just knew he could do 200 miles. The rest of the year was open after these challenges, but something loomed that summer.

* * *

The Frozen Fatass was his first shot at a faster running year. As usual, the weather was bad: this year rainy and windy, with a high of about 40. The wind was coming off the water, so it was hitting Harmon mostly on one side or the other as he ran on or parallel to the beach. He had brought two complete tops: compression shirt, long sleeve tee shirt and rain jacket. He started on the beach near the parking lot at 7:30 a.m. with the heavier of his two rain jackets, with the hood up and a running hat underneath. The rain was coming hard from his right side as he ran west up the beach to the first turnaround. Then he turned south along a tidal inlet and then east, and the rain was hitting him from the left side. Then left again up over a set of steps and back to the beach, this time heading east, the sharp raindrops pelting the left side of his face, as he traced his way through the stones on the beach. Back through the start-finish parking lot and south again to a jeep road along the tidal flats, down four miles east to a left turn back toward the beach, and then west up the beach again to the start-finish area. A big figure eight for 25k, then another lap to go.

Harmon walked to the car and realized his hood had come down, probably when he was facing north heading back to the beach after the second part in the tidal flats. He pulled the hood up and dumped a splash of icy water over his head and down his back. Now he definitely had to change out his clothes from the waist up. He took off the jacket, stripped off the shirts and threw everything in the back seat. He toweled down quickly, then put on a new compression shirt and long sleeve shirt and lighter rain jacket, also with a hood. And he took off west up the beach for the beginning of lap two. The rain had let up some, but the wind was blowing harder off the water. He was staggered by a couple of gusts. The tide was farther up the beach and he had to run in the softer sand by the dunes. Most of the 70 people in the race had stopped after the first lap, except for the fast guys, who were nowhere to be seen. Harmon was again last. He turned and finished the western part of the figure eight. Back in the parking lot, he drank half a bottle of coke and filled his water. He headed to the long jeep road section. The first mile was uneventful, and the dunes broke some of the wind, but he noticed the wind and rising tide had made the water level higher in the tidal flats. Much higher. What was usually grass with channels of water looked like one big pond. He came to a low-lying section of the road, and it was covered with water. He started through and it was mostly ankle deep, but up near the knees in one area. He walked because he was afraid of hitting a stone and stumbling in the ice-cold water. The road rose and was dry again, and he continued. His feet and legs were cold, but soon felt fine.

Then he came to a second low section about 3 miles down the jeep road. This time he waded in and it was deeper, up to the knees then the thighs. Water eddied around his thighs as it rushed from his right to left from the flats into a tidal pond over by the dunes. He slowed and picked his way, mindful that a fall at this point would not only soak him but could carry him into the tidal pond of uncertain depth. He pictured headlines: "Stupid Lawyer Drowns Running Stupid Ultramarathon Stupidly." He decided to try to get out of the water after he passed the open area where the tidal pond was filling. He climbed up a little hill on his left out of the water and walked parallel to the course, pushing through the tall grass and dodging scrub pine and cedar. One more dip up to his knees and he found the left turn toward the beach. That path was also flooded, and he had to skirt around on the grass as much as possible. By this point he was completely alone and his nylon wind pants were soaked as were his shoes and socks.

He got out to the beach and found the waves almost up to the dunes. When they broke the wind-borne spray slapped the whole right side of his body. He slow-jogged up the beach through the soft dune sand and finished the last 4.5 miles in about 1:15. He arrived at the finish and the RD was there laughing at how pathetic he looked, wet and bedraggled. His time was worse, over 7:30, but the effort was greater, wading and bushwhacking his way through those miles. He went into the ranger's building at the finish and had a coffee while he caught up with the RD and what he had been up to. Harmon helped him clean up the race food and pack it away before leaving. It a was a long, wet drive back.

In the following days, Harmon tried to convince himself the exceptional misery of the fat ass would serve him well at Umstead and the fair, that the ability to endure would somehow transfer to those completely different races. Anything that didn't kill him made him stronger. It sounded good, but he knew it was bullshit. The Cape Cod race was an experience in itself. It wasn't training for anything.

Then it was Umstead weekend. Again. At the spaghetti dinner, it seemed like he knew half the people. Emmi and Rich played in the woods and then ate pasta and cake. Lisa herded them and then sat with Harmon. The evening sun slanted through the trees, and Harmon looked out at the start-finish area and the course and the excitement started to rise. By the end of the race, he would have 40 laps on the Umstead course. He could imagine every turn and hill as he thought of the race tomorrow.

They drove back to the hotel and Harmon put out his flat running man on the room floor and then taped his feet. He drank a beer and was in bed by 9:30, ahead of the 4:15 wakeup.

The fifth running of Umstead was part redemption, part just fun. Harmon's only goal was to get faster from the debacle of last year. He and Rufus started out together and stayed together for over a lap, talking about family and life, before Harmon pulled away, running when Rufus took a walk break. Harmon wouldn't end up running with him the rest of the race. Ben was run-walking with a friend, ushering him to his first 100 finish in about 27:30. Harmon had the usual highs and lows, walking most of the 7th lap, running again on the 8th, for a finish of 24:33, missing 24 hours, but finishing before it was light. Rufus was about two hours back in 26:25, again paced by Missy. Harmon was happy to be in the 500-mile club, for five-time finishers. Ben had already done 10. A post-race beer at the hotel tasted sweet.

Starting the next morning, his attention turned right to the fair, six weeks away. He wanted 200 miles in the 72-hour. He gave himself a week to recover from Umstead and then thought of the four and a half weeks till the fair would start: three weeks of heavy mileage, then 10 days to ease off before the Thursday morning start. And while he concentrated on the back-to-back 20-milers on the weekends and enough during the week to average 90-100 miles, most of his preparation was mental. 200 was easy on paper and hard in practice. That he had already learned. He wasn't lowering his expectations for himself. Instead, he wanted to be mentally stronger when he felt himself start to falter. From his one multiday experience, he realized there would come a time, maybe several times, when he needed sleep bad enough that he would do anything to get some, even trick himself into going to the tent for something seemingly innocuous that would lead to an hour nap. To counter this, he decided to plan his mileage in 12-hour blocks. He stopped short of planning all breaks, but he thought this could be an effective partway measure.

On Tuesday afternoon before the fair, he was two states away at young Harmon's high school track meet. Harmon had run cross country every year, but he had never loved it. Track, on the other hand, he embraced. He was a tri-captain at his small high school and ran the 800 meters, which was two laps of the track, and various relays. In three years he had whittled his 800 time down just below 2:10. This day, in the last dual meet of the season, Harmon started fast. He ran smoothly with minimal bounce or arm swing and cruised through the first lap in 1:01 right on the shoulder of the leader. They stayed like that through the turn and backstretch, and then Harmon turned it up on the far turn and drew alongside. He and the other runner hit the home stretch shoulder to shoulder. Harmon had seen his son in this position a number of times over the years. More often than not, the other runner would find that last burst because young Harmon was running a little over his head. This time they roared down the stretch, neither yielding. With 50 yards to go, Harmon edged ahead, first just a head, then a few feet. And then it was over; the other runner yielded enough, and Harmon pushed through the finish. 2:05.2, a personal best by three seconds.

Harmon was at the fence as his jubilant son strode over, still panting. "I've been working on finishing it. The last turn and the home stretch. Just pouring it on."

"Well, that was excellent. Whatever you're doing is working."

Big smile. "Coach had the distance guys doing ladders. That has us doing repeat 400s and 200s at the bottom. He tells us to concentrate on stride length and turnover. I felt fast today."

"You looked fast. That was great." He looked at his son: 16 years old, about 5'9", thick brown hair cut short, thin shoulders and hips, a boy's body. Probably 140 pounds or less. But he could move on the track.

"So, Thursday, I start that 72-hour race at the fair. In time, that's about 2,000 times as long as the race you just ran."

"I'm not gonna lie. That's a little effed up."

"Yes, but it's my kind of effed up, kid."

"Well, good luck and all."

"Thanks. So, I won't see you this weekend. I'll be back next weekend. And no, you can't hang out at the apartment with the boys. It's locked up."

"Hang at the apartment? What do you take me for?"

"A 16-year old kid. I was 16 once. I remember."

"Well, don't worry. I'm not my sister." (Iris had previously broken into the apartment he rented in their hometown and hung out with friends, when she was in high school.)

Harmon gave his son a hug and was on his way. Mind all caught up with the fair and his plans. 85-60-60 seemed so doable, really easy, if you thought about it.

Then he was at the fairgrounds the next night, a Wednesday evening in mid-May. Backing his SUV up to a livestock barn bordering the course just before the last left turn to the start-finish. He set up his tent and unloaded his cot, sleeping bags and supplies. He left the cooler in the car because he needed to buy a bag of ice on the way back to the fair Thursday morning.

Even though the race wouldn't start for about 15 hours, there was a buzz around the fairgrounds. Jim and Jaime were there and had set up the pop-up camper. Ben's one-man trail hiker's tent was set up on the grass behind the bathroom, but he was already gone to a local hotel for a last good sleep. Rufus's massive tent was set up next to the bathrooms. Missy's SUV was parked in the barn near Harmon's tent. She would just sleep in the car. Rufus came out of the kitchen cooler with two beers, handed one to Harmon.

"Something to help you sleep before the big race."

"I still have to drive. You know, I'm staying at my in-laws place across the river."

"Something to calm you for the drive to where you will then sleep well before the big race."

"Right. That'll do."

"Indeed."

Missy arrived with her own beer. They walked over to the pop-up and greeted the guys. They talked about the race. Jim allowed as how he would be happy with 145 miles because he would walk almost the entire time. Jaime was vague. He said something about only wanting 67 a day. "That's 200, right? That's what I want to shoot for."

Harmon noted that Jaime had done better than that last year, even with a lot of sitting the final night. Harmon then told Jaime he had described last year's race to his son, Richie, and Rich had dubbed him "Sneaky Jaime." Jaime loved the new nickname. "Tell him Sneaky Jaime says hi."

After a few more minutes of catching up, Harmon's beer was empty, and it was time to get going, so he could get a full night's sleep. He drove the half-hour across to Pennsylvania to the empty vacation house, arriving just as it was getting dark. He turned on the hot water and organized his gear for the next day. He laid out a running man on the floor and got out his taping supplies. By then, the water was hot, and he took a long shower, his last until Sunday. He toweled off and started taping his feet, putting kinesio tape along the parts that had blistered in the past: the inside of each big toe, the balls of his feet, around the heel cup and each little toe. He reinforced the kinesio with micropore paper tape on the edges. He put on a pair of his expensive socks, so the tape didn't peel in the night, and went to bed by 10. Sleep did not come easily, as his mind raced over the next days' action and strategy.

He woke up from a fitful sleep at 6:16 when his watch alarm went off (the minute of Iris's birth almost 19 years earlier). He had plenty of time to get to the fairgrounds but dithered it away, arranging and packing and repacking, and finally arrived at 8:45. He put the cooler in his tent and walked over to the starting area. Ken and Mark were not running this year, but Jim, Jaime, Rufus and Ben were there. Missy was there. Dan, the guy who wore laundered oxford shirts to protect against the sun, was sharing Harmon's barn. And there were other familiar faces: the blond woman with the all-day smile, the fast-walking woman with the shoulder-length hair, the short woman with curly brown hair, the tall guy with silver hair, the

Canadians, young and old. A lot more people than the previous year, some really fast people. Some studs who could go over 250 miles.

Rufus stood a head above the crowd and walked over. "Bigger group this year."

"Yeah, the RD said there are 250 in all the races together and 74 in the 72-hour."

"Well, nice day for a run."

"You should trademark that. It would look great on a tee shirt."

They both laughed.

At 9:00, the race started with a soft movement forward, so unlike young Harmon's 800 two days earlier. Some people walked right from the start. Others started with an easy jog, many with a run-walk strategy that would have them parsing up the course into run and walk sections each lap. The lap length had been adjusted to a measured mile to ease the confusion of addled runners late in the race. Ben had put flags out to break the mile up into four quarters.

Harmon had a secret plan, an experiment really. He knew it was foolhardy, but it had a simple logic. All of his best efforts from decades earlier came by running the front end of the race. While numerous people had extolled the beauty and power of the negative split, Harmon had never had a good race that he did not push at the start. All personal bests came from going out hard and hanging on for dear life.

So, what if he burned off his nervous energy by running a medium to hard marathon at the front end of a 72-hour? So, he set out to do it.

He started running at a Saturday morning 10-miler pace and found himself near the front of the group. Rufus saw what he was doing and went off with him. They were second and third at the mile mark. He and Rufus talked casually through that mile. Then Harmon told Rufus that he was going to run a marathon without a walk; maybe, if he felt great, a 50k. Rufus replied the obvious: according to all conventional wisdom this was foolish. Harmon stated, "It has been said that a wise man learns from the experiences and mistakes of others, while the fool learns from his own mistakes. Someone has to play the fool in that construct; why not me?"

The second mile came, and they were first and second, cutting the humid morning air at about a 9:30 pace. And they carried that pace around and around, even lapping people who would definitely beat them over time. It was a little crazy to just carry the speed for miles, but it was a cool, sunny morning and the course seemed to beckon to them.

After 10 miles in 1:36, Rufus realized the madness of the thing and fell back to walk a lap with Missy, Jaime and Jim. Harmon was alone in front, determined to run to the marathon point, feeling fast and loose.

At about 18-20 miles, the miles got tougher. This played on Harmon's mind. He knew he could run a 3:40 marathon or thereabouts, if that were truly the finish line. His mind was applying some subconscious governor because he knew this was not just a marathon. He couldn't ditch that. After mile 20, he was still running, still in first, but it was pointless. The miles were clicking off much slower, like 11:00 – 11:30. Finally, he passed the marathon in 4:23, sweated up and feeling beat. He passed the 27-mile mark and jogged around to his tent at about 27.9. He stopped, drank a root beer and took a 30-minute break, sitting in his folding chair in the cool barn. Experiment over for now, Harmon wondered if he would be able to run more, or if the fast start would doom his race. After readjusting to the pace of the multiday, Harmon felt alright, not depleted or slow. He walked and ran and still cranked out the miles okay. 59 miles by midnight (goal was 60 – 65). And after midnight, he was feeling fine and he cranked out another 33 miles to 9 am when the 48-hour started (goal was 30 – 35). In the night he met some of the elite runners, walked and ran with friends and did not go down for sleep. At all. He wanted 90 miles by 9:00 a.m.

He passed 92 miles just before the 48-hour race started and kept going on around the track. The forecast was for drenching rain around mid-day. Harmon planned to stay on the course till the rain came, but was finally wound down to nothing and lay down at 9:45, at just over 95 miles. Within minutes, the rain was pelting the metal roof of the barn and he drifted off in the light and fitful sleep of the race course. He could hear footsteps and conversations. He stayed down for two hours and then went out in the downpour for 10 more miles. Many of the 72-hour runners were down for hours during the storm. Rufus was out mostly running his miles with a big smile. He was soaked and his feet were make squeech, squeech sounds and he was laughing about how awesome it all was. Rufus was fucked up.

Harmon was wet and his feet were soaked through, and he went down again after 105 miles. Took his shoes and socks off and tucked into his cot for 3 more hours down. He feared ruining his feet, running in the storm. Everyone was warning about macerated feet and how they would end your race. Harmon had never really considered how silly the word macerated sounded. When he was at the far end of the course alone, he tried saying it three times. "Macerated. Macerated, macerated." He laughed. Like a fool. In the rain.

It was still drizzling when he went back out with new shoes and clothes. Rufus was still out, looking even more soaked if that was possible, still in good spirits, but not moving as fast. Harmon did a few more miles, but this was not to be a big day with the rain. At about 7 p.m., Lisa and her parents and Emmi and Rich arrived with a Subway footlong for dinner and he took another break. Rich ran a lap with him even in the drizzle. He vowed that he would run the race someday.

Then they were gone, and it was getting dark and still spitting rain. Harmon re-taped one foot, put on dry socks again and tried to stay out there, but the miles were coming slow. At midnight, he was at 121 miles, meaning in the 15 hours between 9 am and midnight he had made only 29 miles. But he felt rested, and his feet were not bad, considering the miles in wet shoes. Not macerated. He re-taped the other foot, got a third pair of shoes, his last dry ones, and forged on in the drying night.

The moon had come out and clouds were scudding across the sky and the weather forecast said no more rain for the weekend. Harmon continued all through the night, mixing walking and running and was at 143 at 9 a.m. Only 51 miles for the rain day. But he wasn't that worn. He could still run and his feet were okay. He would keep the same shoes the rest of the way.

Shortly after the 24-hour race started Harmon went down for another 2-hour nap. Then he plodded through the rest of the day and evening. Lisa came with more dinner and to stay overnight for support. Harmon took more short breaks than he should have. He walked and ran some miles with Ben, who told some stories of other races and other ultrarunning friends. Missy walked with them. Harmon learned that she was an ICU nurse. The miles clicked off. Jaime happened by. He was trying, and failing, to figure the math to get where he wanted to get by morning.

Rufus ran by, chiding another runner, who was in the 24. "Are you going to let a fat fuck like me beat you? Really? Get your ass moving." The other guy got moving. Rufus explained later as they were running a lap together. "Guy, I know. Newbie. First 24. Thought it was gonna be easy. Now he's at 50 miles and he wants to sleep in his car. Fucking newbie. Thought I would shake him up a little." Harmon just laughed. Rufus was a tough coach.

At 10:45 p.m., Harmon was at 176 miles. 200 seemed right there. He was thinking 181-182 by midnight.

It was getting cold as the night deepened. Harmon went to the car for his long pants. Lisa had moved it right into the barn next to the tent. He sat in the driver's seat, determined to pull the pants over his shoes. Then it was 11:40. He had just fallen asleep for 50 minutes putting on the pants. Just fallen out with no warning. He got out of the car ready to go at 11:45, feeling jittery. He passed 177 at midnight and realized all his cushion was gone. This would be a night of pushing for the goal.

He ran two full, slow miles with Rufus after midnight to satisfy the running streak. Then he took the pants off and put them back in the car, careful not to sit there himself. After all that, they were too warm and constricting. Rufus went to bed, saying he would be back up after 2:00. He was closing in on 155 and wanted 160 something. Ben and Jaime and Jim were all out chasing goals. Missy went to bed with 160, promising to get up for the last push. Jim said straight up that 140 was within reach, a good total considering 90% or more was walking. Jaime and Ben were vague about goals and totals. The three came around to the start-finish together, and Harmon saw that they were all within 5 miles of each other, all closing in on the magic plateau. They walked a few more miles together, talking about families, houses, kids, cars. At one point, Jaime was surprised that Ben and Harmon didn't have "extra cars." He had a collection of some sort, including a restored 1960's van. The miles went slow; the 180s took forever.

And then the group fractured, in slow motion, with Ben and Jaime and Harmon sinking into themselves for the last push toward 200 in the late stages of the night. Jaime ran by a few times, turning some miles with one of the elites he always seemed to befriend. Harmon put on some rock music and tried to run, a staggering jog at first, then a shuffle, then an actual slow run. Harmon got the right song on the Ipod and replayed it 5 times to get in the running rhythm. He started singing and pounding around the course, and then was at 190, then 195, and dawn broke and then it was full light. Harmon checked in with Jaime and Ben as they came in contact. Jaime a few miles ahead, Ben a few behind, all closing in on 200.

Then it was about 6:45 and Jaime rang the bell at the start-finish for 200 miles. An hour later it was Harmon, followed by Ben. All kept going around, competing with themselves and each other. Rufus was out after a night's sleep, going over 155, heading to 165. Missy wanted 165 or more.

Then it was 8:20, and Ben started to crank up his Jarvis miles. He and Harmon were on the same lap. They both started running. Ben flew by

Harmon and finished 3 quick miles with time on the clock. Harmon came around with time for one last mile. He saw Ben sitting in a chair at the finish talking up a crowd around him. Harmon yelled to Ben to join him for one more, but Ben declined. Harmon ran that last mile and tied Ben at 205. Sneaky Jaime had racked up 209. There would always be a little fucker ahead of Harmon.

It was a beautiful day and Lisa was there and Harmon's father-in-law had come to watch the finish. In those moments as the clock ran down, he felt elation. Pure elation. He had gotten to and well beyond his goal. He had tied his friend Ben, whom he thought of as a much better, more accomplished runner. Ben had a history of 25 years of ultras. The race had had so many ups and downs, but it had been great.

After the finish, there was breakfast and then the awards ceremony right at the start-finish. Harmon had finished 6th male, but might as well have won, as good as he felt in that moment. He looked around the crowd, saw a group of friends.

He walked over to Ben. "Man, I was trying to get you to go out for one more to stay one up on me."

"Nah, I only have three fast miles in me. Then I'm done. No way I was going for one more. Good race, brother."

"You too. Nice miles."

He walked on greeting and congratulating others.

Missy was all smiles. She had gotten to 170.

Rufus motioned him over to grab a beer from a mini-cooler. "Thanks, man. How're you feeling?"

"I'm pretty much fine. I slept like 7 hours every night. I just don't stay out there all night. But I got 166 miles."

"Nice."

"Did you beat Ben and Jaime?"

"No. I tied with Ben. But Jaime, that little fucker. He beat us by 4 miles. He gets it done."

"Yeah, I saw him running some fast miles with Derek (the male winner) at about 4 a.m. Saturday. He gets a lot of miles when no one is looking."

Sneaky Jaime. Harmon walked on again.

Jaime was asleep in a camp chair. Jim was sitting next to him. Harmon shook hands with Jim, gestured toward Jaime. "Probably won't be much help driving home."

"Never is. He's asleep by the time we get out of the driveway. He'll wake up about the time we get to his house."

Harmon circled back and sat in a chair next to Lisa, slumping lower as the ceremony went on. "You did great, hunny," she said. He smiled and slumped even more.

When he thought about the race later, he felt the elation wash over him again. He described the finish in a race report to the ultralist.

It's about 7:50 am. I walk a few laps with Ben. We are on the same lap, and we are both beaming. We are walking with Liza, who is in the 48-hour and has gone over 100 miles for the first time. We tell her that the way to finish is to summon the last measure of energy and pour it into the race. Don't stop a half-hour early and sit in a chair. Reach for that last mile. And then it's just before 8:30 and we come around and Ben is ready to finish with his typical fast 5k flourish. I gear it up to follow him through the start/finish, which is starting to fill up with people who have pulled the plug. So, Ben goes through just ahead of me and pulls away, and then a few others are running, really running, but most are stopped, and Ben goes way ahead. I run through again, and go out for "fast" mile #2, and then I come around again and the last mile was about 10 minutes and I still have 12 minutes to go. Ben is in a chair; he's done his three fast miles. And it's one more for me and the sky is impossibly blue, the trees and grass lush green and the road is winding a big arc around to the back straight and then through the dirt part and onto the pavement again then the final turn onto the paving stones and up to the start-finish with the crowd now cheering each finisher, as it is really over. And I ring the bell to announce my personal best. And then I'm a spectator. And runners come in and I'm cheering, and there's only one left and it's Liza. And the clock is counting to the finish and there she is coming around the last corner and the crowd is wild and she makes it with seconds to spare having run sub-8 that last lap. Pouring it all in. And another year is in the books. Wow.

He went back to the in-laws for a shower and then a delicious nap in a real bed. Life was not good. It was great. But there was something scratching at the back of his mind. The 205 in 72 hours just made it scratch harder.

CHAPTER SIXTEEN

People use "epic" to describe everything. Going to the end of the driveway to pick up the newspaper isn't epic. Climbing a mountain is. When the time comes that you want to pin the epic tag on one of your running exploits, make it something worthy. Don't be just another tool, who people avoid at cocktail parties.

Underground Runner's Guide

When Harmon had joined the ultralist, he had dutifully filled out the new member questionnaire and shared it on the forum, even though he didn't know shit about ultrarunning. As his fantasy goal race, he listed Badwater, a race that billed itself as the hardest footrace, starting in Death Valley and finishing at the Mount Whitney portal. The people who had done it and won it seemed like legends of the sport. Years passed, and Harmon still respected, even revered, the race. But he no longer cared to do it. It seemed a little overblown in his uninformed, purely-personal opinion. He hewed to something more modest on its face, perhaps even more challenging in the doing. And his reasoning, as unsound as ever, was because of the romance of the race. Not necessarily the course, the romance. The erudite, iconoclastic race director had a way of describing his races in terms that made you believe something transcendent was there for the finding.

Volstate became his fantasy goal. Volstate was epic.

He had mentioned it many times over several years. But the week following the fair, still walking gingerly and running short miles, he brought it up in earnest.

"Hunny, I think it's time to do Volstate."

"Time, like this year? Like now?"

"It's not for 7 weeks, but, yeah, if not now, when?"

She paused just a moment, looked right at him and said, "Okay. If you have to do it, do it."

So, he set about to do it. It was easier and harder than it seemed. Entering the race consisted of sending an email to the RD, saying he planned to be there. The race was a loosely organized road race diagonally across Tennessee from Kentucky to Georgia. It had no official entry or entry fee. You showed up to the last supper the night before and to the ferry the morning of. And you were in.

The preparation was something else. It would be 314 miles along the roads in July. In the heat. And humidity. There were hills, even something you could call a mountain, maybe two mountains. Lisa didn't want him wandering along alone, so he would be crewed. Matt and Lisa would man the crew vehicle, and that was that. Except for training.

He was already in good shape from the fair and he poured on more miles as he tried to get used to the heat. He did a series of 100-mile weeks. He ran at midday. He wore extra clothes. He drove back and forth to visit young Harmon with the heat blasting and a towel on his lap to mop his face. Drove up to his state track championship, heat on full, towel on the lap. Saw Harmon win the slow heat of the 800 in 2:02, and drove back to the apartment with the heat going, shirt soaked and sticking to his body. Drove to Western Massachusetts to the state open meet to see Harmon and his teammates set the school record in the 4x800 relay. With the heat blasting, with the towel in his lap. Was this helping? He hoped so.

Mostly, he thought. He spent part of every day thinking obsessively about the race. Looking at the course on line, studying the elevation profile on Google. He memorized the towns: like precious stones, connected by strings of highway on the map, Hickman, Union City, Martin, Dresden, Gleason, McKenzie, Huntington, Clarksburg, and on and on. Places he had never seen, knew nothing about, except in race lore. All the way to Alabama and then Castle Rock, Georgia. He spent hours just looking at the course on the on-line maps as it stepped down and across Tennessee. Wondering. How far would he get each day? How hard would that mountain be? How long to the Rock?

He concluded that the race was hard. Really hard. But doable. Not like one of the RD's other races that was nearly impossible. But there was great risk of failure. The heat would beat him down. The distance on the hot road would wreck his feet. He would have to do more than ever before. That would be required and assumed.

And then the logistics. Where should they fly? What kind of vehicle should they rent? What should they bring? How often should they stop in hotels? He would do the race in a week or less. It started on Thursday morning, so he booked a return flight for Thursday night a week later. He privately thought 6 days should be enough. That would give him a day to relax before returning.

And so, on the second Wednesday in July, he and Lisa and Matt, his tall, 23 year-old oldest son, found themselves in Union, Tennessee, at one of those buffet restaurants with 60 things, none of which looked that good or fresh, to meet the Volstate crowd. There was the Race Director, who had lived much of his life in Tennessee and was a lover of journey runs all around the state. His assistant stood next to him, a former Volstate winner, looking like he could run and win the race right now (and he probably could). There was Don Dennison, the guy who had run Volstate doubles and regular

Volstates and had recently done a transcon. There was the race runner-up from last year, Stewart, looking very fit. Word was he was going to push or pull some sort of narrow wagon down the road. (Harmon thought that sounded hard, given the lack of a shoulder on many of the roads.) There was a mother-daughter team, uncrewed, Louisa and Anna. Harmon introduced himself and commented on how Louisa had trash-talked Anna on the on-line forum, saying she would be first to quit. And there were some very experienced runners who had finished well the previous year, David and Rick. They were both studs, but Rick was an accomplished multiday runner with a 30-year resume of top races against top competition. And there was Ken from three days at the fair the year before. Harmon knew he was coming and was happy to see a familiar face. He met Ken's wife and daughter.

And there were some veteran ultrarunners, Mack and Stan, who had been running long for decades. Mack could recount New York City area ultras from the 70s.

There was a buzz in the room. Nervous energy for the ordeal that would start first thing in the morning. And would go. And Go. Harmon felt at home and he soaked up the atmosphere. This was Volstate. He was here. He got a page of turn by turn directions on waterproof paper from Mack, a small American flag from Rick, to pin to his shirt.

He and Lisa and Matt retreated to the hotel room. He laid out his running man. Fussed with his stuff, like it was a 100 miler he would do in the morning. But it wasn't. He tried to sleep. But he couldn't. This would be fine. This was okay. But was it? Lisa would stay until Saturday; then it would be he and Matt and the hot roads of Tennessee.

The next morning, he was too jazzed to drive, and Lisa maneuvered the SUV the 10 miles to Hickman, Kentucky, to the ferry. The sun was low in the sky and there were a few clouds. It was already about 80. They parked along the road, where it ended at the ferry landing. Harmon took his water bottle and stepped out of the car.

* * *

Harmon Willow thought he knew something about multiday running, but he was most definitely completely full of shit. He had no idea what was coming. No point of reference for how to endure it. But he did know that epic shit would go down right on these roads. This was freaking Volstate. The race he had read so much about, the race across a whole long, hot state.

He walked to the ferry landing just before 7:00 a.m., with one-dollar bills in the pocket of his running shorts to pay for the three of them to travel across the river and back. Then he was on the ferry heading across the Mississippi. It wasn't much. The road in Hickman, Kentucky, wound down to the river and there was a little barge-like craft there, with room for about 8 cars and people standing around the cars on deck. Ken's car was on the boat. His wife and daughter and new puppy were headed for St. Louis when the ferry reached the Missouri side of the river.

The river was wide and muddy, and the water level was still pretty high in mid-July. They powered over to the Missouri side to the ferry landing that was even less built up than the Kentucky side. A two-lane road just basically ended at a ramp at the river's edge. You couldn't even see any buildings, or anything: just the landing, the road, and some swampy woods. The runners got off the boat and lined up at a white line for cars that might be waiting for the ferry (there were no cars waiting). This served as the official starting line of the race, except that the runners were now separated from the course by a mile-wide river. At about 7:23 a.m. the RD lit a cigarette and the race was on, sort of. The 19 runners shuffled back onto the boat for the return trip, and then waited till they reached Kentucky to actually run (or walk). Ken's wife, daughter and puppy were on the Missouri shore. Harmon talked to Mack about his work in New York before he retired. They talked about horse racing at Aqueduct and Belmont. Harmon went to the bathroom, a porta-john lashed to the rail. As the

Kentucky shore approached, Harmon felt a little jumpy. Castle Rock, Georgia, was 300 and something miles down the road: 8 miles of Kentucky, all of Tennessee, a smidge of Alabama and the finish in Georgia. At the rock.

Back at Hickman about 7:55, the real run commenced. Some people jetted off ahead, really pushing it in the warm morning air—not Harmon. He and Ken talked and basically walked through Hickman with the more modest starters. They walked along with and talked to Stan; he said he used to run a 48 second 440. Ken suggested he bust one out now; he just smiled. They talked to Debbie; she was wearing ballet slippers. The group missed a turn about 2 miles into the race and realized about 100 yards later, so they went back and took the unmarked left to the overlook. Lesson learned. Know the course. As they were heading out of town, Ken was enticed by the smell of fried chicken coming from a convenience store at about 8:10 a.m. He was uncrewed and on his own. He decided to stop and Harmon forged on and did a little running on the road to Union City. He had the crew set up to meet him every 2-3 miles along this stretch, but that would change to every mile as the day got hotter. Every crew stop he got a new water bottle and some food. They made Union City, about 18 miles in, by lunch, and ate at the Subway. Harmon stopped to cool down in the air conditioning. It was about noon: sunny and in the 90's, though there had been a little high cloud cover earlier.

They left the Subway and headed up the road toward Martin, the next town. Matt and Lisa were meeting Harmon about every mile and a half, wherever they could find a commercial driveway or turnout on the busy road. It started really heating up in the afternoon sun. Harmon was on a short stretch of sidewalk, then the road shoulder. Several people stopped to offer him help. One man said the heat index was 110. Harmon wondered what a heat index really was; who knew how hot it felt. At that point he felt good; he was crewed and had a baggie of ice in his hat and a second baggie in a bandanna on the back of his neck. On day one, the race felt doable. He wasn't thinking of the long road ahead, just this day and this stretch of road. As the afternoon slid away, he was mixing in running and walking and feeling hot, but okay. The thought flashed through his mind that he might be competitive in the race. This was generally the thought that preceded disaster.

At a mid-afternoon crew stop, Harmon stepped in front of the car in a turnout near a cornfield to pee. It was dark brown. Like Dr. Pepper—not good. Really not good. After a moment of revulsion, he started to think about his day. He figured he knew what had happened and what it meant, but it was disconcerting, even alarming. He was in the middle of a hot afternoon, somewhere between Union City and Martin, on day one of the race of a lifetime. In self-diagnosis mode, he inferred that in the intense heat his kidney function was low (his blood being used for cooling). He emptied his bladder at the previous pee stop and managed to get it irritated and bleeding inside so that he was passing some blood from the bladder scratch. It was brown because it had an hour or more to bounce around in there. Harmon's immediate solution was to drink a little more water and not empty the bladder all the way when he peed. This helped, but it was not easy to hold some in every time he went.

Harmon headed on to Martin still trying to do some running mixed with walking; Ken caught up. They walked and ran together for a while till Ken stopped for some food in Martin. Harmon joked that this was Ken's solo eating tour of Tennessee. Harmon moved through Martin, past the University of Tennessee branch and on toward Dresden. Ken caught up again, and they walked through that town together in the early evening, following markings painted on the road by a good Samaritan. It started to thunderstorm and Ken decided to head to a motel just off course while Harmon kept going. He wanted two more towns before stopping. Steve from New Zealand and Jacob were a little ahead of them and were also heading to the motel in Dresden.

Harmon headed to Gleason and walked some of the way with Rose. Rose had braids of hair down to her waist. She was a puker. They were walking along and she said, "That food didn't agree with me." She ducked into a church parking lot behind a minivan, then emerged a moment later. "Much better." Amazing. She moved ahead when Harmon stopped with the crew and he didn't see her the rest of the night. She would connect up with John in Gleason and they walked all night.

After Rose moved ahead, Harmon walked alone through the darkness down old Route 22. He decided to test his new pepper spray (highly recommended by the experienced runners for bad dogs). He sprayed a cloud at the ground in front of him and to the side. The light breeze wafted it up and over to his face causing him to cough and tear up a little. Nice. Well, apparently the spray worked. He walked past some fields in complete darkness and heard an exhale, almost a sigh, close by to his left. It spooked him and raised goose bumps on his arms. He wheeled around with his headlamp shining across the shoulder and into the field. There was a Holstein sitting about 30 feet away.

Farther down Route 22 Harmon was overcome with the need to crap. There was nothing nearby, so he thought he would have to do it right on the side of the road. And he did, in the tall grass next to a commercial driveway. He hadn't done something like that since . . . well, ever. Harmon was a grown up; he didn't squat on the side of the road. But here he was doing it because he had to. No cars came. It was a quiet night on a quiet stretch of road. He then moved on through Gleason and then on to McKenzie where they stayed the first night at about 55 miles.

At the motel, Harmon peed and saw fresh reddish blood. He knew it was his bladder, rather than some life-threatening kidney ailment, but he questioned whether it made any sense to go on. He sat 260 miles from the rock. Lisa suggested he sleep on it and decide in the morning. He had put a tremendous amount of mental and physical effort into preparing for this race (not to mention the cost of traveling to Tennessee and getting the rental car and provisions) and did not want to bow out after one day. Like a Yankee who couldn't take the heat.

He took off his new Asics road shoes, his super $25 socks he had bought on-line, the brand everyone recommended. His feet were taped on the heels, balls of the feet and insides of the big toes to ward off blisters. There were small blisters anyway right under the tape. He took off his new triathlon top with three back pockets, purchased just for the race. He took off his long shorts, compression shorts and running briefs. He had some sunburn, but no chafing, with Two-Toms roll-on on his underarms and a mixture of Desitin and Vaseline for the crotch

At this point in his life, Harmon didn't eat meat or dairy, making it a challenge for him to get enough calories in the race. As a result, he would not eat health food on the roads of Tennessee. He drank mostly water in a handheld, with some Succeed every now and then to change the taste. He ate Fritos and mint Oreos as snacks to get the salty and sweet sensations. He ate peanut butter and jelly sandwiches. He ate tropical fruit and nut mix. He had a big apple pie from Costco. Ken coveted this pie; he talked wistfully of it, but he couldn't take things from crewed runners. From the road, Harmon ate mainly Subway—12-inch sub with lettuce, tomato, pickle, olives, avocado, oil and vinegar. At crew stops he drank Coke, Gatorade, Mountain Dew, Chocolate soy milk, V-8 and cran-grape juice. It worked, as long as he was sure to pack in enough calories.

In the morning, Harmon decided to go ahead. He just couldn't bail on the race because of the blood. He minimized the problem to Lisa and she suggested that he should go easy on the bladder by walking most or all of the day. Jogging even a few steps caused the bladder to bounce and gave the sensation of having to pee. He drank a lot of water and peed a lot, trying to stem the flow, so his bladder was never empty. This led to some damp running underwear. His only wardrobe change on day two and going forward was the addition of calf sleeves. They kept the sun off his legs, probably not effective for much else. Just as he started out, he found a quarter. This was the beginning of him finding a lot of change on the road.

On day two, walking through the towns and countryside, he noticed more things. The people of Tennessee were generally nice. Many asked what he was doing and offered help and encouragement. The approaching drivers usually gave him as much room as possible on the narrow roads. Harmon waved to everyone, especially those who moved over, allowing him to continue on the roadway and not the rumble strip. Many of them waved back, the preferred way being a raised pointer finger. Harmon never saw anyone running or riding a bike, except those in the race. He did see a lot of people mowing lawns on riding lawnmowers. There were a lot of small houses with big lawns.

He also noted that Tennessee had a lot of road kill. In the hot humid temperatures, it smelled rank. You could smell death and rot long before you got to a carcass. Sometimes there was no carcass at all, just a mark on the road where the blood spilled and that smell of death. Armadillos were popular targets, and the remains suggested that their armor didn't do much for them. There were pieces of it all over the roads. Turtles were also a common sight—lots of broken shells and turtle parts. As the race went on, Harmon figured he smelled so bad, he fit right in with the road kill.

Ken caught up as the morning wore on and they walked for a bit, both stopping for lunch in Huntington at separate places. Harmon just couldn't keep up and Ken went on ahead, mixing in some running. Harmon was having trouble with blisters, having walked the whole day. He had blisters on the ball of the left foot, the inside of both heels, the left little toe, and the foot pads of both feet—the bottom of the feet just behind the second and third toes. Those blisters were about half dollar-sized and painful, because they jolted the nerve in that area just about every step. Walking made the blisters worse. He kept going.

After an air conditioning break at McDonalds, he crossed the interstate at Parkers Crossroads in the evening—mile 82. He ran a bit in the cooler night on to the motel in Lexington, about mile 92. Not a great day; not even a good day with all the walking. Just before midnight, he walked five minutes with Lisa and planned the next day. They would go to Parsons and he would check into a motel for a nap in the afternoon while Matt drove Lisa to the airport. Then Matt and Harmon could travel at night in cooler weather.

Just before Harmon got to the motel, Steve and Rose walked up. He greeted them enthusiastically. They were going to walk through the night. He asked Steve how he was doing in Vibrams. He said he was fine, but Rose interjected, "Don't believe him. His feet are killing him." They went on and Harmon wouldn't see them again in the race.

At the motel that night Harmon was a little down. The first thing he did was pee reddish brown. He drank an O'Doul's non-alcoholic beer (first one ever) because he had read somewhere that they were good for kidney function. He tended to his blisters and thought about the days to come without his wife, with all those blisters, with the bladder thing, with a lot of miles still to cover. Sleep this night and every night would be fitful.

On day two he also heard that Stewart, one of the favorites, had dropped. He was pulling a narrow cart with his supplies, and it didn't work out. He ended up dropping around mile 108. Rick was now ahead and pushing hard.

The next morning Harmon got a late start, but still had plenty of time to cover 16 miles to the motel for his afternoon nap. He tried to keep a steady walk/shuffle to tamp down the blossoming foot pain. If he stopped for even a few seconds, it started to feel like walking on hot coals. Then he would have to beat down the foot pain all over again. The slow-motion run/shuffle was the preferred pace. He saw Jacob and David on the road. Jacob was young and looked rested. David told him he had hardly slept yet. He looked pretty beat.

Then he was at the motel and it was time for Lisa to go. He hugged and kissed her. He was cool, but inside he was crying. He knew he was in the race right now with the clock running, and she was going back home to the kids. He was hot and tired; he teared up as she left with Matt. His emotions were raw. He tried to rest in the few hours he had, but sleep in the middle of the afternoon was tough, and everything hurt. Too soon, Matt was back. He was tired and wanted to rest a bit. Finally, at about 9:00, they got back on the road, heading for Linden.

This was still part of day three, still Saturday, but it felt like a new day because of the rest stop. It was the fourth running session as the days and nights started to mix and blur. They started at mile 108, heading off past some roadhouses filled with cars and pickups on Saturday night. Harmon crossed the Tennessee River for the first time on a long bridge with a good wide shoulder. The moon was just past full, and it was a warm, quiet evening. On the other side of the river, the road was narrower, the shoulder one of those twelve inchers, with the rumble strip built into the shoulder. Tough going, but little traffic. Harmon heard a lot of barking dogs in the night and had the pepper spray right in his hand, but no dog rushed out.

A few hours after midnight, they came into Linden (mile 125), and they were moving right through—destination Howenwald sometime Sunday afternoon. In Linden, Harmon saw a runner on the road ahead. At first, he thought it might be Steve. It was someone tall and thin. It turned out to be Ken. He had just left his hotel in the center of town and started on the road. It was nice to have someone to travel with and they walked miles together through the night and into the next day. At about 7:30 a.m., Harmon again had to crap on a quiet stretch of road. (Somehow, he had lost all culture and was now a caveman.) They were almost up to Harmon's crew car and Harmon asked Ken if he could send Matt back with some paper towels. Ken continued on and, once again, Harmon couldn't catch up. Ken cruised smoothly up the long hill into Howenwald, while Harmon limped in, literally. He went slower and slower up the hill as he became depleted in the hot morning air. The last 6 miles would take about 4 hours.

On the way in to Howenwald, Harmon got annoyed at Matt—even though he was trying to help. He had a habit of lying to Harmon to make the next stretch of road seem better than it was. They climbed the hill outside of Howenwald. He said it was all downhill after the climb and that the town was close. Not true. It was 6 miles and rolling and Harmon was fading. He explained that he needed accurate descriptions because he was counting on them for every stretch of road. It was deflating to expect something and get something else if that something else was tougher.

About a mile out of the center of Howenwald, Harmon saw a dog, a Rottweiler mix, big and muscular, cross the road and hide in the ditch on the left in front of him. Though Harmon was concerned, he turned out to be really friendly and he followed Harmon all the way into town. Matt gave him a bowl of water in the scorching noontime sun. Later, he rolled in some stagnant water in a roadside ditch and smelled awful, even at a distance. Last year's race winner, Sylvie, stopped by to talk a bit and raise their spirits as did another very nice woman, Carol Ann. The dog was about to jump into her open car door when she closed it. The smell would never have come out of that car.

Finally, they reached the motel in the early afternoon (mile 144). The plan was another rest and another all-nighter. Harmon sent Matt for ice and food while he took off his shoes and rested in the room. He heard moaning at the door. It was the smelly dog. He heard Matt pull up, and the motel owner asking him with an Indian accent: "Did you arrive with a dog, sir?" Matt tried to explain that they were from out of state and most certainly did not own that dog. Harmon could just picture the dog stinking up the outside of the motel. He was a nice dog though.

With Matt back, Harmon put his burning painful feet in an ice bath and put icy cold wash cloths on his shins and knees. He moaned so loud he was afraid that the management would think someone was being murdered. Seriously.

At night, Sunday night, at about 9:30 they started the fifth running session, eyes set on Columbia. The motel in Columbia was on the other side of town, at about the 180-mile mark, 36 miles away. This seemed doable. But it didn't work. Harmon's feet were at their worst. He just couldn't get a rhythm going, stopping in the car and putting his feet up or changing socks. There were five identical pairs of the expensive socks on the passenger side dashboard in various states of damp or drying, and none of them felt right. The miles were passing slowly as the night melted away. At one point in the night, Matt and Harmon sat in the car and talked son to father about Matt's career and business aspirations for about an hour. Matt wanted to go into restaurant management, but was afraid that Harmon would disapprove. It was a great talk; Harmon wouldn't have traded the time for an hour walking down the road, but the clock was running. He needed to move on. He cut a hole about 2 inches in diameter in his right shoe insole to take pressure off the foot pad blister. It seemed to help a little, but the going was still slow, with many breaks. Jacob passed by on the other side of the road. Harmon saw him break in to a slow run. He got out of the car and trudged on. This was the worst night. Harmon made maybe a mile an hour with all the stopping.

As morning neared, Matt and Harmon talked about the real possibility that he might not finish the race. He could barely walk this whole night. The feet were so blistered by this time, and the foot pad blisters felt like they were on fire. Harmon felt he was winding down and in a bad place mentally. He knew from other long races that these periods would pass, but he had trouble envisioning going another 165 miles on the beat-up feet. He was very aware of the blisters on the foot pads, both little toes, the ball of the left foot, the insides of both heels, the outside of the left heel, and the back of the right heel. He tried to push the pain away; he kept walking as dawn approached.

Toward dawn, Matt was wiped. The race was hard on a single crew. There was no one to spell him. Harmon was getting a little energy from seeing the brightening sky. He went under the overpass for the Natchez-Trace Parkway and came up on the car while Matt was sleeping. He banged on the window several times, and Matt finally stirred. Harmon told him to rest and that he could come up and meet him in about two miles. He nodded through the window. Harmon moved on, trying to run as dawn broke. The left foot was starting to get numb under the foot pad; the right was still killing, but he could move better. At this half-running pace, he went a mile and then another. The crew car never passed. He kept going not seeing Matt. They were in a low area of several creeks with small ridges on both sides. There were a lot of dead box turtles there. Harmon observed that when shell was hit apparently the front of the turtle still crawled to the side of the road.

He also noted the exposed ledge at the edge of the highway and the close horizontal lines of the sedimentary rock. He remembered as a child looking for fossils in areas like these when the family visited Tennessee. He picked up a few pieces of rock to bring home to the kids. He also picked up a small piece of turtle shell and armadillo shell. Yes, Harmon was scavenging pieces of road kill to show his kids.

With Matt sleeping and missing his crew stops, it became a game. Harmon tried to speed up and get as far ahead of the crew car as possible before Matt would wake up and find him. Finally, the Dodge appeared around a corner and Matt stopped just ahead, apologetic and a little worried that he had not been attentive enough. It had only been about an hour and a half; Harmon had made maybe 4 or 5 miles in that time.

They were both a little ragged and decided that they would get at least to the halfway point, 157 miles and then drive into Columbia and get lunch, figure out what was next. Harmon thought he may drop out if his feet didn't feel any better. But then he started to feel liberated at the thought of getting off the road and flying home to his family. He went up a long hill to about mile 158 and marked the road with a strip of duct tape, thinking this might be it. In the deepest recesses of his mind, he had to admit that his feet were starting to hurt less and that he moved better when he let go of the mental burden of thinking of the miles ahead. Thinking he might quit after a few more miles made those miles easier—something to contemplate. Maybe he needed to think more like a dog.

They drove into Columbia on Monday, about noon time. Harmon called Lisa and told her maybe he should drop; his feet were making it too tough to walk at any decent pace. It was just not working. He could be home by that night. Home in his house Monday night. In his own bed. Lisa listened to Harmon's pitiful story and then asked if he would be very disappointed about dropping. He replied that he would feel good right then, but eventually, yes. She asked if he would feel it necessary to come back to conquer this. He replied that he very well might. She asked if he really wanted to go through the first half again. Harmon replied that he most certainly did not want to cover the first 158 miles again. She reminded him that they had put a lot into this: training, expense, turning their lives upside down, getting the help of her parents with the kids. Then she advised that he go to the motel, get a room and relax till dinner time, and then get back on the road. He would probably feel better with more food and rest. She made it clear that the best way out of this race was through it, not dropping out of it. Harmon valued her advice, such that there was no arguing; she was thinking clearly, not like Harmon and Matt, the two skuzzy road warriors, exhausted after being baked on the road for four plus days. But he kept thinking, he could be home. In his bed, this night.

There was no question but to follow Lisa's advice. (Years later, Harmon would come to understand the advice was always the same and always correct. Keep moving, go another mile. You'll be okay. You'll finish.) They got lunch and checked into the Richland Inn on the far edge of Columbia. They rested a few hours, but started to feel restless, now with the new plan to continue. They drove back to the tape at about 5:30 p.m. It was over 20 miles back up the course. They passed Don, David, Louisa and Anna around Hampshire. Harmon got back on the course about a mile or two behind them. Matt later told Harmon that he saw Tim in the store in Hampshire and that Harmon should catch up to them that evening. He liked the thought of walking with others, but he was disappointed that he had wasted a day and put himself so far back. He had been solidly a half-day to day ahead and was now behind these five. He caught up to Louisa and Anna and David. They walked along for a while. Louisa and David were talking religion. Harmon edged away. He talked to Anna. She seemed really strong, 160 miles into this race. She walked fast on long legs. She was excited at the prospect of completing this race at age 19. Harmon told her he saw no reason why she wouldn't finish. Harmon began to think Matt liked Anna. He was taking a lot of photos of the race. He took a lot of Anna. She was pretty and there was a height compatibility. She was about 5'9"; he was 6'5".

David dropped back, and Harmon talked with Louisa for a while. She was proud of Anna, as Anna was of her. They seemed to draw strength from each other. As ultrarunners are prone to do, Louisa and Harmon had some no barriers conversations, about life and family and raising children. Harmon walked a little with Tim as well. He had started 14 hours late and was doing great. Tim had a big pack. He seemed very strong. They marched into the outskirts of Columbia.

At the near end of town, there was a convenience store. Tim and Anna and Louisa stopped. Harmon forged on, thinking of the motel, and the luxury of being crewed and not having to hit every convenience store for food or water. But it was still about 5 miles more and he was fading. At the edge of downtown, Anna, Louisa and Tim caught up, and they all walked together through the city past the courthouse. The directions sent them through a sketchy area of town, into a dark neighborhood parallel to the main road. A police car pulled up, and the officer warned them to get to the main road. He said there were shootings and killings here on a regular basis. It was near midnight. They moved on and got to the stretch along the main road. The motel was about a mile up ahead. Harmon was really happy to get there and felt like he was back in the race. He needed a good day tomorrow. He really needed a good day tomorrow. He was thinking Shelbyville, about 46 miles down the endless road.

After the late evening session, Harmon had a slow start in the morning, hitting the road at about 9:00. The sun was already doing its thing, and the first five miles out of Columbia were shade-less highway, with a wide shoulder. While he was ambling down the road, Louisa and Anna marched up. Harmon was delighted to turn a few more miles with them, but it didn't last long. They turned onto the Culleoka Highway and there was a convenience store on the right that catered to the runners. It even had signs welcoming Volstate runners, and it had the iconic "bench of despair" outside. Anna wanted to get some ice cream or a milkshake. She was beaming, saying that only one Volstate runner had ever dropped after the bench of despair. This was around mile 185, but she could feel the true prospect of finishing. She and Louisa entered the store and Harmon walked on, sometimes running in a rumbling shuffle, feeling the pull of the race. The road was narrower and there was some shade from the trees along the shoulder. He passed through Culleoka, which was a small village, and then saw the RD. He was driving with his daughter today. She was very nice. Harmon told him about his wife not letting him quit. The RD laughed and laughed. Harmon also talked about the underfoot blisters and how running was actually easier than walking. The RD told about a fast runner asking him how to run on blisters. He imitated him by walking around on his heels. "I told him, you just do it." He laughed harder.

They moved on toward Lewisburg. Another scorching afternoon was brewing, but Harmon was having a better day. He realized the key was to just do it, just deal with the pain and work to beat it down, overcome it. It was working for now and he would ride it all the way to Shelbyville if he could. He worked his way toward Lewisburg through a long construction zone. Finally, he got into town and really there was not much there; downtown was deserted, except one young man listening to a discman, a relic of the 90's. He moved on to the highway connector on the outskirts of town, and Matt and he went for dinner: more Subway. They were a little past 200 miles, but he needed more tonight. Shelbyville, about 23 more miles down the road.

Just as Harmon was getting out of the car to start on to Shelbyville, he saw Louisa and Anna walk up the road. His spirits rose. He asked them if they were heading on to Shelbyville and Louisa said no. They needed to eat and rest. He would have to go it alone. He wished them well and started on again. He wouldn't see them again in the race.

A few miles out of Lewisburg in the deepening twilight, about 200 yards in front of Harmon, there was a heavy car crash in which a compact car rear ended a farm tractor with some kind of trailer on the back. The car ended up in the ditch with airbags deployed. As Harmon ran up, an older guy exited the car and staggered out of the ditch. His car was smoking from the airbags. A man who lived across the street came running over and assumed control, directing traffic around the debris. Harmon picked up pieces of car and put them on the side of the road out of the way of passing cars, and then moved on.

He turned right on Route 64 and moved on through horse country toward Shelbyville. This day (night now) was going well, and he knew if he could just hold on to the energy, he would gain back some miles. In the gloom he saw big barns and white-fenced pastures. There were dogs. Harmon was running with a handheld in one hand and the pepper spray in the other. Several times overnight he roused dogs that came from a long way off and ran right out into the road barking and chasing him. Harmon would turn and yell at them, and none tried to rush or bite him. He never used the pepper spray. At one point, Harmon was yelling "No!" at a pit bull in the roadway, and a voice from a house set back about 50 feet said, "No, Angel, come home now." Angel, right. So Harmon said, "Go home, Angel." Angel eventually tired of chasing and barking.

At another point, the headlamp picked up a pair of eyes in the road ahead and Harmon thought it was a dog. He yelled "No!" and the eyes paused and bolted away, but in a loping manner. It had been a deer in the road.

They eventually headed into Shelbyville, long after midnight. As usual, Matt misled Harmon as to the distance and made it seem shorter than it was. He was running out of energy and barely walking at that point. The last two miles took at least an hour, even though he knew they were so close to a motel. Finally, he got to the turnoff to the highway at about 3 a.m. But they had made 46 miles. He was back in the game and optimistic. They checked into the Best Western, which was the nicest motel they saw the entire trip.

The next morning, they were moving slowly after the long Tuesday, and Matt went down to load the car. He came back with a note from Ken that they should call him before leaving. Ken was at the same motel, feeling a little down, having taken a long break. Ken and Harmon agreed that they would move along together, and Matt would crew them both. Harmon offered his friend anything he had and a crew. He also offered him a ride to

Nashville airport Friday afternoon, because that's when he now thought they would be going back. Ken expressed his doubts about the schedule, but he accepted. Sadly, there was no more pie.

The threesome moved on toward Wartrace, but they got a late start, nearly 11:00. They saw the RD's wife, then the RD. Then, right in Wartrace they ran into Stan and Mack. They had both started solo and then tried to relay, but they had now dropped. It was great talking to them and they gave everyone a Coke. Stan said he liked to drink Coke mixed with milk. They drank it straight that day. When the roadside visit was over, they moved on through Wartrace through the heat of midday. The sun was baking them as they headed through rolling hills of farm country between Wartrace and Manchester. They wilted in the heat and made terrible time through the afternoon. Harmon enjoyed Ken's company and they talked easily of their lives and families and adventures. The miles ticked by, but not fast enough. Harmon thought they both need more calories, but they were way out in the country. Ken ate a few cookies he had brought from the motel in Shelbyville and some of the food from the crew car, but it was not enough. He was running down.

They were coming into Manchester and it was about 10 p.m. They turned right on the main road about 3 miles from the cluster of motels on the far side of town. Matt was waiting at a closed convenience store. Ken said he was done for the day. He suggested he and Harmon mark their progress at that point and come back on Thursday to start from there. Harmon was thinking they should run for the rock on Thursday and these three miles could blow that plan up. He said he would walk it in to Manchester. Ken could get an early start from there tomorrow and meet him in town. Ken and Matt took off in the car to get food and check in to a motel. Harmon went as fast as he could into town, trying to gather the last energy of the day to make the motel. Eventually, he saw Matt on the sidewalk ahead and Matt directed him to the motel. They would all be bunking together. Ken had made a tentative plan to rise early and have Matt drop him back at the convenience store, so he could meet Harmon near the motel no later than

7:00. That would leave them time to put some good distance in on Thursday.

Harmon took off the foot tape. He had about 15 blisters now, some in clusters and at various depths, some regular, some blood blisters. Some blisters on blisters. For the last two days, the second toe on his right foot had been swollen about twice normal size. He noticed the left foot was now the same. The foot pad blisters now had companion blood blisters and blisters coming up in the skin between the big and second toes of both feet. The feet also felt as if the bones were being pried apart. Really pried apart. He also noticed that his legs were swollen, and the skin swelled out above and below the compression sleeves on his calves. He tried to be quieter during the ice bath so as not to disturb Ken.

Then Harmon took a shower to strip off the road grime, and, all of a sudden, he was sobbing in the shower. He was reaching the end of his strength and composure. He kept it quiet: no need to share this with a fellow competitor and his son. He got back to bed next to Matt and emailed Lisa from his phone. He wrote that he was wiped and he knew this was just too much for him and them, that he missed her and the kids terribly and couldn't wait to get home, and that he was going to stick with less dislocating events in the future. He used email because he didn't want Matt to find this when he texted the RD from the phone with the daily progress.

He lay in bed and thought, "I've got to finish this. I am running out of energy; I am running out of sanity." There was little sleep for him that night. At about 5 a.m., he asked Ken in the next bed if he was ready to get up and head back to his point, so they could put in some good miles. He replied that he thought he was done. Harmon was surprised, but he knew he shouldn't be. Ken had been thinking of dropping for two days. The crewing solution really worked more for Harmon than for him because Harmon was used to the crew rhythm and enjoyed Ken's company on the road. Harmon asked him about 10 times in the next 2 hours if he might reconsider. Ken was a friend and Harmon knew, really now knew, how this race depleted you and left you ragged. Harmon thought maybe if he would just get out there, he could do it. Harmon felt that he knew this too. But in the end, Ken was done; he had probably been done for a few days, just hanging on. So, Harmon offered to have Matt get him to the bus station where he could get to Nashville and get a flight to Denver. It was kind of sad that the alternate plan lasted less than 24 hours, but Harmon and Ken both had things to do that day. They shook hands and hugged and wished each other well. Then Harmon headed back to the road. Ken would be home that night in his wife's arms.

Harmon would be trying to get out by going through. He was a full 100k from the rock. But he felt its pull and decided it was time to make a last run for it before he lost it altogether. He and Matt were worn, but this would be their chance to reach for something big. Even epic.

In Harmon's own words, the last day, an excerpt from his long race report:

My plan is to go to the end, with only short rests in the car. This is an ambitious plan; I am about 100k from the finish. I haven't covered that in any 24-hour period in the race, even the first day when I was fresh. And today I'm a wreck.

As I start the day's run, I take stock. The feet are bad, but I can master them for a few hours at a time. The legs are okay. My spirits are up and down, but the prospect of a run to the finish is intoxicating. I move along and see Don at a convenience store. He waves as I pass. A few minutes later he shuffles up to me and we cover some miles together. It's pleasant and we talk about our running history. I know nothing of Don's life, but I know his mileage from the late 80's; with some people it's just the opposite. I have no idea how much Louisa trains, but I know some of the subdivision regulations of her community.

Don has a Garmin and can tell me our pace, which is interesting to note, for a while. We're walking, doing about 19:00 minute miles for the most part. We have been on the road for a week; I'm fine with this pace. We are getting closer to the mountain. After Pelham, we will climb for three miles to the plateau. Then we will go through Monteagle and Tracy City and then down the other side. The RD has said that the steep downhill at mile 290 something hurts bad. Don tells me he plans a break at the motel in Monteagle and then a midnight start for the rock from about mile 275.

The day is cloudy and super-humid. A storm is building at the near edge of the mountain. Thunder starts to rumble. We're going to get some rain today to cut the overwhelming humidity.

A man in a pickup truck swings onto the shoulder to talk to us. He tells us he heard we are in a race and it's hot and he has a bottle of Powerade for each of us. I thank him sincerely and take mine. Don declines; he's completely self-sufficient. The guy is disappointed. We run into the RD. We move on and Don stops for lunch in a little restaurant. I move ahead as far as I can before the skies open up. The rain would be refreshing, but with the condition of my feet I don't want wet shoes and socks, so I ride out the storm in the crew car on the shoulder. While it rains, I see Don and then Tim walk by. I talk briefly to both. At first Don doesn't recognize me in the car. We are all a little fried by this point. Before I get out, I try to eat as much as I can so I have a surplus of energy for the afternoon activity.

As the storm slows to a drizzle, I get back to it. Soon I'm climbing the mountain. It's a series of switchbacks with hairpin turns, tough for negotiating traffic, but there are few cars in the early afternoon, and I can hear them coming in time to get out of the travel lane. I know it's 3 miles to the top, and I put my effort into it, getting to Monteagle in just about an hour from the bottom. It's all a fast walk/slow jog. I replenish my water and get some snack food at the top and send Matt for food, while I head toward Tracy City. I have been to Monteagle, and I spent four summers as a child in Sewanee, just about 6 miles to the west. Having never been back there since 1965, I would love to just drive through Sewanee again, but I'm in a race and the course goes the other way. And I remind myself for the hundredth time that the clock is running.

I go down a winding road with no shoulder. Soon a police officer pulls up and asks me how I'm doing, but it really comes out like, what the hell am I doing. I explain that I'm not just some scraggly, staggering, homeless meth head. I'm a scraggly, staggering, journey runner and racer, having come over 275 miles from Kentucky and heading 35 more miles to Georgia. He is hardly satisfied. He looks me up and down. He says he has reports of some crazy person running in the road and creating a traffic hazard. I apologize and do my best to seem lucid. He asks me to please stay on the shoulder at all times (the shoulder here is about 8 inches wide and is all rumble strip). I say okay, no problem, and he lets me go. I have a copy of my license in my shorts, but he never asks for id. He does pass me about three more times before I get out of town.

During this time, I am shuffling from Monteagle to Tracy City and waiting for Matt to return with food. He takes over an hour, and I start to think that he is lost. Then I am convinced that he is lost. I consider my options and think I will try to finish with what I have. I take inventory—4 mint Oreos, one Ziplock with some Fritos, a baggie with two Tums and one S-cap, 4 dollars, and some change I have picked up on the highway. I think, if I have to I can make it with this and look for Matt later. Things start to unwind after a week on the road.

Then the white Dodge Journey shows up, and all is well. I tell Matt about my fears and inventory. He thinks it's funny and that it sounds like the scene from "The Jerk" when Steve Martin is leaving home. "All I need is these 4 Oreos, and these Fritos, and this S-cap . . . ."

I move on to Tracy City in the evening. This is a depressed town. Dead. I see an older man at a table outside a closed bakery. He motions me over and we talk a few minutes. He finds out what I am doing and says he would like to do something like that and that he used to walk a lot but the leg has been acting up. He has to be about 80. I encourage him to keep walking; you never know.

Later, as I'm leaving town, a little sub-compact passes me two or three times. Finally, it stops near the entrance to a dirt road and the driver motions me over. He is about 75 and he is driving with a teenager in the passenger seat. We talk about the race and what I'm doing. The man tells me a story about how he used to have a repair shop. He put a small room in the back where he could sleep if he needed to. Years ago, a man from out of town had his car break down and the man let him sleep there while he was fixing it. This is a roundabout way of his offering a place to stay if I need it tonight. I thank him and say that it is a very generous offer, but I have to get to Castle Rock, Georgia, by the morning so I will have to be on my way overnight. He wishes me well and warns me about traffic on the road down to Jasper.

I continue on and it gets dark. I know that the road down the mountain is coming up, but there is a lot of flat road after Tracy City before it plunges down to Jasper. A lot of flat road. Hours at the pace I am going.

At some point shortly before midnight the race changes. Matt reads an update from the RD that says that there is a 4- or 5-way competition for 6th place. Tim, John, Jacob and I are within a few miles of each other heading to Jasper, and Don Dennison is in Monteagle resting before his run for the rock. Matt is excited. He says let's get 6th place. I say to him that I'm really mostly competitive with myself and the goal that has propelled me through this day is to finish in less than 8 days. But . . . it is a race, and if he thinks we should really compete for 6th place, I'm with him. No long rests to the finish, pushing it as much as possible the rest of the way.

For the first time, I reach down inside myself and I consciously summon the strength to push the pace. I do not want to save anything at this point. I tell Matt I am summoning. He thinks it sounds like the occult, but it's really about drawing out my reserves. I think of finishing this race and getting back home. I think of my wife and how much I miss her. I think of how great it will feel to finish. I think of famous quotes about struggle and determination, like the one from Teddy Roosevelt about being in the arena. I even think about Aragorn's speech from "The Return of the King." "A day may come when the courage of men fails, when we forsake our friends and break all bonds of fellowship, but it is not this day. An hour of wolves and shattered shields, when the age of men comes crashing down, but it is not this day." I am about 24 miles from the finish. I am ready to run, to leave it all on these roads.

We move ahead and I start down the mountain toward Jasper. My legs feel great (not my feet, but I'm managing that pain) and I run the whole way down. I know Tim and John are in front of me and Jacob is close behind. About 2/3 of the way down, I pass John. He is moving in obvious pain, walking gingerly, almost sideways on the steep grade. We exchange pleasantries and I run off ahead. Now that I'm being competitive, I don't want him to think he has any chance of catching me, so I disappear as fast as possible around the next curve.

When I reach the bottom, I keep running as long as possible and then shuffle as best I can. We turn right in Jasper at mile 296. I am getting tired again, and I try to eat to keep my energy level up. It's past midnight. I keep the awareness that Tim is now ahead and Jake and John behind. I'm pushing to try to catch Tim. Matt sees him every time he moves ahead. We're less than a mile apart; I envision overtaking him and trying to shuffle past him. I talk to a nice police officer in Kimball cruising up and down the road along the river. He is into the race and the tale of the four runners. At one point he tells me Jake is about a mile behind, Tim a half mile ahead.

The night wears on. Then Matt reports to me that Tim told him he was probably going to stop to rest. He tells me to keep pressing to stay ahead of Jake. I don't want Jake to see me because it will charge him up. He's a lot younger, and I think he's faster than I am. A lot faster. I have to stay out of his line of sight. I manage to stay just out of sight, although I see his crew car a few times. The hours pass and then we're past mile 300 and on the bridge over the Tennessee river, second crossing. It's a big, beautiful, arching bridge and it's empty. Dead quiet. I think of peeing into the river, but realize that in my condition I could fall in over the low railing. Bad way to end the race. So, I pee at the top of the span, right on the road, probably about the hundredth time I've peed on the road in this race. Then I shuffle on down the other side. The road through South Pittsburgh and the rest of Tennessee seems to take forever as the night grows stale. My energy is gone, but I'm hanging on, knowing the end is so close. I see a snake on the road around 4 a.m. I step right over it. I think it's about to become a dead snake, lying there in the road. The terrain is rolling up and down here.

Finally, I turn right and start the climb up Sand Mountain, another 3 miles up. More switchbacks and hairpins. I'd like to say I ran it all, which is a Volstate tradition. That would be a lie. I walk most of it, but briskly. It is just starting to get light. All the traffic is coming down the mountain. I walk some of it on the right side of the road to avoid the cars. About halfway up I turn and see the Tennessee sign, and know I am in Alabama, my fourth state of five. On I go. We see Jack,

Rick's crew. He is driving back down the course to see where everyone is. Rick won a few days ago.

I turn left on the last road. Just a few miles to go. It is morning, but I am still chasing the sub-8 day finish. I see Liz; she has to go somewhere, but wishes me well and offers her house for a shower and nap. This road is rough and hard on the feet. I am trying to run it in.

Finally, there is the gate, and I enter the final stretch. It is actually marked with ribbons. I turn left into the corn field and try my best to keep a good running pace on the soft, sandy soil. I am so anticipating the finish that this section seems to take a long time. I am hot and panting in the humid morning, sweat streaming down my face, the familiar beard of spittle forming on the chin. Finally, I take the last turn and see a motley crew and makeshift camp with a few cars including my crew car parked there. I cruise into the finish and the assistant RD helps me stop before plunging off the rock, which is really an outcropping with a drop on the far side. I look for Matt. He has gone back to direct me and take pictures of me finishing and has taken a wrong turn in the cornfield. He arrives about 5 minutes later, very winded. We have a laugh at this. Two completely wasted warriors. He gives me a bottle of champagne. We toast and I down a big glass. Then Matt finishes the bottle and takes a well-earned nap.

Official time 7 days, 23 hours, 42, minutes and 46 seconds: sixth place. The last 100k takes us one continuous stretch of 23 1/2 hours. We manage to finish ahead of the others that were near us on the road last night. Matt is very satisfied at this. So am I, but I'm happier to get in under 8 days. I tell Steve that we finished around the same time—7 days and something (he really beat me by just about a whole day). We laugh. Finishing feels great. I can turn off the motor now. Can I turn off the motor now?

I accept handshakes and hugs all around, and then Jake sprints in 25 minutes later, and I'm just another guy at the campsite. I sit around for a while, talking to Mack and Stan and the RD and assistant RD and Steve and Rose and Jack and Rich (this year's king of the road—great job, Rich!). I congratulate Jake. I love everyone. Really. It's done. It's a grey humid morning, and I'm sitting on the edge of a cornfield in Georgia, near Alabama and Tennessee, high above the Tennessee River. Life is beautiful.

The Rest

After some talk and a few minutes of rest, I wake up Matt. We are still on the edge of a cornfield in the middle of nowhere. We should get up to Nashville in time to turn in the rental by about 2:00. I give my cooler, bought at Walmart last week for the race, to the assistant RD. I should have tried to give the campers some of the left-over food and stuff, but I'm too spaced out at this point. We say our thank-yous and goodbyes and drive off. We take the same wrong turn out of the cornfield that Matt took running to meet me, and we get the scenic tour on the way out. Then we're at a car wash trying to make the Dodge presentable for return. It was brand new 9 days ago, with 6 miles on it. Now it has about 1,150 and is filthy. It smells like dirty running clothes (surprise). We wash and vacuum and toss some trash and pronounce it okay. Then we go to the airport where we cannot get an earlier flight and end up waiting (sleeping) for hours.

Epilogue

So, I completed my fantasy race, a race I had romanticized with the help of the RD and others and felt compelled to do. There was a great risk of failure and I teetered on the brink of failure, but I did it. I'm pleased. Really, I'm fucking ecstatic! And I haven't supplanted it with something bigger and badder (really there aren't that many races bigger or badder); it's still my fantasy race. And I learned along the way that there is a limit to the amount I should ask of my family to let me do things like this. This race exceeded that limit; I was too long away from my wife and kids and business. So, I can scale back. I can concentrate on races we can drive to, that won't be so dislocating to others. And I am so thankful to Lisa and Matt and everyone who helped me and who had to listen to my growing obsession with this challenge.

Other than that, with the incredible difficulty, the romance of pushing down the road across this state in July, enduring the elements, the hardships, climbing and descending and climbing again, I thought I might have some epiphany, I might get a glimpse of some greater meaning of existence. I would like to be able to end this report with some pithy literary quote, like "I know myself and that is all." I'd like to say I learned something profound out there.

And I did learn something, something simple. Probably something I already knew. I like to challenge myself to be a better version of myself as a runner. But it's really more important to challenge myself to be a better version of myself as a person, a husband, a father. That challenge should happen every day.

But, come on, this is running. It's a lark, a child's sport. I do it just because I love it. It's not opening up some deep inner meaning or showing me how to live my life. And to the extent that I should think that it will, that this race will cause the world or nature to whisper something impossibly profound in my ear as I struggle down the highways of Tennessee, "Isn't it pretty to think so."

* * *

After the flight home, after a final drive with Matt, Harmon dropped him off at his place and continued to the house. It was almost midnight, running streak day 10,797. He unlocked the door and got a drink of water before heading upstairs. He brushed his teeth and undressed for bed. He slipped into his side, and Lisa stirred. "Hunny, you're home."

"I'm home."

"Good." Her voice was sleepy, soft.

He lay on his back and everything hurt. He placed three fingers of his right hand in Lisa's palm as she slept on her stomach, stroking it gently like he always did. He drifted off and dreamed. The race was on; there was urgency to go. The clock was running. There were other runners with him. Men and women. The Volstate crowd was there. The big fucker, Tom was loping along. The little fucker with the green singlet was out ahead. Rufus was there next to Harmon. Another big fucker. Was he bigger than usual? Missy was on the other side of Rufus. She was saying she might want to run

Volstate and something about Limoncello. Hope was running next to Missy. Jaime was sneaking up to the green singlet guy, always a little ahead. How was he running so fast carrying a cigar-box guitar? Ben was running next to Jim, who was moving right along. His knee was fine. Ben was telling a story. About a fox, or was it a dog, or black cat. His voice was baritone honey. Everyone was listening. Laughing on cue. People were all around. Everybody running down the road. The race was on. The clock was running.

He flinched hard and awoke. Lisa was there.

"Hunny, you were moaning in your sleep. Maybe you need an aspirin."

"Maybe."

He got up, stiff-legged, and got an aspirin from the medicine cabinet, lay back down and felt his feet throbbing with his pulse. His voice was cloudy, like it was coming from far away.

"Hunny, it's you, you know."

"I know."

"It was always you."

"Of course it was."

He reached for her hand again. He sank further into the sheets, felt himself drifting. Maybe back to the dream, to the race that was always.

He would run tomorrow.

Cheshire, Connecticut June 3, 2018

Made in the USA
Columbia, SC
11 September 2018